COPPITTS GREEN

A Selection of Recent Titles by Nicola Thorne

THE PEOPLE OF THIS PARISH SERIES

THE PEOPLE OF THIS PARISH (Book I)
THE RECTOR'S DAUGHTER (Book II)
IN THIS QUIET EARTH (Book III) *
PAST LOVE (Book IV)*
A TIME OF HOPE (Book V)*
IN TIME OF WAR (Book VI)*

THE BROKEN BOUGH SERIES

THE BROKEN BOUGH *
THE BLACKBIRD'S SONG *
THE WATER'S EDGE *
OH HAPPY DAY *

COPPPITTS GREEN *
A FAMILY AFFAIR *
HAUNTED LANDSCAPE *
REPOSSESSION *
RETURN TO WUTHERING HEIGHTS *
RULES OF ENGAGEMENT *

* *available from Severn House*

COPPITTS GREEN

Nicola Thorne

This first world edition published in Great Britain 2003 by
SEVERN HOUSE PUBLISHERS LTD of
9–15 High Street, Sutton, Surrey SM1 1DF.
This first world edition published in the USA 2003 by
SEVERN HOUSE PUBLISHERS INC of
595 Madison Avenue, New York, N.Y. 10022.

British Library Cataloguing in Publication Data

Thorne, Nicola
    Coppitts Green
    1.   Romantic suspense novels
    I.   Title
    823.9'14 [F]

    ISBN 0-7278-5988-9

Typeset by Palimpsest Book Production Ltd.,
Polmont, Stirlingshire, Scotland.
Printed and bound in Great Britain by
MPG Books Ltd., Bodmin, Cornwall.

Author's Preface

R e-reading this novel is like making a nostalgic journey into my past. It is one of three 'gothic' novels written over twenty years ago. The modern 'gothic' is usually a novel of suspense with supernatural overtones, and this is very strong in *Coppitts Green*, which is about a girl who is strangely affected by the sinister atmosphere of a house she visits when trying to find her lost boyfriend.

The other two novels in this category were *Haunted Landscape* and *The House by the Sea* (also being reissued by Severn House). For some reason *Coppitts Green* was never published, presumably because the fashion for gothics was over. However, looking at it again after so many years, and having completely forgotten the plot, I found it absorbing and wanted to know, as with any good thriller, what happened.

Writing this preface, I had to transport myself back approximately to the year 1978, when James Callaghan was Prime Minister, the first test-tube baby was born, John Paul II was elected Pope and the tragic Diana had not yet married her Prince. I had yet to write my first big novel *The Daughters of the House*, or really to establish my career. The personal computer, e-mails, mobile phones and all the modern paraphernalia did not exist. My son, Stefan, now thirty-four and a father, was a schoolboy of nine and we lived in a flat in central London whereas now I live in a cottage in a beautiful part of Dorset.

But the location for *Coppitts Green* goes back even further to the Yorkshire Dales, where I roamed as a child, when with my parents I came to England from South Africa, where I was born, to the village of Kettlewell. I have been back many times since and it has scarcely changed. Reading this book, I was visited by a strong sense of nostalgia and imagined I could still smell the delicious odours of the village shop, which stocked everything from wellington boots to biscuits. I can see the brook that ran at the back of our tiny cottage, which my father's brother, my Uncle John, had lent us until we found somewhere to live. It was here that he came as a young man at weekends to fish and play cricket for the local team. Here, also, he wooed the attractive young woman who was to become my Aunt Betty. I can see the village of Kettlewell so clearly in my mind's eye and the village school, where the heroine of the book, Jocasta, comes as a teacher but to which in reality my parents would not send me in case I picked up a Yorkshire accent. Oh, shameful days of political incorrectness!

I should say here that some of the complexities of family relationships that thicken the plot of *Coppitts Green* were not learned in Kettlewell but much later in life when I was older, wiser and perhaps a good deal sadder than in those days of youthful exuberance.

Although the book was written in the 1970s, the setting appears to be a decade or so earlier. Clothes have changed considerably. The young Jocasta wears a 'pretty blouse and skirt', the young men are in 'flannels and tweed jackets' and there is a curious garment called a 'suede hunting jacket', which I can't remember hearing about since. There is no mention of drugs, but smoking is apparently the norm and Jocasta and her friends are forever lighting up.

Things have changed such a lot since my childhood in the Dales. We have all moved on and many of the friends I made are no longer with us. My beloved uncle, who taught my son the art of fly-fishing, is dead and, by sad coincidence, my Aunt Betty died at the age of eighty-eight a week after I had finished this preface. My mother, who loved the Dales, lies buried beside the River Wharfe in the beautiful churchyard at Burnsall, a few miles down the valley.

But although *Coppitts Green* belongs very much to my past, it seems to me it still retains its charm and I hope my readers will not be disappointed.

Nicola Thorne
Chideock, Dorset
March 2003

One

No one knows how Coppitts Green got its name. Maybe it came from a clearing in the great forest that, in olden days, stretched as far as Knaresborough and was a famous hunting ground for the English kings. The little patch of green in the forest, a glade perhaps, would have spread outwards as the wood was cut down for timber to build houses in the growing cities of the North, and now all that is left of the forest is Coppitts Wood, which grows prettily on either side of the River Whern and is filled with bluebells in springtime.

But if the 'Green' part is explained by conjecture, the name of Coppitt remains a mystery. Was he a 'copper' who worked in the old mines, or is it a corruption of 'potter' or 'potholer', because the Yorkshire moors are full of subterranean caverns and caves? Whoever or whatever Coppitt was, nothing remains but the name, and that is abundant. There is Coppitts Fell, Coppitts Raike – which is the Yorkshire name for an old roadway – and Coppitts Beck, which runs at a brisk pace through the cluster of dales-side houses and cottages that form the actual village of Coppitts Green.

My first sight of the village was from the windows of the daily bus that trundles out of Skipton and meanders through the dales at a leisurely pace, letting folk alight or board where they will. My nose pressed to the glass, I saw that Wherndale, in which it lay, was a soft open valley with low hills and large limestone bolders, which, from the distance, looked like the sheep which grazed on the hills. That day, there was nothing grim or menacing about the dale, basking in the afternoon sun of a late summer's day and the melancholy that I was feeling had nothing to do with the scene of rustic tranquility that greeted my eyes and with which I was to become so familiar in the months ahead. For I was the new infant teacher of Coppitts Green school.

Croft House, Coppitts Green. The name had a lovely ring: at the time I'd first heard it, I'd envisaged an exciting arrival with Peter and a bustle of cases and greetings, and dogs jumping up and the smell of hot muffins for tea. I didn't think that after the driver got my cases from the back of the bus I would be stumbling along a dark lane with the sound of the Whern roaring now in my ears and a feeling of foreboding gripping my heart.

Teatime. There wasn't a soul abroad. The sun had disappeared over the hills; there was an autumn nip in the air, much sharper than London, which I'd left only this morning. Oh London . . . what would I not have given for your warm smoky comfort? The sound of traffic instead of this noisy river; the lights of Swiss Cottage as I'd come home on the bus from my school in Finchley. The welcome from my landlady and the rush of people coming and going in the large boarding house where I'd lived. I was a city girl born and bred – what on earth was I doing here? And where was Peter?

Finally a man with a dog directed me to Croft House, which faced the river and was only a stone's throw from the bus stop. It seemed a large house and was approached through an iron gate and a small neat garden. I stood on the stone step several minutes before the door was opened and a woman in an overall peered at me.

'Miss Oaks? You're expected. Please come in.' She opened the door wide and smiled, helping me with my things. I found myself in a pleasant hall, well lit with watercolours on the wall; it was also warm.

'Cold for the time of the year,' the woman said, closing the door. 'I'm Mrs Bargett, miss. The Master and Miss Ryder are not at home . . .'

Ryder; my heart missed a beat. Peter Ryder . . . I was
to stay with his cousins Agnes and Tim. Peter had fixed
everything for me. Where was Peter? I looked anxiously at
Mrs Bargett.

'Did Peter Ryder ring or anything? He was to meet me at
the station in Leeds but didn't turn up. I waited and waited
until a porter put me on the train for Skipton, and in Skipton
the dales bus was just leaving in the station forecourt.'

'Oh dear, miss, and you've come all this way by yourself?
You must be tired, and upset. I'll take you straight to your
room. No, Mr Peter didn't ring and Master Tim and Miss
Agnes sent their apologies. They've gone to York for the
races and won't be back until tomorrow. I suppose they
thought Mr Peter would be with you; it makes it seem so
unwelcoming. I'll get you a nice fire in the drawing room.
Follow me, miss.'

I liked the deep pile of the stair carpet, the gleaming white
of the paintwork. The stairs were steep, the house was old,
and the landing seemed to disappear into a warren of rooms
with stairs leading up to some and down to others.

'You're on the second floor, miss. Miss Agnes wanted you
to have your own cosy little suite; it has a bedroom, a sitting
room and a bathroom. You'll be very comfy there.

The stairs to the second floor were even narrower. I realized
it was a kind of attic; but indeed my quarters left nothing
to be desired – they were small but beautifully clean and
compact. A bedroom with a narrow bed, dressing table, chest
of drawers and chair; a sitting room with a sofa, two chairs,
a table and even a television, and next to the bedroom a
fair-sized bathroom with a big hot-water tank and a large
old-fashioned bath.

Mrs Bargett drew the curtains.

'There, I'll shut out the night; you'll see it at its best in
the morning; but night's a bad time to see a new place. Pity
you came so late. You'll be wanting a cup of tea, miss? Shall
I bring it up while you unpack or will you come down and
have it straight away?'

I shivered.

'Straight away, thanks. Yes, I am cold and . . . tired.' I'd been going to say confused, but the kindly impersonal stare of the good lady somehow prevented me.

I followed her the way we had come and she showed me into a well-proportioned drawing room with a welcome fire in the grate. It was a long low comfortable room, the sort of room in which you imagined people living and spending a lot of time. The sofas were covered with well-worn chintzy material, there were lots of bright cushions, tables with magazines and books and a chess set that looked as though someone was in the middle of a game.

'You sit by the fire, miss, and I'll fetch your tea.' The good Mrs Bargett bustled out. I looked about. There were ornaments of brass, silver and a lot of good china; some nice oils on the walls and a few watercolours of local scenes. I knew nothing about the Ryders except that they were orphans, well off and Agnes was prone to attacks of poor health, which had prevented her from following a promising academic career at Cambridge. Tim wrote books about Yorkshire life. It seemed a strange place for young people to live. What sort of social life was there here?

As if answering my thoughts, Mrs Bargett came in with a well-laden tea tray.

'You'll find it quiet here, miss. The new teacher, I hear. Except for the Master and Miss Agnes, there are few young people in Coppitts Green, not folk of your own kind, I mean.'

I jumped up to help her with the tea tray.

'Oh, thank you, Mrs Bargett. Won't you get another cup and have one with me?'

'Thank you, miss, but I have my tea about four. I have to go shortly and get tea for my own family.'

'Oh, you don't live in?'

'Just around the corner, miss. I have four children, only one at home and my husband works for the electricity board and travels up and down the dale. Master Tim and Miss Agnes

4

usually have lunch and a snack in the evenings when they're here, and I leave them a cold tray; but tonight I've made you a nice stew and some greens. I'll leave it in the hot trolley just ready to eat when you feel like it. You'll be tired, miss, ready for an early night.'

'I expect Peter will ring,' I said, 'when he finds out he's missed the train or forgotten the day.'

I thought that Mrs Bargett was giving me that rather reserved look people have for those they're sorry for. My heart sank. So she knew about Peter too . . . that he was unreliable, always somewhere else but where he should be . . . always full of well-intentioned excuses. Did she even know, or guess, how in love I was with Peter, how he'd swept me off my feet and how it was at his instigation that I had applied for the vacant school post so as to be near him? 'So that we could see more of each other,' Peter had said as his business would keep him more and more in the North and less and less in London.

'It will be his business has kept him,' Mrs Bargett said tactfully. 'Mr Tim always says how hard Mr Peter works. He will be right upset to have missed you.'

'Is it all right if I smoke?'

'Of course, miss.' Mrs Bargett lit a match for me and her friendly brown eyes gazed levelly at me through the smoke.

'I'll ring his home in Leeds a bit later,' I said. 'He won't be in yet.'

Mrs Bargett's level gaze continued. Did she know, could she possibly guess that I didn't even know where Peter lived, so how could I get hold of him? Would a sensible body like Mrs Bargett with four children and a husband who worked for the electricity board ever possibly be able to fathom the mind of a woman, carefully brought up, a schoolteacher by profession, who had thrown herself willy nilly in blind helpless passion at the most exciting man she had ever met, yet about whom she had only a smattering of knowledge?

That he was twenty-eight, an ex-Army man, decided it didn't suit him, had gone into business. (What business? Oh, business.) Who appeared and disappeared like a jack-in-the-box, well dressed, driving fast expensive cars, took one to places one had only ever seen in Sunday colour supplements, made one suddenly fully aware of being a woman . . . that before one had been only half alive, that sort of thing. What would Mrs Bargett know about *that*?

It was exciting to have changed your personality in your mid-twenties. From being cautious to have become reckless, from being rather alone and spinsterly to have blossomed into lover. My practical married sister only the day before said ruefully that it had happened to me rather late and had released in me a lunatic streak buried rather deep in our family. In fact she had recalled our mother, dead long ago and buried in India, and said she'd supposed this streak affected the women, some of the women, in our family (not her of course). I pointed out the Yorkshire Dales weren't as wild as all that or as far away; no, it was *Peter* Sarah meant, the effect Peter had had on me.

Mrs Bargett stoked the fire. 'I'll have to be off, miss. You won't be lonely, will you? If you'll come with me into the dining room, I'll show you where everything is, and I'll be here before you get up in the morning. My menfolk are away before seven. You'll be going over the school tomorrow, I expect, before term starts.'

'Yes, I have to see Mrs Baker at ten.' Mrs Baker was the headmistress. There were only two of us, infants and junior teachers, not more than thirty children; what a change from Finchley.

My dinner left in the dumb waiter in the dining room had been perfect, a lovely brown stew with huge pieces of meat and milky potatoes, smooth creamy vegetables. I'd unpacked and had a bath before it, ate in my dressing gown, carrying the plate in front of the drawing-room fire. Then it had felt nice to be alone even though an ear was cocked for the sound of the phone but somehow I'd known it wouldn't ring. Peter had completely forgotten the day.

I left the plates on the table as Mrs Bargett had insisted I should, some people just didn't like others interfering in their kitchen. I'd creamed my face and brushed my hair, and now I was in bed trying to read, yet the print was a blur before my eyes. It was very still in Coppitts Green; the moon had shone through the trees as I drew the curtains to open the window, and I saw that what flowed past the house was a swift stream, not the river; then beyond the stream was another row of houses. The moon was partly obscured by a great cliff that seemed to hang over the village.

I put my book down and turned off the light. The moonlight flooded the room and I gazed through the trees at that rather fearsome cliff. This was potholing country; people went caving and sometimes got stuck and lost their lives. Why had I suddenly thought of death? I was normally a cheerful person; but there was something about that cliff that worried me. It seemed full of menace.

Yet I slept well and in the morning I felt a completely different person. The sun shone into my room as Mrs Bargett swept in with a cheerful greeting and a cup of tea, and I saw the cliff was obscured by a haze.

'It's a grand morning, miss, did you sleep well?'

'Very well, Mrs Bargett. Thank you so much, what luxury.'

I propped myself up on an elbow and sipped my tea.

'Do you like bacon and eggs for breakfast . . .'

'Oh no, just toast, thank you, Mrs Bargett. I can't take much in the morning.'

'I'm the same, miss; but my menfolk . . . did, er, Mr Peter ring?'

Her tone of voice changed, I was sure, just as her expression had changed last night when she'd mentioned him. The inflection was one of doubt, definite disbelief . . . was it also pity?

'He didn't, Mrs Bargett. I'll give him a good talking to when he does turn up,' and trying to keep my voice light I jumped out of bed.

It was still warm enough for summer clothes and I put on

a skirt and a light shirt. I wore all my clothes long now and hoped I wouldn't be considered an oddity in the village. I didn't see Mrs Bargett again before I left. I ate my sparse breakfast quickly and called to her by the door. I could hear her hoovering on the first floor. I'd decided to spend the day exploring the area after my interview at school and wouldn't be back to lunch. No doubt when I got back all the Ryders would be there and Peter would be laughing into my face, teasing me . . .

I stepped into the street and everything seemed to sparkle about me . . . the brook rushed away, the birds twittered in the branches of the swaying trees and the windows of the houses shone. Although it was warm, little spirals of downy smoke wafted into the very blue sky and from somewhere came the smell of a wood fire.

The village of Coppitts Green inclined gradually up the hill on one side of Wherndale; on the other lay the long winding road along which my bus had come the day before. At Coppitts Green the valley narrowed, and it was on the road towards the next village, Starthrush, that the school lay, a one-storey stone building with a gothic spire, and stained-glass windows at one end just like a small Nonconformist chapel. The gate from the road led into the playground and I saw that the main door was open and that someone was standing beyond it looking at me. Was Mrs Baker appraising the person she'd appointed without an interview, arranged through the Ryders, who didn't know me either?

I reflected that it was a strange set-up as I squared my shoulders and walked briskily to the door pretending I hadn't seen her silent form, watching.

But my first impression of Mrs Baker was pleasing. She was an ample motherly lady with a slight northern accent, a warm smile and a firm handclasp.

'You'll be Miss Oaks,' she said, drawing me into the school room, 'welcome. I hope you had a good journey.'

The school did indeed seem to be an old chapel because it consisted of one long room, partitioned down the centre, and Mrs Baker led me into the part that was presumably reserved for the class taught by her. There were rows of desks – not what I was used to in my progressive infants school at Finchley, and a tall lectern at the end. On one side was a table, and, offering me one of the chairs placed up to it, Mrs Baker took the other.

'There. I suppose it is very different from what you're used to. A real old village school. I've been the sole teacher for years, but now it really has grown too big and the local authority have authorized me to have some help while they decide what to do with the school.'

'Decide what to do?'

'Well, your appointment is only temporary as you know, and I'm getting on. There's a school at Grassington, and they may decide to shut this altogether when I retire. It's very hard to get staff up here, as you know.'

I understood they had advertised the post and got no suitable applicants, which was extraordinary when one considered that there was no shortage of teachers. But Coppitts Green was remote; over twenty miles from Skipton and fourteen from Grassington, the nearest village of any size.

'Also the birth rate is falling. We have fewer younger children than before and your class is quite small. However, I was delighted that a chance meeting with Tim Ryder led to his telling me that you were looking for a job, although I doubt whether you'll see more of your fiancé than in London!'

I saw that Tim had 'engaged' Peter and me to make it seem more respectable. Not only weren't we engaged but Peter had never mentioned marriage. Mrs Baker didn't seem to me to be the kind of woman who would mind one way or the other.

'My fiancé has disappeared,' I laughed. 'I wonder if I'll see him at all.'

Laughter was the only way to hide the chagrin I felt about Peter.

'Disappeared?'

'Oh, I'm joking. But he failed to meet me at Leeds . . .'

'And you came on here alone, and the Ryders are away . . .
Oh, that is too bad – your first night spent on your own.'
'Oh, I didn't mind. Mrs Bargett is an angel.'
'I see you're a sensible, practical girl,' Mrs Baker touched
my hand, 'just the kind to help me. Now let me show you the
timetable . . .'

By the time Mrs Baker and I had considered the term's
programme, it was after midday. We had talked non-stop
without realizing the time. I was excited and impressed by
what I'd seen and heard. I felt as a missionary might feel
in a foreign land; this was all so different from anything I'd
known before.
'And here are the toilets.' Mrs Baker had taken me outside
to the playground. These were in a wooden shed by the side
of the school.
'You've guessed of course that this was once a chapel.
It's very Nonconformist in these parts though I am C of E
myself. As people went into the towns the congregation
dwindled and this has been a school for almost thirty years.
The children from Coppitts Green walk, those from Yoken
and Starthrush usually come by the school bus. Most of the
children of course are from Coppitts Green.'
Mrs Baker looked at her watch.
'Goodness nearly twelve thirty. I must get back and give
my husband his lunch. He's an invalid.'
'Oh, I'm terribly sorry.'
'Parkinson's. He's marvellous though and they do have
good drugs now. Look why don't you come over and have
something with us tonight?'
'Oh, I couldn't . . . the Ryders . . .'
'I understood they were away for a few days. Oh, I see –
your fiancé . . . of course; but if you are at a loose end just
dial 204 and I'll give you instructions on how to reach the
house. Really.'
'Thank you so much, Mrs Baker. I'm going to enjoy
being here.'

'And I'm going to enjoy having you; a brisk modern young girl like you. It will do the school the world of good. Are you going back to the house?'

'No, I'm going to potter. I want to explore; find my way about.'

We parted at the gate, Mrs Baker setting off towards Coppitts Green. I looked up the valley towards Starthrush, but I guessed it was a couple of miles or so to that village and sharp little hunger pains were beginning to gnaw at my stomach. Maybe I'd pop back into the house, have a snack and spend the afternoon exploring. After all, I followed Mrs Baker, who by now was out of sight.

It really was a splendid scene, the soft green hills surmounted by limestone crags, the great cliff overhanging Coppitts Green and the village itself nestling into the hillside, while beyond, Wherndale stretched as far as the eye could see, gradually being enveloped by a heat haze.

When I got to the house it was empty. Mrs Bargett probably went home for lunch to prepare vegetables for the evening meal. I wondered if everyone left their front doors unlocked in this fashion and then supposed that they did; what was there to fear in a small place like this where everyone knew everyone else?

The first thing I noticed was the silence in the house; it hung heavily like an echo, so that one actually listened to it. The sound of silence . . . Everything seemed not only silent but preternaturally still and a sunbeam in the lounge appeared to have ensnared the dust and held it petrified.

I realized that something had frightened me and that my flesh was cold, that I dared not advance a step for fear of I knew not what. I was frozen into immobility, like everything else. I looked towards the window, and through the thick leaves saw the brilliant green backdrop of Coppitts Fell and the chalky boulders that dotted it.

Had I heard something? Was Mrs Bargett there after all? As I called her name, I realized I was trembling and I called it louder to show whoever it was that I was not afraid. But there was no reply.

And then the spell, or whatever it was, snapped and I could see that the dust was dancing in the sunbeam and suddenly the house began to creak and sigh as places usually do and the noise of the brook obtruded again. What had happened in those few frozen moments of time I did not know, but I was no longer hungry; I was no longer happy and eager and looking forward to my new job. The gaiety of the day had gone for me and I felt oppressed and anxious. Why had I forgotten Peter? Where was he? Was this some kind of premonition? Had something happened to Peter?

And then there was a sound at the door and I turned as it opened and saw him and ran into his arms.

Two

B ut it wasn't Peter; it was his cousin Tim. They were so alike it made my heart lurch; but whereas Peter had curly hair permanently ruffled, Tim's was dark and straight. He was also shorter than Peter.

'I'm terribly sorry,' I laughed and drew away from him. He was laughing too and dusting himself in an embarrassed way.

'I thought you were Peter.'

'Isn't he here?'

'Oh, you don't know . . . ?'

'Look, let's say how do you do. How do you do. I am Tim Ryder, you must be Jocasta Oaks. I do apologize for being away when you came; but there's a three-day event at York and both Agnes and I—'

'Don't apologize. How do you do, Tim? It's given me a nice chance to settle down and I've been to the school and seen Mrs Baker, and . . .' I realized I was prattling like a nervous schoolgirl myself. Suddenly I sat down.

'. . . and *I* don't know where Peter is.'

'But he was going to bring you from Leeds. Actually, Agnes and I thought you might like the time alone together – that's why we weren't too fussed about getting back. But haven't you *heard* from Peter?'

'Not a thing and, you know, it sounds absurd, but I don't know his telephone number at home, or at work if it comes to that.'

I stopped abruptly and thought. Yes, it was absurd; but then I'd never had any need to ring him, he always rang me or came.

'Do you know Peter's number?' I asked.

'Of course. Let's ring it now.'

Tim strolled purposefully to the phone, consulted a book and then dialled several digits. I could hear the phone ringing and then Tim replaced the receiver.

'Of course, he wouldn't be at home at lunchtime.'

'And his office?'

'Peter doesn't have an office. He works from home. What *has* he told you about himself, Jocasta?'

'Very little . . .' My voice trailed off and I looked at the floor.

Tim went over to a table and picked up a box.

'Cigarette?'

I took one and he lit it for me.

'Sherry? Yes, I think one for both of us.' He disappeared and came back with a tray and two glasses. I sipped the amber liquid, hoping it would clear my mind, remove my fear and confusion.

'I don't really know Peter very well,' I said at last. 'I know it sounds stupid.'

'But he told us you were going to be married.'

'Did he? He didn't tell me.' I smiled. 'Now that *is* like Peter. I'm beginning to feel he does exist after all; do you know, a moment ago, I wondered if I'd imagined the whole thing.'

'What whole thing?'

'Peter, the house, you. It was the oddest feeling . . .'

'I expect you're upset. But Peter did suggest you came up here?'

'No, I did. He said he wasn't going to be in London much and I told him I'd get a job in the North, in Leeds, and then a few days later he said he'd had dinner with you and Agnes and they were looking for a temporary schoolmistress, and then I went to Greece for three weeks and when I came back it was all fixed up.'

'When did you last see Peter?' Tim inquired.

'A week ago. He wanted me to drive up with him, but I said

I had a lot to do and wanted to see my sister, who has just come back from holiday, and tell her what I was doing, and he said he'd meet me. I caught the early train from London and . . .'

'He wasn't there?'

'No, so I came on by train and bus . . .'

'Bus! Why didn't you get a taxi?'

'Well, they said a direct bus was just leaving, and a taxi was rather expensive . . .'

'True, it would have cost you a tenner. I'm terribly sorry, Jocasta; at least did Mrs Bargett look after you?'

'Oh, she was marvellous; but . . . do you think there is anything to worry about with Peter?'

'Of course not. I just think he's damned inconsiderate. Honestly, a girl gets herself up here to be with him . . .'

'And he isn't there. It's not even near Leeds,' I said reproachfully.

'Oh, yes, it is. It only takes an hour or so by car. You came a roundabout way. Don't worry, we'll soon have everything fixed up. Look, I'm terribly sorry, Jocasta, but I actually have to go again. I only came to get some things for Aggie, she's not well . . .'

Tim looked suddenly agitated.

'Oh, I'm terribly sorry. Peter said she suffered bad health . . .'

'She has these awful migraines. They are absolutely incapacitating, frightening. One minute she's OK, the next she's not. She's tried all kinds of things, treatments, cures. Now she's just resigned to leading as quiet a life as possible. Luckily I'm at home, so I can usually help.'

'Is it as bad as that? That you have to be around?'

'Well, it helps. She seems to rely on me a great deal and gets rather frantic if I'm not around when she has an attack. Excuse me, Jocasta, I promised I wouldn't be long.'

'Can I help?'

'Oh no. I know where everything is.'

I smoked another cigarette and waited thoughtfully in the drawing room for Tim. We teachers all consider ourselves

15

students of elementary psychology, but Agnes' symptoms seemed a classic case of neurosis. If she wasn't ill, her brother might marry, go away. Funny that Peter had never mentioned any of this to me.

Funny that Peter had never mentioned anything much about his home, or his family if it came to that. Funny that I hadn't asked him. What *does* make a person so stupid? Love of course.

Tim was down before I had finished the cigarette, a case in his hand.

'Jocasta, once again, I'm terribly sorry . . .'

'Tim, it's quite all right. It's marvellous that I have a roof over my head. I do hope Agnes is better soon. I'm longing to meet her.'

'And she you. It will be great company for her. She often gets over these attacks in a day or two. I'll be in touch.'

I stood at the door and watched Tim get into his car. I hadn't heard the car draw up during my curious reverie just before he'd come in. What had happened to me? It was a noisy sports car and he shot off, waving, in a cloud of black smoke. Surely I'd have heard it arriving?

I went up to my room and finished unpacking. Stowed the cases away at the top of the wardrobe. The sun had gone round the back of the house and my room was in the shade. I looked out of the window and watched the brook rushing by towards the bridge where it joined the Whern. The bridge formed a crossroads with a pub, the Three Horses, on one side, the local sports club above that and then the roads, one leading to Starthrush, one to Skipton, one into the village and up towards the fell and the other that ran past Croft House and up on the other side of the valley towards Grassington, where the Whern joined the river Wharfe and became Wharfedale.

I had a good view of the village and the valley from my window. The irregular grey slate roofs tumbled over one another at all angles and in all shapes. The church was behind us but I could see the maypole that stood in the small village green. With the sun on it from the south-west, the cliff now looked majestic and splendid, not sinister at all. It really was a sight, growing more spectacular the more one saw of it. Why, if it should fall, it would cover the upper road, the sports club and possibly the pub.

A sudden thump in the bowels of the house made me jump. My heart started to race. I'd known I was listening all the time, for what? The telephone? The door? Then came the reassuring sound of the hoover. Mrs Bargett! I looked at my watch. It was only two o'clock. I combed my hair and dabbed on some make-up. I'd take a book and wander; rest maybe by the river somewhere up the dale.

Mrs Bargett was in the drawing room and switched off the cleaner giving me her cheery smile.

'There you are, miss! Did you have some lunch?'

'I wasn't hungry.' Yet at one time I had been ravenous.

'Could you eat a sandwich now, miss? It's the excitement, I expect.'

'I think I could, Mrs Bargett, if it isn't too much—'

'No trouble at all, dear. I have my lunch here early and then go home to tidy a bit. I've got some nice cold ham. You wait here.'

'Mayn't I came into the kitchen? I don't want to put you out.'

Mrs Bargett smiled.

'I expect you find it more cosy there, dear. Missing your mother, are you?'

'Mrs Bargett, I'm twenty-four! My mother died when I was a little girl.'

'Oh, I am sorry to hear that—' we were walking along the hall towards the kitchen – 'about your mother. There, dear, you sit at the table. White bread or brown?'

'White, please.'

I watched her get out a lovely crusty loaf from the bread bin and slice a whole cooked ham. The kitchen, filled with the afternoon sun, was a homely, pretty place with a large table in the centre and well-scrubbed red tiles on the floor.

'I'll put the kettle on. I can always do with a cup of tea, can't you? There, you tuck into that.'

The sandwich looked marvellous and I realized I was starving.

'Tim was here,' I said, my mouth unpardonably full. Mrs Bargett's back seemed to stiffen but she didn't turn around.

'Mr Tim came and went?'

'His sister's not well . . .'

'Oh, one of her attacks . . .' Mrs Bargett's voice was grim.

'Does she have them often?'

Mrs Bargett poured the water from the huge kettle on the Aga into the teapot, put the lid firmly on it and covered it with a cosy. Then she placed a large capable hand on the pot and looked at me.

'Often enough; especially if anything upsets her. She must have an absolutely quiet life. I say it's not natural myself. She must be about the same age as yourself.'

'Yes, she is, exactly, and her brother is two years older. There's two years between the cousins. Peter's twenty-eight. Oh, by the way, Tim rang him. He's not home. I expect Tim will ring him again tonight, or I will.' I knew Tim had his number. It would be in the book. I was beginning to feel very annoyed with Peter. He'd made rather a fool of me; thank goodness I was going to enjoy my job and being here or I'd go straight back to London. 'Is Agnes pretty?'

'Miss Agnes? Well—' Mrs Bargett poured the tea and brought two cups to the table, setting one before me; then she sat down and stirred hers thoughtfully – 'she's not what you'd call *pretty*. Striking maybe; good looking. But I've never known her have any men friends ever since she came home from Cambridge. It's just her and her brother.'

'And does he have, er, girlfriends?'

'No, no, not that I can recall; he writes a lot, you know – very bookish, always in his room. You can hear the typewriting machine go tap, tap.'

'And what does Agnes do all day?'

'Oh, she reads. She spends a lot of time in her room, resting I daresay. Oh, they have the odd people for meals: Mrs Baker when her husband's up to it – he's an invalid you know and has a wheelchair; the Rector, who is very nice; the doctor from Grassington sometimes. There is a couple from Hammersleigh in the next valley they're friendly with, the Fullertons. She's very nice, a painter, and she comes up alone sometimes to paint in the valley and will stop here a night or two; but she's just had a baby, so I suppose she'll have her hands full for the time being. But no, they don't lead a very social life. They seem to like it. Oh and Mr Peter; he comes quite often in the summer.'

Peter. I got up suddenly. Any minute now she'd start on about Peter.

'I must let you get on, Mrs Bargett. Oh, and don't get me anything for dinner. Mrs Baker invited me. I thought the Ryders would be back. I'll ring her and tell her I can come.'

'Aye, I must get on.' Mrs Bargett, reluctantly it seemed to me – perhaps she was lonely – got up from her chair and washed the things we'd been using.

In the drawing room I picked up the telephone book I'd seen Tim use. Baker, that was it, 204. I was about to ring and thought that no, I'd wander up and see her on my tour of the village. I let the page fall open at R . . . Ryder. I looked down the list of names, no Ryder, so I turned to P. No Peter listed. I turned back to R and went carefully down the list of names; likewise again with P. I couldn't see Peter's number any-where. Yet I'd seen Tim consult the book; this very book.

It was cold in the room, previously warmed by the beams of the sun; now only one corner was still bathed in light. The contrast between the shadow and the sun seemed to me intense as though I was standing in the dark looking towards the light; a very bright beam of light.

There was something about this house I didn't like, this ordinary house standing in a village street. It had an atmos-phere; it had a presence of something I couldn't place. I wanted to be out of it into the sunlight again. In my hurry to get out, I even left behind the book I was going to take with me to read.

I turned left outside the gate and walked up into the village following the line of the stream, or beck as they call it in Yorkshire. The waters of the beck bubbling over the stones was so clear that the myriad colours were intense – greens and greys, blues and dull pinks. It seemed a very normal, ordinary thing, the little stream, and I leaned over the stone wall gazing at it, mesmerized by its swift easy flow. As I continued my walk, the beck soon disappeared between rows of stone cottages and my way was uphill now until I came to the village store on the corner, which I judged to be a good place to ask where the Bakers lived.

Inside the store it was dark and there was a pungent mixture of smells from humbugs to boot polish. In one corner was a grille for a post office and in another a stack of fresh vegetables in boxes. Shelves rose to the ceiling, stacked with every imaginable household need. A man in a green overall was counting change behind the grille and looked up at me over his glasses.

'Good afternoon. Could you tell me where Mrs Baker lives?'

The man continued to look at me without saying a word. Then he opened his mouth and closed it again still wordlessly.

'Baker . . .' he said at last. 'You'll be the new schoolteacher; staying at Croft House.'

'And if you're the postmaster, that's how you know everything,' I said.

The man smiled.

'Not much goes on in this village without I come to hear of it sooner or later.'

'I'll be on my best behaviour,' I said.

The man came slowly from behind the counter still looking at me over his glasses. I couldn't tell if he liked what he saw or not. He stood by my side at the door and began to point. 'If you see the small bridge, and that lane of cottages . . . well, you go straight up and past and the Bakers' house is the one standing on its own in a fair-sized garden. End House, it's called. It's the last house in the village.'

'Oh, thanks, so much Mr . . .'

'Parkin, miss – Parkins Stores.' He turned round and pointed solemnly to the legend above the door. 'Established by my grandfather in eighteen hundred and ninety-seven.'

'I'll be seeing a lot of you Mr Parkin,' I said. 'Goodbye.'

'Good day to you, miss.'

The bridge he referred to was not the main one I'd come over the day before but a smaller bridge that ran over the beck, now back in sight again. The beck was almost the level of the road and there was a grassy bank on either side strewn with shrubs and trees. An attractive row of cottages stood directly on the road, which was cobbled and without a pavement. I was walking quite steeply now and could see ahead to the bottom of the fell and a gate that led into it. And then to one side, enclosed by a high hedge, was the last house in the village, End House. It was perched up against the fell and had an even more spectacular view than Croft House, as it had a perspective of the whole of the village and the valley to either side. The garden was large and beautifully kept with wooden arches covered with climbing rose and clematis and the house itself, of grey Yorkshire stone, was clad partly in ivy and partly in wistaria, which trailed over the white portal of the front door.

There was no sign of the Bakers in the front garden and I rang rather timidly, hoping I wasn't disturbing an afternoon nap. The front door leading into the hall was open and I peeped in. Everything was silent; perhaps they were asleep. I began to creep away when Mrs Baker, spectacles in her hand, appeared from the back of the house.

'Why, Miss Oaks! We're in the back garden, dear, it's so sheltered. Do come around.'

'Oh, Mrs Baker I'm terribly sorry, I'm sure I'm disturbing a siesta or something, but I was exploring the village and thought I'd come to tell you that I would love to come to dinner, if it's still all right.'

'Why, that's lovely, my dear; come and meet Herbert.'

Mr Baker was stretched out on a cane chair, his feet and legs covered by a blanket, facing the sun. He wore a white straw hat and sunglasses and he looked to me as though he'd been asleep.

'Herbert, darling, this is Jocasta Oaks, I was telling you about her. Miss Oaks, my husband.'

He held out a thin, slightly trembling hand, but his clasp was warm and firm. He was, I would have judged, a tall man with a fine craggy face and a thin white moustache.

'Jane was just telling me all about you, Miss Oaks, and what a fine help to her you would be. I'm so glad to meet you. Sit down.'

'Really . . . I'm coming tonight.'

'Sit down.' He pointed rather imperiously to a wicker chair and I sank obediently on to it realizing that, in his time, Mr Baker had been the managing director of a large firm of wool manufacturers in Bradford and was used to commanding.

'We were just going to have a cup of tea,' Mrs Baker said. 'You chat to Herbert while I get it.'

'Let me help you.'

'No, Herbert likes company, especially female company!'

Herbert was indeed looking at me with great interest.

'So you're Miss Oaks – ' he nodded again – 'a fine help to my wife. She's had too much to do at that school, coping with nearly thirty children aged five to eleven, can you believe it. She's in her sixties, you know, I wanted her to leave; but she loves it so much, a born teacher. I can't really force her to give up something she loves so much, especially with me.'

His face saddened and he glanced at his shrunken body.

'Parkinson's, a horrible thing but better than it was with these new drugs. I feel almost a new man, though it's hard to walk. I'm over seventy, I can give Jane a few years . . . ah.' He looked up and smiled at his wife who advanced with the tea tray, a silver service and delicate bone chine, beautifully set out on a lace cloth.

'We don't have any living-in help; you can't get it, you know. But I am lucky enough to have a woman in for a few hours three days a week, Marjory Bargett's sister, Clara Doyle, who lost her husband tragically a few years ago.'

'A road accident,' Mr Baker added, 'drunken driving, not John Doyle, of course, some drunken young idiot racing through the dales after a pub crawl.'

'It was disgraceful. He was merely fined and lost his licence.'

'Should have been hanged,' opined Mr Baker, 'I'd do it meself.'

'Oh darling, don't be so atavistic. You'll shock Miss Oaks.'

'Couldn't you call me Jocasta?' I asked. 'I know it's a mouthful, but so is Miss Oaks! Jo for short, if you like.'

'I prefer Jocasta,' Mr Baker said, looking at me, 'a pretty name for a pretty face. Jocasta, I like it.'

'Don't mind Herbert, he's harmless.' Mrs Baker smilingly handed me my tea.

Mr Baker snorted. 'Have to be! Wasn't always so.'

'Now dear, don't let's have stories about your past, mostly made up . . .' She gazed at him fondly.

They were a nice couple. I knew they had children and grandchildren and I was always envious of families with a lovely elderly pair at the head who lived in houses such as this, in villages like Coppitts Green and had huge family parties at Christmas that exuded warmth and togetherness.

Mrs Baker too had had her feet up and with the tray at her side she went back to her low comfortable cane chair placed out of the sun.

'Oh, this is nice! I don't really know that I want school to begin. What heavenly weather for September. Of course we are sheltered here. People always think the Yorkshire Dales is a bleak place but we're in the shadow of the Pennines; it's north Yorkshire on the moors that you get the really bad weather. Did you know Yorkshire at all before you came up, Jocasta?'

'No, not at all. I've been to Scotland, but apart from that never further north than the outskirts of Birmingham, where I've got an uncle who we used to stay with after we came back from India. My father sent us back to school after my mother died.'

Mrs Baker's kind face creased with sympathy.

'Oh, I'm sorry to hear that. How old were you, dear?'

'I was twelve, my sister Sarah was fifteen. My father was a schoolmaster in Calcutta and my mother died very suddenly of typhoid contracted on a visit to the hills during the wet weather. We thought we were just coming home for a holiday but Daddy decided to send us to boarding school and he went back to India. He died soon after too. I think he died of a broken heart; he was only forty.'

Mr Baker grunted and looked at me sharply. I'd told this story so often that I liked to think I could tell it without bathos, without appearing to be asking for sympathy, which I didn't need. After all, these events took place half my lifetime ago. What I didn't tell them was something we didn't find out until we were grown up, that my mother had told my father she was going to leave us and had gone to the hills with a very handsome Indian, a soldier with whom she had fallen in love. It always seemed to me an awfully harsh sort of justice that what had happened to her had been the result of this amorous adventure. Though we loved my father we knew he was a dull, unexciting man; that my mother was an intense, impetuous woman who wrote poetry and painted rather well. Because, in a foreign country like India, one is brought up by servants, our childhood had been spent in relative ignorance of the lack of passion in our parents' marriage, of my mother's frustration and unhappiness, my father's intense preoccupation with his books and the fauna and flora of the Indian subcontinent.

All these things we didn't know until it was too late to be important. Yet in a funny way it had been important to me and I was filled with a desire to know more about that beautiful but sadly unfulfilled woman whom I had loved but hardly remembered and whom I was said so much to resemble.

Yet in the end, I took after my father and became a schoolteacher and Sarah, always studious and serious, fell in love with a soldier like my mother, and married a member of the regular Army and lived an exciting mobile life here and abroad.

But it was true to say that my father had probably died of a broken heart; broken by my mother's infidelity and death. But what can we ever know of human emotions, now hidden and buried in the past?

Mrs Baker was shaking her head. She had picked up some crochet work and I watched her fingers, long and delicate, bent by arthritis, weaving in and out.

'So your uncle looked after you?'

'He was our guardian and we stayed with him during the holidays. But Sarah got married when she was only nineteen and then she kind of looked after me, though her husband's a soldier and much of the time she wasn't here to do that! Now they're in Caterham and I suppose you can say that where they are in England is my home; my uncle died last year.'

'Well, you look very well on it,' Mr Baker said gruffly.

'Oh, I think I've survived! One adapts in life. It also makes you independent . . .'

Mrs Baker put down her crochet and looked at me over her spectacles.

'But you're thinking of settling down yourself, your young man . . .'

I felt myself blushing in the hot sun.

'I think my young man has jilted me! I am doomed to be a spinster schoolmistress.'

'You haven't heard from him yet!'

'Do you know Peter?' I leaned forward and looked at her.

'Oh, we know Peter very well,' she said with emphasis. 'He almost grew up here, like a brother to Agnes and Tim. He was a very alert young boy, rather a scamp; but we don't see so much of him now. I'd like to think he was going to settle down. It would do him good – ' she looked at me curiously – 'and he'd be very lucky to have you.'

Her tone of voice implied that I was more than Peter deserved and I resented it although I said nothing; but, like Mrs Bargett, Mrs Baker had an odd note in her voice when Peter's name was mentioned.

'What does Peter do now, dear?' Mrs Baker continued in a more normal voice. 'Refresh my memory, would you?'

'He used to be in the Army. I met him through Bob my brother-in-law; they were in the same regiment. We sort of took a big shine to each other almost immediately; but then Peter had to move north. I think his business was in some kind of import-export; we never really discussed it very much. I know it sounds funny . . .'

'Oh, business is like that,' Mr Baker said. 'One of our greatest friends, Jerry Henley – you remember, my dear – would talk to us about everything under the sun but about what he did. It appeared that as long as he made money, and he made plenty, he did almost anything – bought, sold, wheeled and dealt.'

'Yes, I think Peter's like that.' I was grateful to Mr Baker for being so understanding. 'He isn't long out of the Army and I think he's finding his way.'

'But dear,' Mrs Baker broke in gently. 'Shouldn't you know a little more about the man you are about to marry?'

There was an awkward silence as I looked over the roofs of the village towards the valley. From where I was, I could just see the thin line of the road I'd come along the day before. 'Actually, I might as well be honest, we aren't exactly on the point of marriage. I think Tim thought it would sound more . . . *respectable* if I had a "fiancé."'

Mrs Baker threw back her head and laughed.

'Oh, how like Tim! As if I'd care. You are hopelessly head over heels in love with this young man and you just want to be where he is.'

'Yes.'

'Then Tim should have said so. How silly. My dear, are they back? I saw Tim's car just as I was passing the house on my way home. The garage doors were slightly open.'

'Tim has been and gone. Agnes has one of her migraines. They're in York.'

'And of course she'll want Tim by her side.' Mrs Baker's tone of voice had altered and I was intrigued. I looked at her curiously and she understood my expression. 'Agnes is a hypochondriac in my opinion. She can turn those attacks on and off at a whim. She uses them to manipulate people. She never had them as a child. They only started at Cambridge.'

'But haven't they been investigated?'

'They've been investigated all right; but Agnes is a case, you'll see.'

'Oh dear . . .'

'Oh, don't be alarmed. She's a very nice girl; very charming and sweet. You'll like her; but if I were you I would regard living in that house as a purely temporary measure . . .'

And as she continued speaking, it seemed that I ceased to hear her; because already I'd decided that Croft House and I were incompatible, and I wondered what it was about the place that both attracted and repelled me? That somehow frightened me?

Three

I sat late into the afternoon talking to the Bakers, too lazy to leave the lovely fragrant garden. There was plenty of time to explore. They'd only come to the valley when his illness forced Mr Baker into premature retirement, but that was fifteen years ago. The post of headmistress at Coppitts Green school had fallen vacant at about the same time.

'Of course we'd known the Dales all our lives; but we had a big house just outside Bradford and four children to bring up and it wasn't practical to live there then though we always wanted to, especially Coppitts Green. It's remote enough to be quiet, yet it's accessible.'

'But aren't you bothered by tourists in the summer?'

'At weekends they're a bit of a bother; but we stay at home then and we wouldn't know they were here; we see them climbing the Fell but we stay off the roads. Then of course, there are the serious potholing parties all the year round; we're just over the other side of the Fell from Kettlewell, which is great caving country.'

'I'd hate it,' I said. 'I've a horror of dark caverns.'

'I did it a lot when I was a young man,' Mr Baker said, 'but I gave it up when we had a family. It is dangerous; only last spring three fine young men were lost, students.'

'It doesn't bear thinking about,' said his wife, 'such a waste. Oh, look at the time. Stephen will be here any minute.'

I looked up at her.

'Oh dear, you're having visitors . . .'

'Stephen is our son, dear. He's a solicitor in Skipton and has a little flat there.'

28

'But he likes mother's home cooking,' laughed his father. 'He stays here about three nights a week.'

'And he's not married?'

'No.' His mother paused and her face suddenly became serious. 'He had rather a fancy for Agnes once and we don't know if it's over or not; but she'd never have anything to do with him. He'd ask her to the dances and so on, but she'd develop one of her "heads". I think he's given up, though sometimes he'll pop in to see them. Now I must put the beef on; he had business in Pateley and he said he'd be here early.'

'I'd better go and change,' I said.

'Oh, you're fine, dear. We're very informal here; you look pretty in that skirt and blouse.'

'Well, at least let me help you lay the table.'

'If it makes you feel better.'

I carried the tray in for her from the lawn while she helped Herbert into his wheelchair and slowly wheeled him into the house.

Stephen Baker wasn't early after all. He was very late and we had started dinner before he arrived, his mother not wanting to ruin the roast. He rushed into the dining room like a large playful puppy, all arms and legs, hugged his mother and never stopped apologizing.

'Mother, I'm sorry . . . finished early . . . gave Michael Jones a game of golf . . . went on for hours . . . tried to ring you . . . line out of order . . . Oh!'

He saw me and his fingers went involuntarily to his tie.

'Darling, this is Jocasta Oaks, who has come to the school for a year to teach the infants. Jocasta, my son, Stephen.'

Stephen was large and cheerful, but as he shook my hand his face, suddenly grave, made him look more thoughtful and mature. He was dressed in flannels and a tweed sports jacket, a green shirt and some sort of club tie. He looked the very epitome of the successful young country solicitor: extrovert and uncomplicated.

'Forgive us for starting, Steve. Your father does like his roast pink . . .'

'Oh yes, wouldn't do for Dad to have overdone beef: I'll just wash my hands.'

When Stephen came back he glanced at me before sitting down and I returned his friendly grin.

After he arrived, talk was mainly about sport and local gossip. I listened with interest but I was tired and after a while I looked at my watch, wondering if I could decently go.

'Do you mind?' I asked. 'School tomorrow. I need a good night's sleep.'

'My goodness, does term start tomorrow?' Stephen got up and looked at his mother. 'How the summer holiday has flown. Mother, I'll walk Jocasta home.'

'That would be nice, dear. The Ryders are away.'

I looked at Stephen but his face betrayed no expression. Had he been hoping to see Agnes? I was more and more curious to seet this woman who seemed a classic case of neurotic frustration. I imagined her as some sort of Brontë-like creature, yet she had excited the interest of this extrovert young man. Outside, the moonlight had the luminosity of day, so that the contrast with the dark shadows made by the buildings we passed contrived an eerie, ghost-like effect. There was a lovely smell of wood smoke lingering in the air together with a heaviness that was almost like midsummer. However, I shivered.

'Cold?' Stephen sounded suprised. 'We'll soon be there. It's been a glorious summer. Hope you like it here; it will be very different from London.'

'Oh, I think I will. I shall have lots to do at school and Agnes and Tim—'

'You haven't met them yet of course.'

'I met Tim briefly today. They were in York and Agnes had one of her attacks. He came back to get some things for her.'

'What sort of things?'

'Clothes, I think.'

'You'd have thought she had enough things with her. What could she need if she was in bed? Besides they always stay with a friend who is her own age.'

'I don't know what he could have wanted,' I said. 'It didn't really occur to me to ask.' We were walking across the small bridge over the beck.

'I had a great old thing going for Agnes at one time. She's an amazingly attractive girl; but she's very cold . . . nothing came through. Got nowhere. I hear you're engaged to Peter?'

'Well, not officially engaged.' We hadn't mentioned Peter all night. Every time I thought about it, the whole thing seemed so extraordinary that I put it to the back of my mind.

'But you have an understanding?'

'I don't know that we have, really.'

Stephen sensed that I didn't want to talk about it and tactfully remained silent until we got to the door.

As usual, it was unlocked. As we pushed open the door, the moonlight so illuminated the hall that at first I thought someone had put on a light. I stood on the threshold listening. Stephen seemed to stiffen beside me.

'What is it?' he whispered.

'Can't you hear it?'

'What?'

'The silence. You can *hear* the silence in this house.'

As he moved past me and switched on the light, everything came to life again; the beck babbled, the house creaked and the trees sighed in the garden. Stephen was looking at me oddly, his hand still on the light switch.

'You can *hear* the silence?'

'Yes. It's odd. It's happened to me a couple of times since I arrived. Oh, it's silly; it soon passes. I expect I'm not used to the country. In the city, the infernal din shuts out everything else. Will you have a drink before you go, says she, offering largesse in a house that doesn't belong to her.'

I didn't want Stephen to go; to be alone . . .

31

I think he sensed it because he took my arm and led me into the drawing room.

'The Ryders are very hospitable; I'm sure they won't mind. Just a weak whisky and water if I may?'

'Would you get it? You must know better than I where everything is. Oh . . . !'

Propped up on the mantlepiece was a small buff envelope. At its side was a note written in the untutored hand of Mrs Bargett: 'Miss, this came for you this afternoon.'

'Oaks, c/o Ryder, Croft House, Coppitts Green.' I could feel Stephen's presence beside me as I tore open the envelope.

> SORRY DARLING ABOUT CONFUSION. BUSI-
> NESS DIFFICULTIES NECESSITATE PRESENCE
> ABROAD. WRITING. PETER.

The words seemed to dance around and I sat down heavily.

'Bad news?'

'It's Peter. He wasn't here to meet me yesterday.'

I handed him the telegram. Stephen read it silently and then disappeared. When he came back he had two glasses on a tray and a jug of water.

'Have a snifter. Good for the nerves. A shock is it?'

'It's awful. I came up here especially to see more of Peter. Why on earth would I have come otherwise? Now he's not even in the country . . .'

'It's nice for my mother. She's very arthritic in the winter. Think of that.'

'Yes, but I'm staying with people I don't know, in a house I don't like . . .' I trailed off and saw he was looking at me with concern.

'You don't like this house?'

'No. It's spooky . . . I . . . I don't know what it is. I feel it's cold and unfriendly . . .'

'Like Agnes,' Stephen murmured. 'Perhaps she imprints her personality on the house.' He sounded bitter.

'Oh, I'll get over it, but I can't stay here for ever.'

'Move in with my mother and dad, they'll love it.'

'No, I can't do that! No, if I stay, I'll get rooms or a small cottage to myself . . .'

'*If* you stay. But surely . . .'

'Oh, Stephen. I feel so confused. It's such a mess. Of course I don't want to let your mother down. But without Peter . . .'

A cold Yorkshire winter stretched in front of me. I could imagine the fell covered with snow and the roads impassable.

'Look, he says he's writing. He may be back very soon. Cheer up . . . Peter's a bit like this, you know. A law unto himself.'

I shook my head refusing to be cheered.

'I'm very worried about Peter, Stephen. I feel there's something not *right*. I've tried to keep it from myself but now I can't . . .'

'How do you mean not *right*?'

'The whole thing's funny. He was perfectly all right a couple of weeks ago in London. *He* arranged all this. I thought at first it was like him not to be at the station. Now I'm not so sure. Peter's impulsive, but I don't think he's thoughtless; not so thoughtless that he would make me give up my room, come two hundred miles for nothing. I think Peter would have make a very great effort to be there. Something's wrong.'

'With him?'

'I don't know. I think he's in trouble. I never knew what he did. Now I wonder if it was something shady, you know . . . illegal. He always had a lot of money; yet he only left the Army two years ago.'

'How did you meet him?'

'At my sister's. He was staying with them in Caterham for a regimental reunion.'

'Well your brother-in-law should know if he's doing anything shady. I never see him myself.' Stephen reflectively poured another Scotch. I hadn't touched mine. 'You care a lot about him I suppose, to have come all this way?'

'Yes, I do. Oh, I was restless, needed a change. I'd been at my last school since I finished my training. But Peter was exciting; utterly different . . .'

'From all the dull young men who'd courted you before?'

'All?' I gave an ironic laugh. 'I was the proverbial spinster teacher, coming home at night to my chaste bedsitter, going on courses in the holidays. I remember meeting Peter at Bob and Sarah's and thinking he would never notice me; but he saw me looking at him and came straight across the room to me and from that moment I was transformed.'

'Fairy princess . . .' Stephen said softly.

'What?'

'You're so pretty . . .'

'I was t-terribly shy,' I stammered, 'Unsure of myself. Although it attracted men, it put them off too when they found how shy I was, how uncertain of myself. They were usually shy like me. Then Peter . . . Just his love and warmth and confidence. Sarah said she'd never known anyone change so much in such a short time. Sarah's very practical,' I added, thinking how much my sister disapproved of my having an affair; she still belonged to the school that believed there was some hidden virtue in 'saving oneself' for marriage, or perhaps she didn't like to think of anyone enjoying themselves purely and simply, without fear or responsibility. Yes, we had been carefree.

Stephen was looking at the clock on the mantlepiece, which had just chimed eleven.

'I must be getting back or Mum will be wondering what I'm up to. Would you like to come back to us for tonight?'

'Oh no, I shall be all right.'

'But the house . . .'

'Oh, that was silly. I shall be perfectly all right, and thank you Stephen, for listening to all this nonsense. I'll feel quite differently tomorrow.'

We both got up.

'I hope so, and that you hear from Peter. Will you . . . will you let me know if I can do anything. If he doesn't turn up? If you're unhappy?'

'Yes, of course I will and thank you. Tim will sort everything out, I expect. After all, he and Peter are first cousins.'

'Well, don't forget, I'm always buzzing about if you want me, and if you don't want to tell Mother, you can ring me. I'm in the book. Stephen Baker, Solicitor, 42A Sheep Street, Skipton.'

I saw him to the door and after a polite goodnight and thank you, I locked it behind me and, putting out the downstairs lights, mounted the stairs to bed.

The moonlight streamed through the landing window, so bright that it looked like a sunbeam as the dust danced and whirled about in it. I paused by the window and was aware of the beck crackling below and, looking out, I at once saw the cliff rising huge and stark and seeming so near that I felt I had only to put a hand out to touch it. It was an illusion, of course, the base of the cliff was about half a mile away; there was the village, the beck and the River Whern itself between me and the cliff . . . and yet. I pressed my face to the window and stared at it and as I did, a cloud obscured the moon and I was plunged in darkness. I stood there petrified, freezing terror numbed my body and I knew I could move neither upwards, nor down to regain the safety of the street. It was as though a great weight was pressing on me and I closed my eyes and started to sob. Then silence, and all I could hear was my sobbing, and the moon was out again and the cliff – why, now it was at its proper distance, and all the village, well a good half of it, lay between me and it, and the bough of the elm tree in the garden tapped on the window, wafting gently like a fan. I wiped my eyes and my fingers were wet. I felt ashamed and crept on upstairs to bed.

'SORRY DARLING ABOUT CONFUSION.' I awoke with the words reverberating in my brain. I was hot and had been tossing in the bed; some of the bedclothes were on the floor and my nightdress was sticky. CONFUSION, CONFUSION, CONFUSION, said my brain. 'BUSINESS DIFFICULTIES', it thumped out. What difficulties? Was Peter going to go to prison? But Peter was an Army man, used to strict discipline. I could no more imagine him doing anything dishonest than my brother-in-law. Besides, everyone here knew him. They would know if he was up to no good. Of course he'd often had to slip abroad, to Frankfurt, Basle, Lyons, just for a few days. But why had he had to go abroad now?

I heard the church clock strike three. If I didn't calm down and go to sleep I'd be a wreck in the morning. I covered myself, lay on my back and started taking deep breaths. One, two, three . . . one, two three . . .

The sound came from inside the house, from underneath me. I listened and then I heard it again. It was an irregular bumping sound like someone walking with a limp very softly across the floor, back and forth, back and forth . . .

My flesh started to crawl again and I broke out into a sweat – I could feel it on the palms of my hands and I tugged compulsively at the sheet.

Well, said my practical self, if there was anyone in the house I'd better see . . . why, they left the front doors unlocked in these parts. I sat on the side of my bed listening, but the noise had stopped, all I heard now was a little furtive rustling that seemed to come from a cupboard in the corner. Mice! No, no mouse had made that limping sound. I went to the door and then my courage faltered. I could no more go exploring in that dark house than . . . I locked the door of my room and took a flying leap back into bed.

I listened for some time longer and I heard the first early morning birds break into the dawn chorus before I fell asleep.

Four

The school term started on a Thursday. I could see it was an inconvenient day for parents, but for staff it was marvellous. Two days to get over the torture of registers, new pupils, new curricula, to sort out the trivia of the beginning of term, and then a beautiful weekend break. In Finchley we'd always started on a Monday, and by the Friday there was not a member of staff who didn't feel like, and indeed sometimes resembled, a wet rag.

In my first two days at Coppitts Green school I almost forgot everything about my previous life except my job as a teacher – getting to know my charges, making myself familiar with the routine, dividing duties with Mrs Baker. In a large London school we had all kinds of help: dinner ladies who also supervised play, secretaries, assistants of various kinds. Here there was just Mrs Baker and me. Some of the children went home for lunch, and others brought a packed lunch as there were no facilities for cooking, nor eating either if it came to that. As this hadn't occurred to me, the first day Mrs Baker very sweetly brought enough sandwiches and coffee to share with me as we supervised play. We had no time at all to ourselves until at four o'clock on Friday she plugged her electric kettle into the socket in the wall near her desk and actually put her feet up on a chair.

'Five more pupils this term! However would I have done without you?'

'I don't know how you did without me before.'

'But they're good children. They're nicely behaved, aren't they?'

'Surprisingly well behaved,' I said.

'You didn't expect it?'

'I thought children were pretty much the same every-where.'

'Oh, but in small country communities there is more discipline. Most of these children have done a few hours' work on the farm or in the house before they come here in the morning, and they go back to the same thing at night. There are very few children here whose parents are not farmers or farm labourers, and those who are not seem to assimilate the atmosphere of hard work and discipline very well. The Dabroe children for instance; you'd never know they were different from anyone else.

'Dabroe?'

'There's Natalie Dabroe in your class and Sebastian Dabroe in mine; their parents are so keen for them to assimilate.'

'I recall the name but not the girl,' I said. 'Oh, wait, tiny and very dark with bright blue eyes.'

'That's the one.'

'What's special about the Dabroes?'

'Well, if we had such a thing as a local squire it would be Jonathan Dabroe. They live in a large house across the river between here and Starthrush. There's a small bridge along the Starthrush road that leads across the river to Felton Hall, the home of the Dabroes. They've lived here for generations and Jonathan Dabroe has huge business interests and is in every way a pillar of the local community. Tessa, his wife, is on every board and committee you can imagine. But they're very nice people; amazingly simple except that Jonathan is something of a ladies' man. He's so incredibly good-looking he can't help it, though I've never heard of any real scandal attached to his hame.'

'And you would know,' I laughed.

'Yes, I should think I would.' Mrs Baker smiled and sipped the tea I had just brewed in her large brown tea-pot.

'Mrs Bargett told me I should be lonely here. I wouldn't

find anyone of – horrid phrase – my own kind. The place seems full of my own kind.'

'Oh, I suppose she's thinking solely in terms of eligible young men. People can't help thinking like that, you know, when they see a pretty girl.'

'But she knew I'd come to be with Peter!'

Mrs Baker was silent and sipped her tea looking at me.

'No other word from Peter? Stephen told me you'd had a message.'

I shook myself. I'd hardly thought of Peter for two days and unlike the previous night I'd slept like a log the night following my first day at school. There was nothing like school routine to normalize the emotions, I decided, feeling extremely self-concious and ashamed of my nervousness.

'Oh, I expect Tim will sort something out this weekend. They're back tomorrow. Mrs Baker, I really can't go on living with them you know. Would you keep your ears open for rooms or a little cottage.'

'My dear, they're like gold dust! A room, yes, maybe; but you have a suite there, you told me, and really Agnes is quite a pet, you'll see. I'm sorry this happened, because you'll find her very sympathetic, I'm sure. See how you get on with the Ryders before you move. I think they're looking forward to having you. Well, that was refreshing! I must get back and put on the dinner. Stephen is away at his old school playing rugby for the weekend.'

'Is he the only unmarried one of your children?'

'No, there's Anne, my youngest, who is a research student at Cambridge. She's in America for the summer; she'll be home in a week or two. Bill and Hilda, the other two, are married. Hilda is the next youngest to Anne and she's married to a farmer near Pickering on the north Moors. Daniel, who's forty and a doctor in Scotland, is married with five children! You'd think he'd know better, wouldn't you?'

'Perhaps he likes them.'

'You remember that book, *The Pumpkin Eater*, about the woman who was always broody? Well, Jess, his wife, is a bit like that; she's never happy unless she's got one under her arm and one in her tummy. However, they're a sweet couple and the children, are all blissful, so I can't complain. Will you come back and have a bite with us?'

'No, Mrs Bargett has cooked me something, thanks, Mrs Baker. I also want a very early night.'

We walked back together to the village, parting at the door of Croft House.

Mrs Bargett bustled towards me as soon as I turned the door knob, beaming with excitement. My heart leapt in anticipation.

'He's rung, miss!'

'Peter?'

'It was ever so faint. He said he was in Germany.'

I felt a terrible pang of wretchedness. I'd missed him.

'But why did he ring during the day? He'd know I was at school.'

'He said he'd try and ring again, miss! It was getting to the telephone, he said. He wanted you to know all was well and he'd missed you and loved you.'

'Did he say when he was coming back?'

'He said in a few weeks.'

'A few *weeks*. Oh no!' I slumped into a chair. The weeks stretched out endlessly; me entombed in this remote Yorkshire village, and soon it would be getting cold. Why were people so irrational? Why did they ring when you weren't there and say stupid things?

'Shall I make you some tea, dear?'

'No thanks Mrs B. I'll have a bath and an early dinner. I'm absolutely whacked.'

I drifted disconsolately upstairs. On the way, I looked for the door to the room under mine, the room from which I thought I'd heard the noise coming two nights before. The corridor was a long one with a great oak chest against the wall and pleasant Indian rugs on the highly polished floor. A large urn of flowers stood on the chest and two sets of brass candelabra without candles. At one end of the corridor two steps led into a smaller corridor; at the other end was the wall. There wasn't a door. It must, I thought, be in the smaller corridor at the end.

The house was a most peculiar construction, as though it had been added on to over the years. Inside it was large and irregular with passages, corridors and staircases that one didn't expect. I went down the two steps at the end and sure enough there was a door. When I pushed it open I found that it was a bathroom, with a large airing cupboard, a big old-fashioned bath like the one I had, and a loo with an ornate wooden seat on a sort of pedestal. Yet the bathroom didn't take the whole length of the corridor! Maybe it was an outside wall and the noises I'd heard came from the bathroom.

This obvious solution came to me with a flood of relief. I was certainly becoming neurotic about this house. It really was a rather nice house, and my suite was very cosy. The night before I'd watched television in bed and tonight I would do the same. It was luxurious after my Swiss Cottage bedsitter.

When I came downstairs after my bath Mrs Bargett had gone. My dinner was in the trolly. It was after seven. I'd stayed in the bath for ages. I had dinner on a corner of the dining-room table – chops, mashed potatoes and cauliflower; home-made trifle to follow. I was hungry and, I realized, relaxed at last. I was glad I'd solved the problem of the noise. My room must be over the corridor and that wall was the back outside wall. Or was it? Well one of these days I'd look and see; with a house the shape it was it was very difficult to tell anything.

I washed up carefully and then took my coffee upstairs. I knew I was half waiting for the phone to ring and I knew I didn't think it would. I had a feeling, almost of hopelessness about Peter. He was obviously safe and well, there was nothing I could do, and yet . . .

When the phone did ring I scarcely heard it above the ITV ten o'clock news. I opened the door to be sure and then charged down the stairs, all two flights, two steps at a time. I grabbed the receiver and shouted, 'Hello!' I could hear static on the line but no voice. 'Hello, hello,' I shouted down it. 'Peter is that you?' The static suddenly stopped and I shouted again, 'Peter!' Then there was a click and that awful dialling tone, which sounds like a knell when you'd been expecting a call.

I replaced the receiver. After all that, he hadn't got through.

The Ryders arrived quietly after lunch the next day, Saturday. One minute I was dozing in the drawing room in a patch of sun and the next moment they were there. I got awkwardly to my feet, feeling I should have been in my own rooms; but this was the sunniest room in the house in the afternoon.

They came in so silently that I had the feeling Agnes Ryder had been looking at me half asleep for some time before I was aware of her presence. But as soon as I looked up, she smiled and came over to me, both her arms extended in greeting.

'Jocasta! Isn't this too bad of me? You've been here four whole days. If only I'd known I was going to get sick I wouldn't have gone.'

Then to my surprise she kissed me on the cheek. I was surprised because she was supposed to be a cold person; yet here was this warm and smiling welcome. Nor was she the least bit Brontë-like. If anything, she was rather voluptuous; not fat but with a full figure and the sort of bust that I'm always envious of, not too big, but not tiny like mine. She had a creamy complexion, wore lots of make-up and had a positive mane of jet-black luxurious hair, which cascaded over her face.

In fact she took my breath away. She could hardly be more unlike what I had been led to expect – a pale, insipid, slightly waspish hypochondriac.

She threw herself into a chair.

'This *head* of mine! I am determined to have it all looked into again. Now they have new information on migraine, haven't they? I was *so* looking forward to seeing you.

Tim, could you pass me a cigarette, darling? Jocasta, do you smoke? Oh, the journey from York. Tim took what he thought was a quiet way, and the people . . . the road was choked over the Buttertubs, how I *loathe* the Dales at weekends.'

I smiled. 'Buttertubs?'

'Oh, it's a pretty way over the moors from Wensleydale. We had to call in at Ripon for some things, so took the Hawes Road. It's a long way round but Tim thought it would be quiet.'

Tim was bending over his sister, lighting her cigarette. He was smiling at her as though he suffered gladly a good deal of this chafing. I sensed an immediate rapport between them, which, again, I hadn't altogether expected. I had rather anticipated that one, the brother, would be dominated by the other – the invalid sister. Again, that notion went for good.

'Now, tell us what you've been doing. Tim, give Jocasta a fag.'

'No thanks. Oh, I've been . . . well, school started on Thursday, so I had two full days. The day before I arrived, and today – well you're here.'

'And Peter? Did you hear from Peter? I think it is a most extraordinary way to behave. I don't think I shall ever speak to Peter again; not that we don't love having you. But it is so *beastly* for you. Did the wretch ring at least?'

'He rang yesterday, but I wasn't in. He told Mrs Bargett he was in Germany. He telegraphed the day before and, I think, phoned again last night just after ten; but the line went dead.'

'It is *so* inconsiderate, and we were going to have such a lovely time. Oh well, we shall still. But that Peter . . .'

'Aggie, won't you go upstairs and unpack?' Tim said mildly, 'Don't get yourself all het up.'

'Really, he's like a nanny.' Agnes smiled and got obediently to her feet.

'And talking of nannies, you should have a rest, the doctor said. We'll call you for tea at four.'

I then saw that Agnes' face had indeed gone rather pale and there were shadows under her eyes. The first impression of blooming health had gone.

'Why don't you two go in the garden?' she said. 'There's a lovely sheltered spot Tim will show you on the back lawn, Jocasta. I imagine you were in because you thought it a bit chilly; but this is a suntrap.'

'I'll do that,' I said. 'I'll wait for Tim. Have a good rest.'

'She's really not well,' Tim said to me an hour later after we were comfortably ensconced on long wicker chairs in what Agnes had justly described as a suntrap. There was a high wall to the east and it trapped the afternoon sun; we were in an angle between the wall and the house, a sort of paved patio that I guessed they used a lot. Beyond us was the lawn with an ornate pool in the middle interestingly clogged with weeds. At the very end was a copse, which blocked out the view of the houses beyond. It was through the leaves of the trees in this little wood that one could see the broad slope of Coppitts Fell.

'I thought she looked awfully well at first,' I said, 'then she sort of faded.'

'She does. It was the excitement. She's all keyed up to meet you. She'd been looking forward to it, someone of her own age. She needs rest, rest, rest, and we must remember it all the time; but don't think of her as an invalid or behave towards her as though she were one. She hates it.'

'I wouldn't dream of it, I'll help you in any way I can,' I said earnestly, wanting to reassure him that I was on his side.

We were silent for a while, and I lay half dozing in the long wicker lounger heaped with comfortable cushions. The tall house loomed up on one side of me and I found myself gazing at it through half-open eyes. Tim was reading the *Yorkshire Post*, yet he seemed restless to me and, instead of concentrating on any one item, was forever turning the pages backwards and forwards until he tossed it to one side and gave that spasmodic wriggle that people do when they're conciously trying to relax. Tim seemed to me to have something on his mind. Was it worry about Agnes? Was she really ill? 'How old is the house, Tim?' I thought I'd try to take his mind off his sister.

'Oh it's old, Jocasta, old. They say it was the oldest building in the village and stood all by itself as a croft, into which the shepherds herded their sheep at night and in bad weather. There were, of course, no roads out here in those days, only rough tracks, though Hubberholme church is twelfth century so the dale must have been sparsely populated even then. Of course, the Conqueror laid waste to a good part of Yorkshire in his wars of revenge after the conquest as a lot of the opposition to him came from these parts.

'But Coppitts Green really begins to have records in the fifteenth century. Parts of the church are fifteenth century and it was then that it first took its shape as a village. The croft here became a farmhouse and then a house and my family moved in in the eighteenth century, the Ryders being sheep farmers. There's always been a Ryder on the parish registers since records began. They prospered over the next century and in the nineteenth century one of the Ryders went up to Oxford and subsequently became a politician and a junior minister in one of the Gladstone governments. But it was William Ryder, a brother of the politician Jeffrey Ryder, who made the family fortune. He took his wool to Bradford and started one of the first wool mills there; and he became a great paterfamilias and Ryders went all over the place and achieved varying degrees of eminence – nothing *very* remarkable, but mostly respectable and to do with making money! One of the younger Ryders always stayed here keeping an eye on the family farm, and then gradually as the village built up, the house stopped being a farm and became a home. I suppose a weekend home as many people have now. But it was my great-great-grandfather Matthew Ryder who lived here all his life, and it is through him that Agnes and I are directly descended. Since him, we Ryders have always been rather bookish, regarding money with a fair degree of scorn. Peter's an exception in that, I might add!'

'And are there Ryders all over the place now?'

'I suppose so. We don't keep up with them much, except for Peter, who was the son of my father's brother, Rupert. Rupert and my father, Charles, were the only two children and were very close. My father only died two years ago.'

'And your mother?'

For a moment Tim didn't reply. He lay looking up at the sky, shielding his face from the sun with a hand cupped over his eyes.

'Well, my mother ran off with someone else. It's something we're rather sensitive about.'

'Oh, I'm sorry. But if it's any comfort to you, my mother did the same!'

'Really?' Tim sat upright. 'And they say men are the philanderers.'

'Well, she didn't actually run far, poor thing. She just spent a week in the Indian hills with a rather handsome major from the Indian Army; but she got typhoid and died soon after. However, there's no reason to think she would have come back to us. My father never thought she would. I was twelve.'

'Oh, that's too bad. We were so small, we hardly remember my mother; it's worse when you have memories. She was always terribly restless in the Dales. Coppitts Green stifled her. She was a London girl. My father was a dalesman and all he wanted to do was to come back and settle here. This was the last thing my mother wanted to do, though at first she liked the parties and the gay social life of these parts. However, she met someone else and she ran away with him; and my father never allowed her to see us again.'

The sun had gone over the roof of the house and I shivered.

'What a sad story, Tim. At least my mother was dead. But to know your mother is alive and not to see her . . .'

'We never thought about it, to be honest. I was sent to

boarding school in the South, eventually to Winchester; and Aggie went first to the Mount in York and then to some exclusive girls' school in the South, whose name I've forgotten. My father usually took us abroad in the holidays. In fact it wasn't until he died and Agnes had to leave Cambridge because of her migraine that we really had any home life at all. I suppose that's why we both love it so. Look, it's getting cold. Shall we go in? I'll take Aggie up some tea.'

'Let me do it, I liked her so much.'

Tim paused in the act of gathering up cushions and looked at me.

'Do you? I'm glad. Aggie is two years younger than you, yet in many ways she is very mature. Pain sometimes does that, you know, and Aggie has a lot of pain and interior suffering as well. She needs to be taken out of herself.'

'Perhaps she should go away, Tim. Get a job some-where—'

Tim interrupted me with all the savagery with which the pure of mind pounce on a rude word.

'Go away! That would be the end of her. She would end up in a home; she cannot take stress, of any kind, any worry, anything to disturb her equilibrium. I know she looks very fit but you saw how tired she got and how quickly. No, we've had all the medical opinions and treatment we can get. She must have peace; but that doesn't mean her life should be dull . . . far from it. That's where you come in.'

I wondered, sarcastically, if I was supposed to read to her. The image of Elizabeth Barrett Browning superseded that of the tubercular Brontës. *There* was a beautiful girl, a spirited one . . .

Yes, I told myself, as I thoughtfully followed Tim back to the house, and there might be a parallel there too. Did Agnes need love to cure her?

Agnes was still sleeping when I tip-toed with the tea into her room, which looked over the back garden and was obviously chosen because it was so quiet. The bathroom that I had seen the day before was next to her, down the

47

smaller, darker corridor. So Agnes' room was partly under mine too. Or was it? It didn't seem long enough to go the length of the main corridor; it was rather a small room and her double bed took up quite a lot of space in it. She seemed lost in the large bed with its white counterpane tossed casually back. Her face now looked very pale and the dark hair lay dramatically on the pillow almost as though she had been posed for a painting.

I was staring at her as she opened her eyes and looked at me, at first not appearing to know who I was. Then she smiled.

'Jocasta! Have I been asleep for ages? I guess I was more tired than I thought. It's those crowds on the road. Did you bring a cup for yourself? Oh good. We can have a nice chat.'

I was only too pleased to have a nice chat and I perched on the side of her bed after giving her the tea. She sat up against pillows that I piled behind her back and sipped at the hot brew.

'Nice. Did you have a good rest in the garden? Did Tim entertain you?'

'He told me about the house; about your family . . .'

'Oh.' Agnes frowned. I guessed she was thinking about her mother. Wondering if Tim had told me. People could be very sensitive in matters of this sort. I did not know how sensitive about it Agnes was.

'He said Ryders had appeared in the records of Coppitts Green church since the fifteenth century and that this house was once a croft.'

Her brow cleared. She didn't want to talk about her mother. One could hardly blame her. What girl wouldn't resent it? I only didn't because I was a lot older when I found out the truth and my mother had been dead for years.

'Oh that, yes. Yes, it's a very old house. That's why it's such an odd shape; it's been added on to willy nilly. We like it.'

'Oh, I like it too. It's very quaint. I wondered . . .'

48

'Yes, you wondered . . .' She was sipping her tea, not looking at me, as though she was thinking about the house.

'Well, I just wondered which room was under mine. I thought I heard noises the night I was on my own.'

Agnes didn't move a muscle, nor did she cease her steady rhythmic sipping from the cup. Yet I knew that her whole body had gone tense, as though it had had some kind of inner shock. I could almost see her brain ticking over in the effort of thought; it was weird and I too gulped my tea.

'Now, let me see, under your room . . . I'll have to work this out. The bathroom is under your room, of course, and my room. Yes, this is under your room.'

'But I feel a lot of space is unaccounted for. As I see it, your room and the bathroom are off the small corridor which is at right angles to the main body of the house. You form the horizontal bar of an L. I'm on the vertical upright part, and my room and the sitting room are about the length of the long corridor. Yet there's no door off the corridor.'

'Of course there isn't! This is an awfully old house, Jocasta. There are all sorts of bits and pieces you don't have in a normal sort of place.'

'But you wouldn't have a room over nothing!'

'Oh well, I don't know what it's over; you'll have to ask Tim.'

Here was the little girl again, going all truculent on me. Tim would have to get her out of every and any sort of hole. But what was wrong about telling me where my rooms lay in relation to the rest of the house? She was looking at me, and I carefully cultivated an expression of unconcern, although the presence of the house had somehow begun to close in on me again and I felt that dull sense of foreboding.

'How's the school?' Agnes said brightly, holding out her cup for more tea. I seized on the subject avidly.

'It's lovely. It's a real tiny old-fashioned village school. We have to do everything: dole out the milk, supervise sandwich lunch and then play, and teach! No wonder Mrs Baker needed help.'

'Yes, she did. She's a martyr to arthritis, besides having to look after Herbert. Mind you, he was a lot worse until they discovered this marvellous new drug that helps Parkinsonism. He's an angel, isn't he? Oh, I do hope you stay. Mrs Baker really does need help.'

'But why shouldn't I stay? I have a year's contract.'

'Oh, I don't know. It's very lonely out here; miles from anywhere really. In the winter we can be entirely cut off. Some people can't stand it. Tim and I were born to it; we love it. The Dales are in our blood.'

I supposed she was thinking of her mother when she turned towards the long low window and looked over the village roofs towards the Fell.

'I think I shall love it too,' I said quietly. 'I'm a bit of an outcast, you know, looking for roots. I was born in India; brought up half there and half in England; and the last few years of my life has been spent in a bedsitter in Swiss Cottage, with occasional visits to whatever Army camp my sister's soldier husband happened to be stationed in. I already love the warmth and intimacy of the Dales. I can feel it growing on me.'

'And Peter?'

'What about Peter?'

'Well, you came here to see more of Peter.'

I thought her tone was rather accusatory; rather sharp and it surprised me.

'Well, I suppose Peter will turn up sooner or later.' I felt embarrassed and I suppose I sounded it. Yes, Peter had behaved badly and I could have been in a very awkward position if his cousins hadn't been so kind to me. 'But I feel I have a job to do here. I love the place, the school and . . . I like you and Tim.'

Agnes glanced at me wryly, sitting up in bed in a white slip, looking rather fragile.

'Let's hope that lasts,' she said.

Only a long time afterwards did I realize she was being prophetic.

Five

M y last headmistress had always been very complimen-
tary about my work. She had said I was a gifted
teacher, born to it and so on, and it hadn't swelled my
head because I'd known it was true. I'd loved teaching
and the contact with children, especially small ones. I'd
loved the developing mind from five to seven, the almost
daily acquisition of new skills as the child gropes towards
understanding and maturity. What a long process it was
compared to animal development.

But above all, I'd loved teaching and young company
because it banished all my shyness. I was never tongue-tied
or embarrassed with children. It was only with forceful,
awkward older human beings that I'd become confused and
forgot what I was going to say.

What had arrested my development (because I knew I
was immature in many ways)? Was it being brought up in
institutions, being an orphan from a relatively early age with a
childless uncle and aunt as very remote guardians? Had I been
thrown too much on my own resources, so that the outside
world was a challenge and not always a pleasant one?

Or was it sex? Had it inhibited me, and had my experience with Peter, my blossoming into womanhood given me
confidence I'd hither to lacked? One couldn't generalize;
it was very dangerous. I knew some very mature people,
including some nuns I'd trained with, or taught with from
time to time, who were remarkably mature though one must
suppose their sexual knowledge was limited. So it wasn't sex.
It was Peter. Peter had given me confidence; made me wanted,

acknowledged I was a fully grown-up and responsible person. Where was Peter now? Yet, did the very fact that I could carry on without Peter mean that some peculiar maturing process had been taking place all the time, like vintage wine left for years in casks while the mysterious fermenting process went on?

I was very happy at the school in Coppitts Green. With few exceptions I liked the children, and I adored Mrs Baker. What a pleasure to work with a woman of such experience, so resourceful, so capable. Except for the new ones, my class could almost all read; they knew their numbers and could tell the time. How she'd done it, I didn't know.

Of the sea of faces in my first days, names, identities and characters had emerged and I must say that among my favourites was Natalie Dabroe. She was adorable: astute, wise beyond her years and a gifted comic. When we weren't working hard, which was most of the time, she could have the class in stitches with her antics. There was no one really to touch Natalie when it came to sheer ability, yet I had to be impartial and gave to the rest of the class as much care and attention as I gave to her.

After school, some of the children walked home, some took the Dales bus, others were collected by their parents, those who lived in remote farms for the most part. I used to see an estate car waiting on the other side of the road pointing in the direction of Starthrush with a woman at the wheel and it was towards this that the Dabroe children ran after school each day. In the middle of my second week as I stood at the gate seeing them safely on their way, the woman got out of the estate car and came over to me.

She was about thirty, tall with streaky blonde hair and a rather hard but still beautiful face. She was one of those unfortunate women who must have been absolutely stunning in their teens and to whom time had been rather cruel even though they were still young. She wore a lot of make-up to conceal lines on the forehead and round the mouth, and her eyelashes were long and thick with mascara. But she had a

superb figure and was light and athletic on her feet. She wore
a camel-hair trouser suit and a red silk shirt. I knew she was
the Dabroe children's mother, and Sebastian, who was fair,
took after her. Dark little Natalie must have favoured this
very handsome father I'd heard about.

Mrs Dabroe came up to me smiling as the children charged
towards her.

'You must be Miss Oaks. I thought I'd let you get settled
in before I introduced myself. I'm Tessa Dabroe.'

'How do you do, Mrs Dabroe.' I knew I was blushing. My
shyness again. People like Tessa Dabroe made me feel about
fifteen years old. They seemed to have such a rich store of
experience compared to the meagreness of one's own – five
years in a bedsit in Swiss Cottage.

'Yes, I'm beginning to give names to all the faces now.
The first days are awful.'

'But you're very popular. You've made a hit with Natalie.
Sebastian of course sees less of you being in Mrs Baker's
class. Ah, there she is. Mrs Baker, I was just introducing
myself to Miss Oaks. Saying she was a hit with Natalie.'

'She's a hit with everyone, including me.' Mrs Baker
laughed and took the younger woman's hand. 'She makes
me feel my age. I don't know how these children put up with
me. You should see Jocasta at rounders!'

'Jocasta! What an unusually pretty name. You must come
and have tea with us, Miss Oaks, when you've settled down.
Are you staying with Mrs Baker?'

'No with the Ryders . . .'

The change in the atmosphere was so sudden that once
again I had the feeling I'd uttered something obscene. Mrs
Baker actually blushed and the smile left Tessa Dabroe's face
as though some invisible person had taken an invisible cloth
and physically wiped it off.

'Oh, the *Ryders* . . .' Mrs Dabroe said at last. 'I didn't know
they took paying guests. Or are you a friend of theirs?'

'Jocasta's fiancé is Peter Ryder.' Mrs Baker's voice was
terribly wooden as though she were reciting the alphabet.

'Oh, is he? How interesting. We shall look forward to getting to know you better. 'Bye Miss Oaks. Come on children.' The social smile returned automatically; but the warmth had gone. As she saw the children into the back of the car and climbed into the front herself, I stared after her.

'Well what did I do wrong?'

Mrs Baker slipped an arm through mine.

'It isn't anything you did. It was done a long time ago. Ryders and Dabroes have never got on. There's a family feud that goes back about a hundred years, and then there's something more recent than that, that was very unpleasant for everyone concerned. I don't want to gossip. I think these things are best not talked about. You see, Tessa isn't even a Dabroe, she only married one; yet the feud affects her. You see how she looked. It is just that Ryders and Dabroes don't talk. It's idiotic but its a fact. Thank goodness the Ryders don't have small children at my school, that's all I can say, because no doubt the feud would be continued each day on the playground of Coppitts Green school!'

'But I've never heard anything like it. A family feud a century old?'

'It is rather Sicilian, isn't it? But emotions are very deep in this part of the world. There's not much else to occupy folk; they give a lot of time to feuds and disagreements that to outsiders seem ridiculous. They feed on them; they enjoy them, if you ask me. Tessa Dabroe took to the feud like a duck to water. You'd think they'd all be more civilized. However, the young Ryders aren't very sociable and don't go in for St George's dinners and flower-arranging in the church and the like. If they did, there'd be clashes all over the place. But they feel it very deeply. Just you mention Dabroe and see what happens!'

'I don't think I should at the moment,' I said. 'I can see what you mean about Agnes. Charming but edgy. She doesn't like being asked questions; either about her family or the house. Now I just leave all conversational openings to her.'

'How odd.'

54

'I think she thinks I'm prying. I'm not, of course; but what can you talk about?'

'Yes, conversation is limited and it is a lovely house. One of the oldest, if not *the* oldest, in the village.'

'So they say, and I think the Ryders are very possessive about it.'

'Ours is in a better position and I think prettier in every way, but Croft House has some fifteenth-century timbering, It's been added and added to over the years. Ryders have always had a deep and irrational love for Croft House. It's a characteristic of the family.'

'Did you know any of the rest of the family. The father?'

'Oh yes. Charles Ryder was a nice man; a real scholar. He and Herbert had lots in common and used to talk about the history of Old Bradford as though they'd lived in the nineteenth century. He only died a couple of years ago of some heart ailment; premature. It was a great pity and I think it made a difference to the lives of those children. He'd never have tolerated Agnes' nonsense.'

We'd closed and locked the school gate and were walking along the road to the village.

'I'm not sure that Agnes *is* nonsense. Her illness is real, if psychologically inspired. None the less genuine for that. Did you know her mother?'

'Oh no, that was before we came here. And now we don't see them as much as we did; they seem to have withdrawn into themselves.'

'Come in now, say hello!'

We stood at the gate of Croft House.

'Oh no, Jocasta. I couldn't! We don't just pop in in these parts. It really isn't done. I know they do it in the South but they don't here. Not really. Not even if you know someone very well. In Wharfedale, which is very pubby, they meet all the time in the local; here we tend to have fewer pubs and more formal invitations to tea, coffee, whatever. I'd never dream of popping in to see anyone without notice that I was coming unless one of the children were ill.'

Well and truly chastised, I smiled my goodbye and opened the front door, thinking what a funny closed environment it was and wondering what I'd let myself in for. It seemed to increase the claustrophobic feeling that entering the house always gave me, and as it was a dull day, the hall, when I got inside, was almost dark. Of course it was now mid-September, and the days were noticeably shortening. I was on my way upstairs when Mrs Bargett came into the hall, buttoning up her coat.

'Oh, it's you, dear. I wondered if it was Miss Agnes coming back. She's been out all day.' Her face looked anxious. 'It's not like her.'

'Oh, Mrs Bargett! Don't you think all the fuss Agnes gets contributes to her illness? She's probably having a perfectly lovely day in Skipton or somewhere.'

Mrs Bargett's pleasant face assumed an expression of hostility that took me by surprise; it was almost venomous.

'No, I do not, miss! It's all very well to talk like it was something that went on in her mind; but believe you me, miss, Agnes' illness is very real indeed. We have seen her very close to death, Master Tim and myself. Nursed her through many a crisis. If you ask me, there's something wrong with her brain and the doctors don't know what to do about it. I've seen her go out a healthy young woman and come back a physical wreck, having to be helped into the house.'

I felt suitably chastened; but I was interested. This was a most extraordinary illness indeed. I wished I knew someone medically qualified to discuss it with. She just seemed to collapse for no apparent reason.

'I'm sorry Mrs B,' I said contritely. 'Please forgive me. I meant no disrespect, I assure you. But did she never have symptoms like this as a child?'

'I never knew her well as a child. She and Mr Tim spent most of their childhood at school; but the symptoms really got bad at Cambridge and she came home then, just before her father died.'

'And that must have been a shock.'

'It was terrible,' Mrs Bargett quietly said. 'Ever so quick. Terrible. Those two young people thrown on their own. Terrible.'

I leaned on the bannister, a thought playing in my mind. 'I met Mrs Dabroe today. She came to pick up the children from school . . .'

Mrs Bargett stiffened and her face set impassively, as Mrs Baker's had.

'We don't talk about the Dabroe family in this house, Miss Oaks. We never mention their names.'

'But why, Mrs Bargett?' I came down the stairs and stood opposite her. She seemed to have grown in her indignation and dwarfed me.

'I can't say, miss. It's none of my business. But remember what I told you. I'm off early now, miss. My youngest married daughter is coming to tea with her children.'

Mrs Bargett closed the door firmly after her. I had never seen her so cold and unfriendly towards me. I turned and thoughtfully went up the stairs.

On the first floor I paused in the corridor. Outside rain had begun to fall and the thick black clouds hovered over the hills in the distance, a pall of damp mist shrouding the cliff. A wind had sprung up as we were walking home and the scattering of leaves reminded me how near we were to winter.

Winter. Could I stand winter here, with all this uncertainty, all this insecurity? Oh, I loved my job and I liked Mrs Baker; but how did the Ryders really feel about *me*? The warmth of that initial greeting had vanished and they were both polite, but rather remote from me. What would I do in the long dark evenings that would stretch interminably until the spring?

The branch of the elm tree knocked sharply against the window, almost a sinister knocking instead of that gentle tap-tapping I had heard a few days before. There was something about this corridor; this particular part of the house. The long window on the landing gave such a clear view of the cliff that it seemed to dominate the hallway like a huge prehensile hand ready to grasp . . . I stood in the corridor wishing I'd put a light on, the stairs up to my floor seemed very dark. I grasped the bannister and realized my hand was sweating profusely; the hair seemed to be rising on my scalp. I couldn't move. I couldn't go forwards or backwards, and then I heard it, the slow shuffling as though someone very old and tired was limping along. It seemed to be coming from down the corridor towards me and I shut my eyes for fear of what I should see. Nearer and nearer it came and I thought I was going to scream but the sound stuck in my throat, and my mouth just opened and nothing emerged. There was a smell now, an awful smell, and I had never felt such terror, such apprehension in all my life.

Suddenly the hall light came on and Tim called up to me from the bottom of the stairs.

'Is that you Aggie?'

I was breathing very hard as if I had been running in a race. I gulped and caught my breath, swallowing hard to try to make my voice sound normal:

'No Tim, it's me. I was just on my way upstairs.'

'Are you all right?'

'Of course.'

'I thought your voice sounded shaky.'

'Oh, I was just tired after school. I'm going to have a rest. Shall I see you at supper?'

He didn't answer my question.

'I wish Aggie would come back. It's nearly dark. I'm really worried about her.'

'Where was she going?'

'She didn't say. She just took the car and went off; she does that; I was working in my study.'

'I'm sure there's nothing to worry about.'

I climbed up the rest of the stairs like a tottery old lady, glad of the light. I was trembling when I got into my room and sat heavily on the bed. This was absolutely absurd, I told myself. I was frightened to death. Of what? Of a house, of a cliff, of sounds. I lay on the bed and took a cigarette from the packet on the bedside table. The smoke tasted acrid and made me cough. What I needed was a drink to steady my nerves; but I could hardly go down and get one. I tried to relax and analyse what was the matter with me.

I was afraid of this house. There was something about it I couldn't place and I didn't like. There was an atmosphere, a mystery, a sense of menace . . . It was connected with the Ryders. I wasn't at ease with them. Something about them worried me, no, not worried, left me feeling deeply disturbed. The angry hostility with which Tim and Mrs B defended Agnes. I could sense already they were beginning to dislike me; because I was trying to treat Agnes like a normal girl?

I knew then that I couldn't stay in Croft House; that whether I remained in Coppitts Green or not, I had to live somewhere else. I'd begin looking tomorrow.

I must have dozed off to sleep after this resolution – perhaps it gave me peace of mind – because when I woke it was quite dark. I hurriedly washed and changed and went downstairs. Everywhere was in darkness and the silence seemed heavy and unnatural. I switched on the hall light, the lights in the drawing room and went into the dining room, where cold meats and salads were laid on the sideboard.

Tim's study was at the back of the house. It was one of the many extensions. I had never been into it and I didn't quite know where it was. Between the dining room and the kitchen was a short corridor. I'd always gone into the kitchen but indeed the corridor continued and I decided Tim's study might lie along this. At the end was a door. I knocked and receiving no reply went in: it led into the yard! I felt foolish and laughed at myself, and then from the yard I saw a light in a downstairs window. This came from beyond the drawing room. There must be another warren of corridors to navigate. I went back into the hall and indeed there was a door next to the drawing room that I'd assumed was a cloakroom. It was a small hallway with two doors leading off it. Again I knocked. The door was flung open and Tim stood eagerly looking out. His face fell when he saw me.

'Oh, it's you, Jocasta! I was about to ring the police about Aggie.'

'Tim, come and have some supper. You're overwrought. Then if she's not here, we'll do something.'

'Do you realize she might be dead?'

'I don't think she's dead, Tim.'

'Lost on the moors, a car crash, fallen into a valley . . .'

'You'd have heard.'

'You don't really care, do you, Jocasta?'

'Oh Tim!' I looked at him angrily. 'Of course I care, if there was anything to care about. But Agnes is a grown-up, a young woman of twenty-two; you're treating her like a child!'

'You don't know what we know.'

'Well, I'm sorry.' His study was a book-lined room with a large table and several easy chairs. I sat on one of them.

'I think I should go, Tim, anyway. Look for somewhere else to live.'

His expression changed immediately.

'Oh, come . . . you've only been here a short time.'

'Yes, but . . . I don't know how to say it, but I feel I'm a nuisance, an intrusion, yes, that's it, an intrusion. If I felt I could be of more help, do something; but I feel useless. I'm not paying you and, well, I'm worried to death about Peter. Where does he live, Tim? Can't I go to his flat?'

Tim turned to the window so that his back was towards me.

'I'm sorry,' he said quietly. 'I don't think we've made you feel at home. We meant to; but you know it is strange when you're not used to company. As for Peter – ' he shook his shoulders and turned to fiddle with something on his desk – 'I don't know what to say about him. He seems to have vanished abroad.'

'Do you think he had anything to hide, Tim?'

'Hide?'

'Anything dishonest in his business?'

Tim seemed to be deliberately avoiding my eyes and fiddled with his paperknife.

'Maybe . . .'

My heart jumped and began an uneven pounding in my chest.

'You mean you *do* think he had something to hide?'

'I don't know; but we must face it, mustn't we? It's a possibility.'

'But Tim, then we must find out; do something.'

'What can we do?'

'Well, at least look around. He must have had some business friends. There will be clues in his flat. Peter can't just vanish. Besides,' I said slowly, realizing something important for the first time, 'why would Peter have let me come up here if he was about to disappear? He would have stopped me. Peter wouldn't have wanted me to worry. He loved me. I know that . . .'

Did I? Was I sure? Was Peter as evasive and as devious as his cousins?

'No, it is odd. But things sometimes do get out of control, don't they? I don't know. He may just have decided he had to leave the country for a while.'

'I don't believe it. I can't believe it.'

'Well, I think it is a possibility. You must face that, Jocasta. As for staying here . . . well, you're welcome, very welcome, as long as you're in Coppitts Green, to remain with us.'

Now he'd said it. '*As long as you're in Coppitts Green.*' '*Oh, I do hope you stay,*' Agnes had said. Why shouldn't I stay? What made them think I'd break a year's contract? What made them so sure there was something impermanent about my stay?

We were standing in the study, aware of each other but not looking, the atmosphere decidely tense and uneasy, when the telephone shrilled sharply on Tim's desk. He grabbed it. I couldn't hear what was being said at the other end – it was a woman's voice, I assumed Agnes' – but his face first appeared relieved and then anxious.

'Oh, could you, Karen? Is she all right? Until tomorrrow? I could come over but we only have one car . . . Are you sure? What about the doctor?' There was more talk on the other side. It wasn't Agnes. Something had happened to her. I realized then the meaning of the expression 'heavy hearted'. My heart did physically feel as heavy as lead. It was a weight in my chest; a repository of anxiety, insecurity and yes, why not admit it, fear.

When Tim put the phone down, the look he gave me was almost one of triumphant vindication.

'There was something wrong. I knew it. She was on her way home and collapsed outside the home of some friends of ours, at Hammersleigh Hall. She managed to stagger up the drive and they put her to bed. Dead with fatigue, Karen said, blinding headache. Karen wanted to call the doctor but Agnes felt better as soon as she was lying down; said she was exhausted. They're keeping her overnight.'

'Oh, Tim, I am sorry . . .'

'Yes, Jocasta, but you said there was nothing wrong with her, a normal healthy girl you said . . .'

'But I only thought, Tim . . .'

'You only thought "she makes it all up" . . .'

'No, I didn't . . . Oh Tim, I am sorry you should think that. I wanted to make friends with you and Agnes. Now you don't trust me.'

He didn't reply. His silence was a condemnation. Yes, he was saying, I was in the way, I was a non-believer in the reality of Agnes' suffering. I was an alien to this claustrophobic little world of worry and anxiety they had built for themselves, which afforded them some kind of protection against I knew not what, into which they drew sensible people like Mrs Bargett. But not, I thought, Mrs Baker . . . she would be my ally.

'I'm going to eat, Tim, will you join me?'

'No, thanks,' Tim said. 'I'm not hungry.'

I turned to go and stopped at the door.

'Tim, will you give me Peter's address?'

'I'm not sure that I have it,' Tim said coldly. 'He moved recently.'

A cold anger seized me.

'Tim, if I don't find out more about Peter, I'm going to the police. You have his telephone number. I don't believe you haven't his address, or – ' I looked at him and walked slowly towards him – '*did* you have his telephone number? Were you just making it up?'

'What on earth do you mean?'

'I couldn't find it in your book. I looked the day after you phoned.'

'Oh, Christ!' Tim shouted. 'The man lives in a hotel! The Morecambe House Hotel, just outside Leeds. Go and look under "M" in the flaming telephone book!'

I was stunned. Why hadn't Peter told me he lived in a hotel? There was nothing wrong with it. I lived in a boarding house. Lots of people, especially if they travelled, lived in hotels. There was nothing to be ashamed of. Perhaps he thought there was. Poor Peter. I loved him. I didn't care where he lived. But where in the name of heaven was he now?

Six

During the night I remembered Stephen. He'd asked me to let him know if I wanted help. Well, did I? I could just go to the Morecambe House Hotel myself. They would tell me Peter had left and then where would that get me? But it wasn't only Peter's disappearance that made me feel I needed help. There was the awful aching uncertainty of my relationship with the Ryders that now, at least between Tim and myself, bordered on hostility. I could understand that in his concern for his sister, Peter didn't seem very important; and that I now was a nuisance was only too apparent.

But I'd been here no time at all. I couldn't go now; let Mrs Baker down, disappoint the children I'd already grown to care for. I must give it a chance.

Gradually the sinister face of the cliff came into view with the light of dawn. It was still enveloped in mist. I got out of bed, dog-tired but still unable to sleep, and gazed out of the window. It was pouring with rain – heavy, leaden drops that seemed to have come from a great distance, almost the size of hailstones. The grey slate roofs of the cottages glistened, and rivulets of water ran along gutters, jets spluttering out of the tops of drainpipes. I couldn't see the valley at all; it was as though a thick impenetrable blanket had cut us off from the world.

This was what I had dreaded. Supposing this had been snow and I couldn't get away! I'd be here all winter, trapped in this isolated, unfriendly place. I was a city girl. Even in Calcutta you had had the feel of a great city. I seemed to be alive in

64

a city, breathe through its clogged-up, smokey pores. What
on earth was I doing stuck in this place a dozen miles from
even the nearest small town?

It was cold. I turned on the electric fire, but still the keen
wind rattled the frame of the sash window and huge drops
of water were shaken on to the window pane.

I went back to bed and lay shivering under the blankets. I
still couldn't sleep.

'Goodness child, you look ill! Whatever is the matter?' Mrs
Baker and I liked to get to the school half an hour before
it opened, officially at nine. But today I got there just after
eight, an hour before, and found her, to my surprise, there
too. I asked her why.

'Oh, Herbert couldn't sleep. He gets a lot of pain at times.
I made us an early breakfast and decided to come and mark
some books.'

'I couldn't sleep either.'

'You look wretched. Is something wrong?' Mrs Baker's
voice sounded anxious. Sweet, concerned person though she
was, I imagined a fear of losing me would give her added
cause for anxiety.

'A lot's wrong actually. I'm worried about Peter and . . .
I don't really get on with the Ryders. Tim Ryder, at least.'

'Oh, that does surprise me. You said you and Agnes . . .'

'Well, the first day was fine. Since then, there's been a sort
of deterioration, even Mrs Bargett has changed her attitude
towards me since they've been back.'

'She's very loyal of course.'

'But I haven't *done* anything . . .'

Mrs Baker put out a restraining arm.

'My dear, I'm sure you haven't! Don't fret. Agnes must
be worse than I thought.'

'They persist in considering her very ill. I think they
think I don't believe it. Whereas I don't really know what
I believe . . .'

I was walking up and down trying to get warm. The central

heating was kept low at night and the school hadn't begun to heat up.

'Would you like to stay with us, dear?' Mrs Baker said gently. 'Stephen said you weren't very happy in the house.'

'Oh, did he tell you? That was silly. Just lonely, I suppose. No, Mrs Baker, thank you, but I can't just leave *now*. Besides, I think Tim should do something about Peter. He's been lying to me about him.'

Mrs Baker looked astonished. She had been vaguely scanning childish essays all the time I'd been talking and now she put down her pencil and looked at me.

'Lying . . . about Peter? What can you mean?'

'I think he knows where Peter is.'

'But why. How?'

'Something he said. You know, I don't like to say this, but I did mention it to Stephen, who was very kind to me that night, so perhaps he told you, but I wondered if Peter had had to disappear because he had done something dishonest. Something that might be found out. Now, Peter told me he had a flat in Leeds. He kept on talking about "the flat"; I remember it quite precisely. I wondered what sort of flat it was, you know how one does. He even said I couldn't live in the flat with him as it wasn't big enough.'

I noticed Mrs Baker's eyes widen in the realization of what our relationship had been.

'So . . . now Tim tells me he lived in a hotel!'

'How very strange.'

'He even gave me the name, so it must be true. You know what I think.' I went over to the large table and sat on the edge of it, my feet dangling in front of the small electric fire.

'No?' encouraged Mrs Baker.

'I think Peter was in trouble. He moved out of the flat and into a hotel . . .'

'Ready to flit if he had to?'

'Exactly.'

'Without telling you?'

'Quite, and letting me come on up here all in ignorance of what was going on.'

'It sounds very funny, dear.'

'It doesn't sound like the Peter I knew,' I said softly. 'Mrs Baker, do you think, would it be too awful to . . . ?' I searched her kind face anxiously. 'Do you think I could ask Stephen to help me?'

'But dear, he'd like nothing better. He knew you were anxious about Peter and he said he'd offered to help. I don't think he thought the chances of Tim doing much were very great. Tim's too vague. Stephen and I are very close, you know, my baby boy . . .' I thought of great big six-footer Stephen and smiled. Mothers never changed. 'Stephen has a very kind nature. Why don't we run into Skipton after school today? I have to do some shopping and you can have a talk with him. Then he can take us to dinner if he's free.'

'Oh, that sounds marvellous! Are you sure?'

'Yes, and we both need an outing. I'll pop home at lunchtime and get something ready for Herbert, and I can leave a note for the Ryders.'

'Agnes has had one of her turns. She collapsed outside the home of some friends of theirs – Hammer something?'

Mrs Baker looked interested.

'Hammersleigh Hall? The Fullertons live there. Karen Fullerton is a noted Dales artist; but there were some funny goings-on in that place a year or two ago.'

'What sort of goings-on?'

'Oh, the usual thing, very common in these parts . . . affairs and I don't know what. No one ever got to the bottom of it. Karen is Hugh Fullerton's third wife, and they've only just got married . . . just in time for the baby's christening!'

Mrs Baker pursed her lips severely and looked very school-marmish.

'Well, you told me people here had nothing else to do!'

'Oh, I didn't mean *that*. I was talking about . . .'

'I know, intrigues. I was just teasing you. I must say though the country is positively alive with activity, isn't it?'

67

'You notice it more in the country,' Mrs Baker said, glancing at her watch. 'In a village, you may have a few hundred. In the city millions, even in Bradford . . . Everything looms much larger in the country.'

'Oh, by the way, I was told by Mrs Bargett I must never mention the name Dabroe in the house. I said I'd met Mrs Dabroe picking up the kids.'

'There, I told you, didn't I? Now I'll phone Stephen and see if I can fix it up for today. Would you go and unlock the main door, dear? They should be arriving any moment.'

As I opened the heavy main doors of the schoolhouse, I saw that the rain had stopped and the sun was struggling to come through the thick lowering clouds, so that a curious light suffused the valley. Yes, it was beautiful; the colouring was like nothing I'd ever seen before, and the air after the rain was so fragrant and pungent with delicious earthy odours. In front of me, the valley broadened towards a low contour of hills; to the left was the cluster of houses that lay on the outskirts of Coppitts Green and to the right the long straight road that led into Starthrush. A flock of swallows had gathered on the wires of the telegraph pole; they'd left things a bit late but it had been a warm September, the rain must have decided them on a prompt departure and they swung and chattered on the wire, bending it precariously.

I exhaled deeply. Peace. Things couldn't go too badly in a setting like this.

A long sleek black Jaguar stopped outside the school gates. A very tall dark man got out and opened the rear door and the Dabroe children tumbled out, kissed the man and ran laughing through the gates. He looked after them and waved. Then he looked at me, bowed and smiled.

I gave a foolish awkward sort of bob. Jonathan Dabroe was one of the most striking men I had ever seen, but as I gazed, mesmerized, he leapt into the car and drove off.'

'He's nice too,' Mrs Baker said beside me, 'as well as handsome. Oh, don't be ashamed. Everyone reacts like that; people stop and stare when they first meet him. But then his niceness comes through and you realize he's not a god. Still, with looks like that in the family you can see what Angela Ryder saw in his father . . .'

I turned to her slowly.

'You mean the Ryders' mother went off with . . .' Mrs Baker nodded.

'Sam Dabroe. Oh dear, and I said I wouldn't gossip. But it all happened so long ago. Good morning, Neil, wipe your feet on the mat, dear! Hurry up, Sandra, and don't step in that puddle!'

Mrs Baker nodded and smiled as the children ran past us into the school.

'Oh, and Stephen says it's fine for this afternoon. I'll leave you at his office while I do some shopping.'

But I only dimly took in what she was saying. No wonder the Dabroe name was forbidden in Croft House; and no wonder the mother's behaviour left a mark that still hurt.

'But it wasn't really the mother's fault,' Mrs Baker took up the subject as we climbed the hill out of Coppitts Green towards Skipton. 'Sam Dabroe made such a set at her that she couldn't help herself. We knew them vaguely because we've always been up in the Dales. The war changed people's attitudes, you know. After it, the Ryders and Dabroes forgot the old family feud and spent a lot of time together – Charles and Angela, Sam and Rebecca, all newly married.'

'Did they farm then?'

'Oh no, the farming stopped a long time ago. Croft House became purely a family home. Charles and Angela didn't start a family at once, I think there was some difficulty about it, but Sam and Rebecca already had Jonathan and Douglas. They kept Rebecca to the home; you couldn't get help and she was very maternal and domesticated anyway. Sam was just the opposite. He felt trapped by the Dales and spent a lot of time in Leeds, where the Dabroe family had a business. Then he'd flit off to London, and whenever he came back he always seemed to be seen about with Angela, less and less with Charles. Anyway, finally Angela had a baby, who was Tim, and then another baby who was stillborn and finally Agnes. Charles seemed to be determined to try and tie down his wife to domestic concerns; but she wouldn't be tied down and behaved just the same as ever – London, the Continent, anywhere but Coppitts Green, the children left in the care of a nanny whom they had to have living in by that time.

Anyway, Agnes was still a baby when Angela left for good. She'd arranged to rendezvous with Sam on the Continent somewhere and after it was all over wrote to tell Charles all about it. At the same time Sam told Rebecca. He'd arranged to leave the running of his business to his brothers – he had three – and he made Felton Hall over to Rebecca for her lifetime. Thus as far as these things go, he behaved very decently.'

We were driving through the woods, still hung with the mist, which hadn't lifted all day. Through the trees, I saw that the River Whern had widened. Mrs Baker saw me glancing down. 'Lovely, isn't it? We call it Bluebell Wood. It's a mass of bluebells in spring time. I used to pick them when I was a little girl. Now that road leads to Wharfedale and Grassington, and here we turn right for Skipton.'

'It must be marvellous to have childhood memories of the place where you still live. I never even *feel* I want to go back to Calcutta. Anyway, go on. So Rebecca stayed and brought up the children?'

'Yes, three by the time Sam left for good. The baby was Dora, who is training to be a nurse in London and is a very nice girl. They all grew up to be very responsible too; mother was quite a martinet.'

'Is she still alive?'

'Oh yes, but she had the sense to leave the nest when Jonathan married, and she has a little cottage up the dale beyond Yocken. She's very active in doing good works too.'

'So she and Charles remained single for the rest of their lives?'

'Yes.'

'Sad.'

'They were very similar types too; both quiet and dutiful; but they avoided each other's company and Charles took care they should never meet the young Dabroes, who came to this school, by sending Tim and Agnes away.'

'Is their mother still alive?'

'Oh yes, and Sam, but Charles would never divorce Angela, he didn't believe in it and whether that was a reason or not I don't know, but Sam eventually left her and married someone else, because Rebecca gave him his freedom pretty soon after he left. They had this civilized arrangement. With Charles there was no forgiveness and a bit of revenge. I think she lives in Brighton.'

'And the children never saw her again?'

'Not that I know of.'

'I wonder if they want to?'

'I shouldn't think so. Ah, here we are. Now let's see, where can I park?'

Now that I know Skipton so well, I forget the impression it first made on me. Certainly that day it was not at its best in the rain, and the dusk of evening made it hard for me to form any idea of it at all. But now that I know every inch of its streets and alleyways, its backwaters and canals, I love it dearly, and I always feel a sense of exhilaration from whichever way we approach it, whether from our home in the Dales or after a visit to Leeds, or coming back home from the South. At the top end of the town, the castle surmounts everything, the home of the Cliffords steeped in blood and wars. There's the church with the Norman tower and then a sturdy main street with stalls on either side on the market days, and the main shops and the high front of Manby's corner, where you could buy anything from a packet of seeds to an Aga. Manby's shop bisects the street because parallel to the main street at this juncture runs Sheep Street, which is narrow and cobbled and cars go down it at their peril. Lots of little arches lead off Sheep Street down to the labyrinth of canals where Skipton boasts a proper marina and a cluster of boats of every description, from heavy barges that ply the inland waterways, to flighty little skiffs used for week-end fun.

I remember going to Stephen's office that dull September evening and being surprised that the black oak door lay just under an archway and we climbed up the narrowest stairs you ever saw until we came to a sort of Dickensian suite of offices with stained floors and highly polished furniture, and a proper clerk at a high desk with a pince-nez on his nose and a prim-looking secretary typing at an old-fashioned upright machine. In the polished black grate was a coal fire and even the lights were dull as though they were lit by oil, which in fact they weren't.

Stephen was beyond a glass door sitting at a large desk littered with papers and smoking a pipe that smelt as though it had been filled with peat.

I remember Mrs Baker left me there and said she'd call back at the hour we'd decided and that Stephen, seeing the expression on my face, knocked out his foul-smelling pipe and saw me to a chair by another huge coal fire and offered me a glass of sherry.

'Or would you prefer tea?'

'Perhaps, if I'm to keep my head clear. I do love your offices, Stephen.'

He went pink with pleasure. This surprised me and secretly pleased me. I decided that Stephen was shy like me, gratified by flattery, but that he concealed it better than I did.

'I'm glad. I bought the practice and decided to keep it as it was, only changing it to my name. I didn't see why I and my children and my children's children, should they choose to follow law, should bear the name of Alder-man and Briggs, Witney and Co., none of whom as far as I can see survived beyond the end of the last century! Excuse me.'

Stephen went to the door and asked his prim secretary to

be good enough to prepare a tray of tea and to fetch some cakes from the baker underneath. Then he closed the door and took his seat opposite me.

'I'm glad you came. I didn't like to think of you being so unhappy.'

'Did I seem so unhappy?'

'Yes. Oh, I know you think we solicitors might be thick, but some of us are really quite human. I like to think the best ones are and that they care about people.'

Now I blushed.

'Oh Stephen, I'm sure there's all the difference between someone like you and one of those awful London sharks who do nothing and charge high fees.'

'Did you have a bad experience with a solicitor?'

'Not really; but a lot of my contemporaries were getting married and buying houses and things and solicitors always seemed to be more of a hindrance than a help.'

'Let's see if I can change that image.'

I smiled gratefully at him. Yes, he was nice. He was really a normal, healthy, extrovert and rather a kind young man who wanted to make his way in the world by plying law. That he favoured a tweedy sporty look probably reflected his personality, and I thought it was rather nice that he wore a sports jacket and flannels in the office instead of that awful grey pinstripe one saw in films with a stiff tight collar rising up to a bulbous Adam's apple.

'Now tell me,' Stephen said, 'all that has happened and what Tim said to you about Peter, and go back to how you met Peter and what you know about him.'

I took a deep breath and began, going back to the weekend when Bob jokingly said they were having a bloke to stay for the regimental reunion who would send me into raptures. I always think Bob thought of me as rather a sexless individual, a virgin schoolmarm if ever there was one, and it was a great and probably tasteless joke on his part. But he was right. In forty-eight hours, Peter transformed my life and I had never looked back.

'So you saw each other pretty constantly over, how long, six months?'

'Well, nearly a year now. The regimental reunion was just before Christmas last year.'

'Did Peter live in London? I don't really know much about him.'

I looked steadfastly at the fire and reminded myself I was speaking to a solicitor, a professional man who would, or should, be used to hearing all sorts of tales.

'No he stayed in a hotel until . . . we got to know each other better and then he would stay with me.'

'Oh. It was really as intimate as all that?'

'Yes; very intimate.'

'But you never discussed marriage?'

'No, we never mentioned it.'

'Did you want to marry him?'

'Oh, yes, of course. I thought it was just a question of time, but that he wanted to be sure. I was sure straight away.'

'Hmm . . .' Stephen frowned then as his secretary came in with the tea, motioned for her to pour for us and while she did, he offered me a plate of cakes, which looked so delicious I had to have one. After the door closed, he started fiddling with his pipe.

'Do you mind terribly if I smoke? It does help concentration.'

'Of course I don't.'

'I can't understand why in such, if you will forgive me, intimate circumstances, you didn't know anything very much about him, where he lived for instance.'

'Oh, I knew a lot about him. I knew his father was killed in an accident, and that his mother married again and had another family. But he was a good bit older than his eldest stepbrother and he always felt a bit of a loner. He was close to his cousin Tim, and he loved their house in the Dales, so he used to spend a lot of time there.'

'At Croft House, in fact?'

'Yes. His uncle Charles seemed closer to him than his

mother, and Tim and Agnes like brother and sister. So there was nothing mysterious there. But no, I didn't really know what he did. I vaguely thought he had some sort of office and he was so seldom in the North that I never even thought very much of his flat as his home, if you know what I mean. I was more interested in and curious about Croft House, and I loved the sound of the Dales and the way Peter talked about them.'

'And *Peter* suggested you came up?'

'Yes. He said he was going to be much more in Leeds and his flat was too small. I then saw by chance an old advert in one of our professional teaching papers about a post in Coppitts Green. I thought it would be filled; but Peter found out it wasn't and that they were desperate for someone.'

'So you had an interview?'

'No, I filled in all the forms and had references and so on, but I was leaving for a summer school in Greece. I also had the problem with my school; but they were quite happy to release me, because they had been told to make cuts with the new axe on government spending and fewer people in London are having children, so the classes are getting smaller.'

'Is that so? The things you learn. Anyway, that was settled and you went to Greece?'

'I left Peter to settle it, yes, and went to Greece for a month. I came back a month ago, and went to my sister in Caterham, because I'd given up my bedsitter in London. Peter came down there and said everything was fixed and stayed with us and we arranged to meet at Leeds station a week or so later.'

'Did you speak to him in the meantime?'

'No; but this was not unusual. Peter wasn't sentimental. He seldom rang and never wrote letters.'

'*Never* wrote letters?'

'No. There was no need. We saw such a lot of each other.'

'But did you write letters to him?'

'Of course not.'

'Not a card from Greece?'

'Oh yes, several.'

'And where did these go to?'

'The London address. Peter kept on the room for a while.'

'So there was no real mystery about the address in Leeds. It just never cropped up?'

'That's it. There was no mystery at all. But with Tim there has been a mystery.'

And I went on to elaborate about this to Stephen and by the time I'd finished and we'd discussed all this and more, there was tap on the door and Mrs Baker, laden with parcels, stood there.

'All finished?'

Stephen got up and helped her unload.

'We've hardly begun, Mother. All I've got are the facts as the American lawyers say on the telly. Over dinner we shall decide what action to take.'

Seven

The Morecambe House Hotel was pleasantly situated in a tree-lined drive in a leafy suburb on the outskirts of Leeds on the Skipton road. It wasn't at all the seedy sort of commercial hotel that one might be ashamed of and wish to hide from one's girlfriend, even supposing her to be a superior type, which I was far from being.

Mrs Baker had again taken me into Skipton the following Saturday, two days after my talk with Stephen. We didn't want to be secretive, but in view of Agnes' health – she was still in bed at home – we didn't want to get all alarmist. Nothing seemed more natural than that I should appear to be spending the day with Mrs Baker, who actually did want to shop in Leeds. Stephen drove us in his car and we left Mrs Baker in the middle of the town, arranging to meet her for tea at the Queen's Hotel or even sherry if we were later. She said not to worry, she'd want to put her feet up anyway.

At first everything at the hotel seemed perfectly straight forward. A uniformed desk clerk told us that a Mr Ryder had indeed been a guest at the hotel. P. J. Ryder. Peter James Ryder.

'He had a room and bath on the second floor, sir. Is anything wrong?'

Stephen had already told the man I was Peter's fiancée and he was a solicitor.

'Well, he does seem to be missing and this young lady is worried. He arranged to meet her and never turned up.'

'I'm sorry sir; but he did seem a busy gentleman. He was hardly ever here.'

77

'Oh?'

'We don't normally notice these things, you know, sir. This is quite a large hotel and people come and go all the time. It was just that, er, Mr Ryder gave me an unusually large tip for a short stay, so I have reason to remember him. Nothing wrong with that, is there, sir?'

'Nothing at all as far as I can see; but it was unusually large?'

'I think ten pounds is a very large tip sir for a stay of less than a week.'

Stephen and I looked at each other.

'Mr Ryder was only here a *week*?'

'Well, less than that, sir, but nobody ever saw him. He paid for five nights bed and breakfast. Oh yes, he once dined in the hotel.'

'Alone?' I asked timidly.

'He does not appear to have had a guest, madam.'

'Do you think I could see the dates?' said Stephen and the clerk pushed the ledger towards him.

'Mr Ryder registered on the night of September seventh, sir; it was a Friday and he checked out on the twelfth, a Wednesday, just under the week, sir.'

'The day after I arrived,' I said to Stephen. 'I came up on Tuesday the eleventh. He was supposed to meet me.'

'So he checked out the day after you came?'

'Apparently.'

I felt embarrassed with the good-natured desk clerk's eyes on me. Another young female crossed in love, he would be thinking.

'Do you want to see the room, sir?'

'I don't think there's any point, thank you,' Stephen said. 'Do you, Jocasta?' I shook my head. 'No? Well, thank you. You have no idea where Mr Ryder went?'

'No sir, I don't recall his departure.'

'Would anyone else know?'

'If I went to a lot of trouble, sir, I *might* find someone who saw him go, but I doubt if it's worth your while, sir, if you'll forgive me saying so. We do have a lot of custom, in and out. I don't even think I would recall what Mr Ryder looked like.'

'Oh!' I said, fumbling in my bag. 'I do have a snap. Not a very good one. Peter on holiday in France the year I met him.' I fished out the treasured snap. The only one I had of Peter. He was leaning over a wall, smiling in that vacuous way people do for the camera. It was taken from some distance and was altogether not a good likeness at all. However, I pushed it under the clerk's nose.

'Is that him?'

'Oh, well, miss . . . yes, this does ring a bell. I think it might be the gentleman.'

Stephen produced a card from his wallet and gave it to the clerk together with a one pound note tucked discreetly under it.

'Thank you so much. If you could ask around and if you do come up with anything useful I would be obliged if you would ring me and your trouble will be recompensed of course. It's just that the man concerned may be ill . . .'

'I understand, sir, of course.' The clerk took the card and the note and bowed to us, heaving another ledger over as he did so. The day's work must go on.

'At least we know he's alive,' Stephen said in the car.

'Did you ever think anything else?' I couldn't keep the bitterness from my voice.

'Oh, I don't know . . .' Stephen's voice trailed off as he looked at me, hunched up in the seat, the picture of a rejected woman. 'I'm sorry, Jocasta.'

'I want to know where he lived,' I said suddenly.

'But why, what's the point?'

'I want to see his flat. He must have had belongings. There may be clues.'

'My dear, I think Peter probably had an idea this was on the cards. It all looks very prepared to me.'

'I want to know who he worked for, where he went . . . what happened. I must know, don't you see, Stephen? Don't you think his relatives would want to know what's happened to Peter? His mother! If Tim and Agnes don't care, surely his mother would care? Can't we find out where she lives?'

'It will take time,' Stephen said a little weakly – I don't think he'd quite bargained for this. 'And by that time, you may hear from him again.'

'Well let's start,' I said firmly. 'And I've money if you need it.'

'I don't see why we should need money. I should have thought Tim had no reason to withold his mother's address from you.'

'You don't know Tim,' I said grimly. 'Oh Stephen, how I hate to go back to that place.'

'Come and stay with Mother.'

'No! Don't you see, the Ryders are the clue to Peter?'

For all my bravado, the muscles of my stomach tightened as Mrs Baker dropped me outside Croft House shortly after seven that night and I saw the light in the drawing room. She pressed my hand as I got out of the car, and in the dark I gave her a courageous smile I didn't really feel.

Did I look white and frightened as I opened the door and forced myself to go inside? The house always seemed to be still and silent these days, an invisible wall of unwelcome. But today there were noises from the drawing room and suddenly the door opened and Agnes stood there smiling.

'Jo! I thought I heard the car. Come in and meet some friends of ours. We're having a dinner party, I forgot to tell you.'

'Oh dear.' I felt confused. 'Please let me go and change, Agnes.'

'No, everyone's informal, come on. The men were shooting and Karen and I have been spending a girlish afternoon chatting and crooning over the most adorable baby.'

I felt my interest quicken. These were the exciting Fullertons, over whom that whiff of scandal hovered.

Tim was getting drinks when I walked in and I thought

the Fullertons looked at me with as much interest as I felt about them. Karen was a dark beauty but her face, I thought, showed signs of tension, and her body was too thin. She was very taut, as though all her nerve endings were straining for any nuance in the atmosphere. I was introduced to her and shook hands and then literally a huge paw grasped mine and nearly pulled me off my feet.

'This is Hugh, my husband,' Karen said. 'Yes, he's got a bearish grip, hasn't he? Doesn't know his own strength.'

'How do you do?'

Hugh Fullerton nodded, but didn't smile. He looked to me the sort of man who hardly ever smiled; a huge man with a piercing, rather unnerving stare. I decided I didn't like him very much. He made me feel shy. They both did, in fact; a strange electric pair.

'I'll just go and wash,' I said, thinking that as the women were in slacks and the men suede hunting jackets it would be absurd to change.

'Oh, let me show you the baby – ' Agnes joined me smiling at Karen – 'may I?'

'Of course; don't wake him up.'

'He's in the spare room.'

Excitedly, Agnes ran up the stairs ahead of me. I was astonished at this demonstration of a maternal instinct I hadn't expected her to have. She shot down yet another dark passageway I hadn't seen, and quietly opened a door.

The baby was tiny, very new indeed and was all wrapped up in warm shawls.

'Isn't he an angel? Gavin. Six weeks old, imagine! Isn't he like Hugh?'

I peered through the gloom but thought it was difficult to decide which parent the baby resembled.

'I can hardly see him,' I said.

'He's just been fed. He's on the breast; she's very earthy, you know; paints. In fact, she's quite famous. Do you like her?'

'I can hardly say in such a short time.'

'She's my best friend, really. She understands me.' Agnes looked at me rather reproachfully as though to say I had been weighed on the friendship scales and been found wanting.

'But isn't she a lot older than you?'

'She's in her thirties, I suppose. So?'

What I really meant was that I thought Karen Fullerton looked very much more mature than Agnes; there was a steely knowing quality about her eyes that made you feel she knew most things and would miss absolutely nothing. What did Karen make of Agnes' turns? I'd give a lot to know.

We left the sleeping baby and went downstairs and I spent a leisurly twenty minutes in my room washing, reapplying make-up and smoking a cigarette, thinking back on the day.

When I went downstairs they were about to begin dinner and Tim rather crossly thrust a glass of sherry at me.

'Mrs Bargett's come specially in to cook,' he said. 'We don't want to be late.'

'I'm sorry, Tim.' I gulped my drink and followed them into the dining room. The table was beautifully set with silver, crystal glasses, and starched white napkins. The meal was simple, but very satisfying: soup, smoked salmon and good Yorkshire roast beef. Before the beef we had Yorkshire pudding on its own with gravy, a custom that I knew about but found strange. Of course, I really was the outsider here. Or was I?

'Are you from Yorkshire?' I asked Karen. Hugh had a very definite Yorkshire accent, so there was no doubt about his origins.

'Yes. I was born in Hammersleigh; but I lived abroad for a long time.'

'That's why she sounds so refined,' Hugh said brusquely.

I decided I really didn't like him at all, but his wife gave me an affectionate mocking look.

'How are you liking it here, Jocasta?'

'Oh, I love the country . . .'

'It's the people she's not so keen on,' Agnes said lightly. I thought too lightly. Dangerously lightly.

'That's not true,' I said colouring. 'I like the people very much.'

'Poor Jo! My head has been bad almost ever since she arrived. She must think I'm some useless idiot.'

'That's *not* true, Agnes. I wish I could do more to help.'

'You could help by being more understanding,' Tim said.

The embarrassment was almost palpable. Even Hugh seemed to feel it and stopped eating to look around the table with a puzzled frown. Then he glanced at his wife, shrugged his shoulders and resumed his meal.

I knew my face was flaming and I longed to get up and run from the room; but willpower coupled with a strong desire not to look foolish kept me in my place. I decided not to answer. I thought Karen was looking at me with approval and as I met her eyes she smiled encouragingly.

The rest of the meal I forget, so overwhelmed was I with a longing to be out of Croft House.

It was afterwards in the lounge that Karen made a point of trying to speak to me and eventually brought her coffee to where I had been sitting alone on one of the sofas.

'You must come and see Hammersleigh Hall. Hugh and I have been refurbishing it with a grant from the state! It's not actually an ancient monument, but it was falling to bits, so someone we know on the council pulled some strings.'

'I'd love to.' I knew my voice was flat and unenthusiastic. For one thing I could see Agnes looking at me and I didn't want her to be jealous of me talking to her 'best friend'.

'And how do you like the school?'

'Oh, I love it. It's charming. Very different . . .' I stopped and cocked my ear. 'Isn't that your baby crying?'

'Oh, what good ears you have! Don't say he's hungry again. We shall have to go soon anyway.' She got up, seeming reluctant to leave me as though she wanted to say something. I caught her eye and understood.

83

'I'll come up and have another look at your lovely baby if I may.'

Agnes was turning over some records with Hugh and didn't see us go out. For that I was thankful.

Karen swiftly and competently handled the screaming baby as though she had six more. Yes, she was a very competent woman; capable and so kind. Secure.

'Oh, he's only wet.' She got a nappy out of a bag on the floor and did complicated things with pins and talcum powder. 'I wanted to have a word with you about Agnes. I can see you're not happy here.'

'Is it as obvious as that?'

'To me it is. You came into the room as though you were going to the dentist.'

'Well, what is wrong with Agnes?'

'We're trying to find out; that is, her doctor and her close friends are.'

'And Tim?'

'Tim is almost as bad as she is.'

'But he doesn't get headaches . . .'

'I mean he's *so* neurotic. He's obsessed by Agnes and can't talk about her logically. I like the girl, I like them both, and I want to try and help her. I got drawn into this by our doctor; but of course I can't do anything much. We really live too far away and with Gavin and Tina, my stepdaughter, I have my hands pretty full.'

'Does the doctor think it is psychological?'

'He's baffled, but – ' Karen looked at the door and lowered her voice – 'physically they can find nothing wrong with her. She was thoroughly examined at the Radcliffe. It is completely normal.'

'But does migraine *show*?'

'This is the point. It's more than migraine. She seems to collapse. She really does. It's quite frightening. The other day outside our house I thought she was dying . . .'

'Tim said something about her being dead—'

'Yes, but she's nowhere near death, I mean she just looks

awful; but the doctor has examined her during one of these spells and finds pulse, breathing, everything quite normal – *during* an attack.'

I sat on the bed. Karen was gently rocking Gavin and he seemed to be dozing off to sleep again.

'I can't do anything for her. She doesn't like me.'

'But she does. She wants to. She told me. She says you're shy and difficult to know . . .'

'Yes, I am shy; but I thought . . . I thought it was her, and there's definite dislike from Tim.'

'Look, you know they're an odd pair. The had no mother and . . . well, you might know something about the family background. I think it would be very nice if you could try and befriend Agnes.'

Her warm, concerned voice touched me but failed to move me deeply. Did Karen know, or care, anything about my problems. About Peter?

'Frankly, it's difficult to befriend them,' I said at last. 'They're both so terribly selfish. Do you know that my boyfriend, their cousin, has disappeared and they're not the least bit concerned about him?'

Karen was gathering up the baby's things and paused. She turned slowly and looked at me.

'You mean Peter? Peter Ryder has disappeared?'

'Yes.'

'But we saw Peter only a couple of weeks ago. He was looking forward to coming up. He was going to meet you. In Leeds.'

'Yes,' I breathed excitedly. 'When did you see him?'

'Well, I can't remember exactly when, but I do remember it because . . . well, there is a silly feud going on here which you probably don't know about with another family in the valley. It's typical of the Dales.'

'Yes, I know, I do know,' I whispered. 'With the Dabroe family.

'That's it. Well, Peter was having dinner with Jonathan Dabroe and he nearly had a fit when he saw us and begged us not to tell the Ryders. He came especially over to our table to ask us. We were at a funny little Chinese restaurant in Leeds which has marvellous food, but the last place you'd expect anyone else to know about. The last place Peter would have expected to see anyone from the Dales.'

'But why was he having dinner with Jonathan Dabroe? Why?'

'I don't know . . . I . . .'

And we both stopped guiltily as the door opened and Agnes came swirling angrily into the room.

Eight

On Monday morning I waited eagerly for the black Jaguar to bring the children to school. I got there early and stood by the gate. I was determined to see Jonathan Dabroe. But to my dismay, the blue estate car came along instead, and Mrs Dabroe got out and started to shepherd the children towards the school gate. I watched their progress, trying to decide what to do. Mrs Dabroe made up my mind for me by coming right up to the gate with the children and wishing me a good morning in a very civil voice. The children ran towards the school house and their mother was about to turn away.

'Mrs Dabroe!'

She stopped and looked quizzically at me detecting, perhaps, the strain in my voice.

'Miss Oaks, you wanted to speak to me?'

'I'd like to talk to your husband actually.'

'My husband!'

'It's something personal, but it is important.'

'Could you tell me what it's about?'

'Well, I'm afraid I can't, here. Please, Mrs Dabroe . . .'

'Certainly, why don't you come up to the house this evening? Say about seven? He left for Newcastle early today, but he'll be back about then.'

How could I get to the house at seven without anyone knowing? Yet if I refused, it would look so strange. Stephen! Maybe this was one of his nights at home.

'That would be fine,' I said. 'Thank you so much.'

'The house is along—'

'I'll find it. There's the bell. 'Bye.'

I could sense her eyes on my back as I dashed into the classroom feeling extremely foolish but rather brave at the same time.

As it happened, it *was* one of Stephen's nights at home. I told his mother at lunchtime I wanted to see him but I didn't tell her why. I felt that, much as I liked her, Mrs Baker was so involved with the life of the village that my meeting with the forbidden Dabroe family might upset her.

'I'm sure Stephen will do anything you say, dear. He's very keen on this knight-errant role. Phone him now if you like.'

Stephen was in his office. He'd be delighted to pick me up at six, and would I have dinner with him?

'I've something to tell you too,' he added. 'I've been on the phone all morning on your business.'

'Oh Stephen—'

The bell rang for afternoon school and I shut the door of my little classroom and got out the elementary reading books we were doing.

'Now children, can we look at our big alphabet books.'

A rustle of paper and my obedient pupils had their large books open in front of them. Besides each letter were some words and a little story.

'Now, Henrietta. "A is for . . ."'

'"A is for Apple", miss.'

'Good, can you go on?'

Henrietta, one of the youngest, began in her tremulous little voice. '"The apple is, r . . . r . . ."'

'Anyone know?'

'"Red", miss,' shrieked the precocious Natalie. '"A is for Apple; the apple is red; some apples are green . . ."'

'That's enough, Natalie.' I held up a hand, laughing. Natalie was a fluent reader and it really was unfair to have her show up my dear rather backward little Henrietta.

'Can you go on, Henrietta?'

'". . . r . . . r-red",' said Henrietta doggedly then, unaware that Natalie had read the next section for her, stuck over 's'.

I sighed. Outside, the rain had started again. Our beautiful

September had gone for good. It seemed curious to have my mind buzzing with a thousand thoughts about Peter, the Dabroes, and the Ryders, both of whom had been very civil to me during Sunday, as though the approval of Karen Fullerton had improved my image in their eyes, and then the contrast with this tranquil village school and the timeless ancient beauty of the Dales outside.

After Henrietta had finished mauling A to bits, I turned to Simon Hinchliffe, a bright little boy whose father was the village policeman.

'Now, Simon, can you do "B"?'

'"B",' said Simon carefully, '"is for Button . . ."'

Agnes was in the drawing room when I got home. She was pouring tea and on the sofa beside her was an open book.

'Jo, there you are. I've just taken Tim a cup. You can keep me company. Had a good day?'

'Very good.'

'You're liking the school?'

'Loving it. And the children are such dears.'

'I often wished we'd gone to the local school, everyone else did. But our father was keen to have us away from the village.' Her voice sounded bitter and I thought she was about to tell me what I, after all, already knew; but no.

'I had a wandering childhood too,' I said, sensing she was looking to me for that companionship Karen had described. 'You look better today, Agnes.'

'Oh, I'm fine. I'm not always ill, you know, Jo; just when I'm disturbed.'

'I suppose me coming was a sort of disturbance?'

'Yes, I suppose it was. It's difficult to adjust to someone in the house, a stranger, you know.'

I stirred my tea thoughtfully.

'Agnes . . . would you prefer it if I found accommodation somewhere else?'

For a moment I thought Agnes looked intensely relieved

and was going to say yes, but she frowned and lowered her eyes.

'Of course not, Jo. As long as you're here—'

'But, Agnes, you and Tim keep saying that! "As long as I'm here". I'm going to stay here for a whole year. I'm under contract.'

'Yes, but will you stay if Peter . . . if Peter doesn't come back?'

She looked at me timidly. This was the first time she'd mentioned Peter. It had come into the category of subjects, I'd assumed, that gave her a bad head. Even now she passed a hand over her brow as though anticipating one at any moment.

'I'm expecting Peter to come back. I don't know what has happened to Peter or why, but everything has a logical explanation, hasn't it, Agnes?'

'I suppose so . . .' Her voice trailed away as though she were getting tired. Maybe she was as worried about Peter as I was.

'He must turn up sometime, Agnes, mustn't he? He can't just *disappear*?' I realized my voice was rising and Agnes was looking more and more fraught, almost scared, with her large dark eyes gazing at me.

'What the hell are you doing?' Tim's voice behind me was thunderous and when he grabbed my shoulder I felt like slapping his face, such was the fury his gesture engendered in me.

'Take your hand away!' I snapped. 'How dare you touch me!'

'And how dare you speak to my sister like that!'

'I wasn't speaking to her any way at all.'

'You were. You were threatening her.'

'I was not!' I knew my face was blazing and my hand still had hold of his wrist. I thought any moment he was going to strike me.

'Why did you raise your voice to her?' He let go of my shoulder and rubbed his wrist, which I was glad to see was good and red.

'Tim, can't you see I'm frantic about Peter? Don't you understand that, you and Agnes, or are you so bound up in your own affairs?'

'We're not bound up in our own affairs. We're worried about Peter too; but we don't see what you can do about it if a man chooses voluntarily to disappear. Peter has done this kind of thing before, you know.'

Immediately the rage inside me abated, like a sea suddenly calm after the wind had dropped.

'Has he?'

'Of course he has.'

It would be typical, of course. It was a Peter-like thing to do. He hadn't ever done it to me before, presumably because he'd been in love with me; but he'd certainly gone off abruptly and then not appeared for days until he phoned or turned up out of the blue.

'Peter has actually gone off for a long time without saying anything?'

'Frequently, abroad, often for weeks. Then we have a phone call and he's back again, or he suddenly turns up.'

I looked at them both, suddenly contrite; each seemed to be looking at me anxiously, Agnes very pale now.

'I'm sorry,' I said. 'I think I've been the victim of hysteria.'

'Well, it's understandable,' Tim said, the tone of his voice placatory. 'Isn't it, Aggie?'

'Of course. She doesn't know him as well as we do. Peter is *very* unpredictable, Jo, even unreliable. That's why we were so pleased he seemed smitten with you. We thought he might settle down, get married maybe. But then he doesn't turn up to meet you. We think it's rather symbolical . . .'

'You mean that he doesn't love me?' I said quietly. The ground was beginning to move under my feet and I sat down abruptly. 'He suddenly decided he didn't want me after all. Couldn't face me?'

Neither of them said anything. Agnes lit a cigarette and exhaled vigorously.

'You hadn't wanted to tell me,' I went on.

'He did it once before,' Tim said gently. 'With a girl. He just took off and didn't even tell her. He never saw her again. We know him, you see, he's our cousin. He seems to go so far and then decides he can't face the responsibility.'

'That's why we thought you mightn't want to stay . . . when you knew the truth about Peter,' Agnes said, putting a hand on my knee and patting it gently.

'We wanted to be sure it was the truth first,' Tim continued.

'But after a week or so it looks—'

'Nearly two,' I said bleakly. 'I've been here nearly two weeks. It's so cruel. Such a cruel thing to do. I can't believe it.' I realized I was close to tears and searched for my handkerchief in my bag.

'You can stay with us as long as you want to,' Agnes said, her hand still on my knee. 'But we understand if you want to go.'

'What will Mrs Baker say?'

'I'm sure she'll understand. But what would you do for a job?'

'Oh, I'd get a job supply teaching or something,' I said morosely. 'It doesn't really matter. I've got a bit of money. I never spent very much on myself.'

I gazed at the floor, staring into the future. The bedsitting room in Swiss Cottage with its impersonal furniture, its well-worn carpet with the bright Marks and Spencer rug by the gas fire, the small Belling stove in the corner; the lodgers who came and went and the few who remained for a long time, like me. The permanent fixtures, without family, who would perhaps grow old and even die there. Every day I'd got the 13 bus up the Finchley Road and changed at Golders Green. The school was large; the staff young and for the most part friendly but they had their lives to lead too, and they always seemed more interesting than mine, at least on a Monday morning. Their weekends seemed to have been packed full of exciting happenings, visits and parties, whereas mine had been spent largely in bed or at the Odeon Swiss Cottage for a film on Saturday afternoon, not evening because that made me seem more lonely with all the couples around me.

Then Peter had come . . . and suddenly I'd had a lot to talk about on Monday mornings too. Now no Peter. What was life going to be like without Peter? What was I going to go back to without him?

The doorbell rang. I put my hand to my mouth.

'Oh! I'd forgotten. Stephen Baker has asked me out for dinner. That will be him.'

'Oh?' Agnes' voice was curious.

'I suppose he wants something to do,' I said awkwardly.

'Perhaps he wants to take your mind off Peter,' Agnes' tone was unmistakably malicious. 'Maybe it's just as well.'

'I'll let him in.' Tim went to the door and I was aware of Agnes' by now malevolent gaze. Well, what did she want? Did she think I was as fickle as Peter? That I didn't care? Should Stephen and I take them into our confidence; tell them what we were trying to do? Or would it seem absurd now in the light of what they'd told me; of what they undoubtedly believed; that Peter had jilted me. I'd better keep silent.

Stephen came eagerly over to Agnes and took her hand. 'Agnes, it's good to see you, and you look well!'

She smiled up at him, a rather languorous and, I thought, flirtatious smile. Maybe she'd change her mind about him now. Stephen was looking down at her eagerly.

'I'm much better, Stephen, and how well you look too. Positively prosperous.'

'Oh I get by.'

'Sherry, Stephen?' Tim stood by him with a decanter. 'Or whisky?'

'No, a sherry would be nice, thanks.' Stephen looked pleased by his reception. He was glowing. Well, I didn't mind. Let him have Agnes if she wanted him. If Peter had indeed jilted me I couldn't really see I'd be here for long, in a place I hardly knew, in a house where I wasn't really wanted.

Suddenly all these people seemed part of a closed world, alien to me; they'd all known one another since childhood; grown up together; their parents had known one another. Where on earth did I fit in?

But Stephen was looking at me, his eyes speculative.

'Ready Jocasta? I've booked at the Bridge in Hammersleigh, over in Esterdale.'

'That sounds lovely.'

Suddenly it occurred to me there was no earthly reason why we shouldn't suggest a foursome. The way Agnes was looking at Stephen I wondered if it had occurred to her too. What would I do then? How could we refuse? What pub would be booked up on a Monday? The anxiety must have shown in my eyes because Agnes smiled at me mockingly, as though she could read my mind.

'We must have a foursome one night,' she said, 'but not tonight. Tim is engrossed in his new chapter. That's if you'd like to, Stephen?' She lit another cigarette and glanced at him. She was definitely making a play for Stephen.

'That would be marvellous, Agnes. I'll fix it with Tim later in the week.'

'I'll just run up to my room and get a coat,' I said and as I went out I could hear a babble of sound as though they'd all started talking at once.

I thought Stephen's face was rather pink as he started the car.

'Where to, madame?'

'Felton Hall,' I said.

'The *Dabroe* residence?'

'Yes.'

'Is it something about the children?'

'It's about Peter,' and I told him what Karen had said.

'But the Ryders and the Dabroes haven't talked for years.'

'That's what I want to know. Why they were talking then.'

'And you didn't tell Agnes and Tim?'

94

'Not a word.' I looked at him. 'The lady was making a play for you Stephen.'

I couldn't see in the dark but, I imagined, from the sound of his voice, that Stephen's face went pinker.

'That's what I thought. Dammit!'

'It's very flattering, Stephen.'

'Is it?' He looked at me. By the lights from the dashboard I could see his mouth was grim. 'If she thinks I'm interested in someone else, she thinks she'll have a go at me? No fear. I tried and I got nowhere.'

Now I felt pink. Could Stephen possibly be interested in me? But surely he knew that Peter, why Peter . . .

'She's very attractive. Maybe she's changed her mind.'

'Well, I haven't, and no was no.'

'We'll see. Maybe things will change.'

'Nothing will change. I'm not interested in Agnes Ryder any more.'

And I felt by his voice that he meant it, or wanted to mean it.

'Here we are.' Stephen turned off the road and went slowly over a small hump-backed bridge. 'I've only ever been here for parties and the like. They give one a year for the local dignitaries, of whom my mother is counted as one. One can't say she knows them. I knew Douglas Dabroe better than Jonathan becase he played rugby for our club, The Dales United side. However, Jonathan plays a fairish game of cricket for the local team in the summer. I must say I wouldn't mind a bit of business from him.'

'Well, maybe if he gets to know you better he'll give it.'

'Oh no. They'll have their family lawyers. These old families always do. You have to start on a new generation. No, I'm doing nicely really in Skipton; quite a lot of legal work from the Dales farmers, land and stuff like that. There's the house, I think anyway. Hope we don't get stuck up a mud track.

'No, it says "Felton Hall" on the stone lintel.' I was peering out, fascinated. 'My, it's quite a place.'

'It *is* a place. It's a very cold place too, I believe, if my mother is anyone to go by. She's on committees which meet here.'

There was a shortish drive to the house, which seemed to rise up, a noble pile at the end of the drive. There was a light on in the porch and lights behind drawn curtains at various windows. But that's all I could make out for the moment. The gravel crunched beneath our feet as we approached the porch and I waited behind him, looking about, as Stephen rang the bell.

Jonathan Dabroe opened the door to us himself.

'Why, Stephen Baker,' he said, his face breaking into a smile, 'and Miss Oaks behind him! I hope I haven't committed an offence and this is a legal matter.'

'No,' Stephen smiled and shook our host's hand. 'I'm merely giving Jocasta a lift. She's carless. However, I do know what she's come to see you about and wonder if I may sit in.'

'Certainly, certainly. Come this way. This is all rather mysterious.'

Mr Dabroe took us across a broad hall and opened the door into a pleasant long room with fires roaring in two grates.

'Them, do sit down. My wife's at some committee meeting or another, so we're on our own. Natalie and Sebastian are in bed. I didn't dare tell them Miss Oaks was coming or we'd never have got rid of them. You're a great hit with the children, Miss Oaks.' He looked at me and smiled warmly. Jonathan Dabroe was quite a hit with me. He had looks that though striking, were not obtrusive. Some people are so good-looking, you feel uncomfortable in their presence; not Jonathan. They were friendly good looks and seemed contoured out of the land of his native Dales, an almost rugged face with deep-set dark eyes and straight black hair that sprang up from his head and lay naturally in place.

He stood easily with his back to the fire, hands in the pockets of the trousers of his fine tweed suit.

'Did you find us easily? Of course you've been here before, Stephen. Lots of times.'

'Well, once or twice. My mother comes here quite often . . .'

'Ah, committees. They're a way of life in the Dales. I think I must be on twelve at least. How would country life suit you, Miss Oaks?'

I'd been soaking in the atmosphere of the lovely room, barely listening to what he was saying, and his words took me by surprise.

'Oh. I don't really know. So far I like it.'

'London, was it, where you were before?'

'Yes.'

'Well, I hope you'll stay a long time with us, although there's talk of shifting the school after Mrs Baker retires. I'm on that committee too.' He laughed. 'May I get you a whisky?'

'We were drinking sherry,' Stephen said. 'Maybe Jocasta would like one; but I won't drink, Jonathan; we're dining out and I'm driving.'

'I quite understand.' Jonathan turned away and said in an aside, 'I'm also the chairman of the Bench, Miss Oaks!'

'You are busy,' I murmured. 'I suppose your family have been here generations.'

'Well, we're sort of well dug in – ' he gave me my sherry in a small exquisite glass – 'although we're not an old Yorkshire family. My ancestors were French – Dabroe is a corruption of d'Arbre, tree appropriately enough. They were furniture makers from Lyons and came here in the late eighteenth century when fine furniture was so much in demand; established themselves in Leeds, did well, prospered. The Dales connection is not very old, only about a hundred years. My great-great-grandfather built Felton Hall in 1850, so it's not an old family home.'

'Of course, d'Arbre,' I said, thinking of the well-known business organization. 'You've still kept the French.'

'It's still officially called d'Arbre Père et Fils and we have

97

that on all our furniture and machinery. Now, as I don't want to keep you from your dinner may I know . . .'

Now that it came to it, I felt awkward and looked at Stephen for help. But a gesture from him told me he thought it was my business.

'It's about Peter Ryder,' I began and stopped when I saw Jonathan's reaction. He closed his eyes and the muscles of his face tensed as happens when one has a shock. It was momentary, however, and when he looked at me again his expression was quite calm.

'My wife told me you were his fiancée. I did wonder if it was about Peter. I couldn't think of anything else. How is Peter?'

To an ear strained for every nuance I could detect nothing untoward in the tone of his voice.

'Peter seems to have disappeared,' Stephen said. 'We wondered if you might know where he was.'

Now Jonathan Dabroe looked astonished.

'I? Why should I know the whereabouts of Peter? He comes and goes, as far as I know.'

As he spoke, I had that heavy-hearted feeling that was by now becoming so familiar whenever there was talk of Peter. I hadn't yet told Stephen about my talk with the Ryders, there hadn't been time, and to have cancelled the appointment would have seemed too strange. Jonathan was confirming what the Ryders had said.

'As a matter of fact, I don't know him very well,' Jonathan continued. 'I only say this because the Ryders and the Dabroes haven't very much to say to each other. My father, as you may or not know, Miss Oaks—'

'Please call me Jocasta,' I murmured.

'Thank you, Jocasta. Well, my father ran off with the Ryders' mother. It's an episode none of us is very proud of, but it happened. So in fact, the Ryders don't talk to *us* . . . and I can understand why though it had nothing whatever to do with me. In fact we here suffered as much as they did. However, they keep up the feud. Peter Ryder thought this was as stupid as I did and he sought me out in my office about six months ago with a business deal. He wanted to import a new kind of multiple wool-shearer manufactured in Czechoslovakia, and which he thought might have a future in Yorkshire and the North if he could market it well. He thought we could and I agreed with him.'

'Peter wouldn't market it himself?' Stephen interposed.

'No. Peter had no organization as far as I knew; he was simply a dealer, a middle-man acting on commission. We would import and sell the machines and he would get a percentage. Peter's skill came in knowing where to go to buy what and to whom to sell it. Our only public meeting was in a Chinese restaurant in Leeds where we were spotted by the Fullertons. Peter said it would get around. I presume it has?'

'I don't think the Fullertons told the Ryders,' I said.

'Karen told me because she knew I was worried about Peter.'

'But why are you worried about Peter?'

'He arranged for me to come up here, stay with his cousins and failed to meet me—'

Jonathan threw his head back and gave a mannish laugh that I resented because I knew what it meant.

'You don't think it's important, do you, Mr Dabroe?' I knew my voice was chilling and Stephen looked at me approvingly.

Jonathan stopped laughing abruptly.

'Oh, forgive me, Miss Oaks, Jocasta – and you must call me Jonathan if I'm to call you Jocasta, but you know Peter is a very dedicated businessman.'

'And so meeting me wouldn't be so very important compared to importing sheep-shearers?'

'I see I've angered you, Jocasta.' His voice now was solemn.

'I've just been through a lot of worry!' I said. 'I think that for Peter to do such a thing was extraordinary; but now perhaps the more I hear about him, it isn't.' I got up. 'You

99

think I'm a nervous, silly woman, and perhaps you're right.
I'm awfully sorry we troubled you.'

Stephen looked rather puzzled and got up quickly.

'It's no *trouble*, Jocasta.' Jonathan took my elbow and
steered me to the door. 'Don't think that: but please don't
tell the Ryders if you haven't already. It would upset Peter.
We agreed to do business on this basis.'

'What basis?'

'That it was and remained as far as possible a secret. He
was very concerned about the effect on his cousins, especially
Tim, if they found out.'

Nine

O ver dinner, I was still simmering despite all Stephen had done during the drive over the Dales to Hammersleigh to calm me down, assuring me that Jonathan Dabroe wasn't a bad bloke and didn't despise women.

'Well, he despises me. I could feel it. He is such an important man of affairs, chairman of the Bench to boot, that to worry about my boyfriend is a silly girlish pastime. Anyway – ' I speared a portion of hors d'oeuvres and looked at Stephen – 'maybe he's right. I just wished he hadn't shown it so obviously. Peter is apparently adept at letting women down once they are involved with him. According to his cousin Agnes, he does it all the time. He can't take the responsibility of permanent liaison. I think that is why the Ryders have been so odd with me: they were simply embarrassed.'

Stephen had put down his soup spoon and was staring at me.

'I'm sorry, Stephen. It was a wasted journey. But they only told me just before you came. The hunt is over, and they seem to think, and I feel too, I should go back to London . . .'

'But my mother . . .'

'I'm sorry about your mother. I really am. I like her and adore the school. But I'm not wanted here, Stephen. I'm out of place. I've been jilted and I'm embarrassed and everyone will know it . . .'

'Oh, don't be silly!'

'Yes they will. You yourself know how gossip travels in the Dales. I'd be conscious of everyone looking at me and

101

saying, "That's the girl Peter Ryder let down and she's still hanging around."'

Stephen was gazing at me with an expression of almost comical intensity.

'Jocasta, you've got it wrong. People around here are kind people. If they thought about it at all they'd think you had guts; you just go on normally and forget about Peter. Yorkshire people admire steadfastness and courage; they don't go in for emotion very much. It has its good points and its bad, this attitude of theirs, because at times it makes them seem insensitive to one's problems. But pity you, never! They'd admire you.'

This hadn't occurred to me.

'You mean I should stay on?'

'Of course, and teach.'

'But I can't stay with the Ryders now!'

'They seemed to like you, I thought.'

'And Peter comes back and I'm still there? No fear.'

'I see your point. Jo – ' Stephen looked down at his plate of, by now, stone-cold soup – 'I am very sorry about Peter, for your sake. I know how you must feel; but I think that the best thing is to put him out of your mind. I'll talk to Mother about somewhere to live, there's sure to be some farm, and if you let me take you about . . . why . . .' he faltered.

Yes, I did like him. He was like me; shy but not paralysingly so. It was becoming, if one can use such a word about a man. He was different. Of course I could never feel about him as I felt – had felt? I wasn't sure – about Peter, but he was nice. He was a good friend. I sighed.

'What was it you were going to tell me?'

'Oh well, that's irrelevant now, if you think Peter's disappearance is natural. I just found out where he lived.'

'Oh?' He was right; my curiosity was perfunctory.

'Not interested?'

'Not really.'

'Brave girl because there is one thing. He has kept on the flat; he didn't give it up.'

'He is a swine,' I said, 'isn't he?'

Stephen screwed up his face, crumbling bread on the table.

'I'm not sure. I can't fathom one thing: why did he go to that hotel? It's the one thing I can't understand. Everything else, yes.'

'I think now that Peter was so devious, most of what he did had no logical answer. He took me in well and truly. I'm not going to think about him again, Stephen; but thank you for your help. Thank you.'

Stephen looked into my eyes and in them I saw tenderness, perhaps a hint of passion? I couldn't look at him like that. Not yet. Not after . . . oh Peter.

The hall was in darkness as I let myself in shortly after eleven. One would have thought they'd have kept a light on for me. I fumbled for the switch but as my eyes gradually became accustomed to the dark I realized that a light was coming from under the door next to the drawing room. Tim would be in his study. Maybe now while I felt brave and strong, still angry about Jonathan Dabroe and Peter's fickleness, I should tell Tim I was going. I felt it would help them to relax. They hadn't been very nice to me but I wished them no harm, after all.

Yes, the light came from the little hall. I knocked on the door of Tim's study. No reply. I couldn't be sure if the light was on there or not. Timidly I opened the door. A dim light was on in the corner of the room. Tim was slumped in a chair, a book fallen one the floor beside him. For a horrifying moment, in the oppressive atmosphere of the house, I imagined he was dead; but then he gave a snort and shifted in the chair. I thought he was about to waken and I moved back to the door on tip-toe. I don't know what drew my eyes to the desk; there was no light on it and apart from the fact that it was so tidy nothing exceptional about it at all. It was, I think, the gleam of metal in the light that attracted me, and as I looked, I became mesmerized and moved closer, fascinated by what I saw. A solitary bunch of keys gleamed in the middle of the desk. A large, fat bunch of keys, such as I'd never seen in possession of either of the Ryders, the front door remaining open most of the time. The car keys, used by both of them, lay on a tray on the hall table. Could they be Peter's keys? Why not? The keys to his flat.

Suddenly Tim stirred and a dread of him seeing me overwhelmed me. I tip-toed quickly to the door and crept out, leaving it slightly open so that he would not hear me. I shut the hall door quietly behind me and crept upstairs in the dark, not daring even to put on a light while all around me the heavy atmosphere of the house lay like a pall. Inside my room, the moonlight fell unevenly on the carpet; looking out, I saw the moon was partly obscured by the cliff – that evil, menacing cliff that, as I stared, came nearer and nearer like a predatory hand. It would engulf the whole house and me with it; it would crush us all. Why was I so frightened, so chilled in this house? Did some sort of presence of evil lurk here?

Not surprisingly, I slept fitfully. At one time, I sat bolt upright in bed, thinking I heard banging coming from under me, somewhere in the bowels of the house, my heart hammering against my chest. But no, it was the bough of the great elm buffeting the window pane in the landing downstairs; outside the wind howled and the next time I woke, rain was lashing down, drowning the sound of the tree.

I was cold and stiff in my bed and grateful to be up early and sipping tea made with the kettle in my room. In fact I never breakfasted in the house but slipped out after my tea and ate the delicious soft buns Mrs Baker brought for the children's milk break. She was late to school that morning – there had been something wrong with her car – and the pelting rain slowed down her pace as it had mine, but I could tell she wanted to speak to me. The chance came as we sat at the table eating our buns and drinking coffee while the children played indoors during break.

'I think I've somewhere for you to stay. Mrs Pagett who runs the farm outside the village on the Conistone road would let you a room for—'

I shook my head, my mouth still full of bun.

'You don't want it? You're *not* going? Oh dear . . .' Her sweet face crumpled and I hastened to reassure her.

'No. I'm staying, and I'm staying at the Ryders'.'

'Oh good, you're friends.'

Again I shook my head.

'Nothing to do with friendship. I think they know much more about Peter than they admit. They know where he is, I'm sure, and I do think there's something wrong – with Peter I mean.'

'But, my dear, why?'

'The jilted story was very convenient, maybe for them all. But I think Peter is in trouble and the Ryders are helping him by shielding him. I think they've got the keys of his flat. I saw them on Tim's desk. I'm sure they must be Peter's; if so, Tim is looking after the flat, why?'

'And you know they're his keys?'

'Not for sure, but they were a large bunch, and I've never seen the Ryders with keys like those – car keys, flat keys, you know the sort of thing.'

Mrs Baker wiped her hands on a sticky napkin.

'These buns are super, no wonder I'm getting fat. Well, my dear, it all sounds very inconclusive to me.'

'Oh, I agree there's nothing positive to go on. But I think they are hiding something. He didn't live in a hotel, he has kept his flat on . . .'

'Why don't you just ask them?'

'Somehow I don't think that's the right thing. I don't know why. Maybe I'm being too secretive . . . like them. But I want to stay on there, much as I hate the place, until I know where Peter is and why he went. That's all. If he wants to be rid of me then I want to know; let him tell me. If he's in trouble I want to help him. Whatever it is, I want to know.'

'You still love him, don't you?'

'Of course. I'm hurt and I'm bewildered, but you can't just toss love aside like that . . .'

'Of course you can't.' Mrs Baker looked at me, her eyes brimming with sympathy. 'Poor Stephen. He's quite struck, you know.'

'I know and I don't want to hurt him, or use him.'

'He wants to help you. I think he wants to know about Peter too. It will make it easier for him.'

Her eyes gazed appealingly at me and I smiled.

'He's awfully sweet,' I said. 'I'm lucky to have him, and you.'

She reached out and touched my hand.

'Ring the bell, dear, will you? The children have already had an extra ten minutes.'

We were doing crafts that morning. I'd had the children out the previous day collecting twigs and leaves from the surrounding fields, and they were doing collages on hardboard or scraps of cloth. Watching their young heads bent so carefully over their work, I felt a momentary sense of tranquility and hope and I busied myself with glue and cotton as they came to me individually for help.

Natalie Dabroe never needed help; she was a competent little creature and when she did come to you, it was more for attention than anything else. It was almost as though she knew she was my favourite and I had to be careful not to show it. This particular morning she wanted a lot of my time and was forever marching up to my desk with a misplaced twig or a handkerchief soaked with glue.

'Natalie! What is the matter with you today?' I thought she looked pale with dark circles round her eyes. Suddenly they brimmed over with tears and I put out my arms and took her on my lap. 'There, there . . . what is it, Natalie?' The others gathered around with interest and I gently shooed them away. 'Don't you feel well?' I stroked her forehead and pushed the hair out of her eyes. She sobbed on to my bosom, great heaving sobs, and I became alarmed and wondered if she were ill.

'It's Mummy,' she sobbed. 'She told Daddy she's going to leave him.' There was an enormous wail, which startled Mrs Baker in the next class and she looked across at me through the partition. I signalled to her and she came through the door, Sebastian with her. As soon as she saw her brother, Natalie stopped crying and she put her hands out to him. In a sweet protective gesture, he put his arms round her shoulders and squeezed her.

'What is it, Jocasta?' Mrs Baker whispered.

'Get on with your work, children,' I called to the fascinated class and spoke quietly to Mrs Baker. 'I think the parents have had a row.'

'Really? How unusual.' Then to Sebastian. 'Something at home seems to have upset Natalie, Sebastian. Do you know what it is?' Sebastian's eyes were full of knowledge but he solemnly shook his head.

'No, Mrs Baker.'

Of course at ten he was old enough to want to keep family secrets to himself.

'Perhaps if we leave them,' I murmured. 'Sebastian, would you like to take Natalie to Mrs Baker's table and talk to her?'

'Oh yes, miss.'

He led her over to the corner, and wide-eyed, I looked at Mrs Baker who pursed her lips. Silently she went back to her room and I tried to collect my wits and apply myself to the graphic art of collage as practiced by the under-sevens of Coppitts Green school.

Stephen was pleased with himself. He not only knew where Peter lived; he had acquired a set of keys to his flat. I hadn't seen him since my discovery at the house, but I'd told him on the phone, at Mrs Baker's house, what I wanted. It was out of the question for me to somehow try to get the keys from Tim's study. The last time I'd looked they had gone from the desk. It seemed too much like the heroine of a late night television movie to go creeping round, trying to smuggle keys from Tim's desk.

We'd had to wait until the Saturday following my decision to try to find out more about Peter. The week had passed uneventfully enough. I was very busy on preparation for school – the concentration on country things was very different from our school in London; even the books were oriented to subjects of interest to country children and I had a lot of swotting to do. Except for the evening meal, I saw little of the Ryders. Agnes seemed well and headache-free. I could see she was becoming accustomed to me and that the fact we'd got down to an even routine had settled her.

But it hadn't settled me. I seemed to dread going back to the house a little more each day until I would begin to look for it apprehensively as I walked along the road from school. It first came into view as one rounded the bend by the pub and the bridge and then, like the cliff, it grew bigger and darker, almost menacing, as you approached. It was absurd, I knew that. It was absurd to be frightened of a house, to feel threatened by a cliff.

As before, Mrs Baker drove me into Skipton and Stephen then took us both into Leeds where he dropped off his mother.

The flat was in a road off the Wetherby road about three or four miles out of the city; in the very opposite direction, interestingly enough, from the hotel.

'How did you get the keys?'

'I knew the agent. Peter rents it unfurnished on a five-year tenancy. He's been there eighteen months.'

'You're quite the detective,' I said lightly. 'How did you discover where he lived, by the way?'

'By finding out if he was a ratepayer. If you rent an unfurnished flat or own one you pay rates. His name and address were on the electoral register. I then went to the block, found out who managed it and, presto! I don't think that you'll find anything though.'

'I want to know why he went to that hotel.'

Stephen changed gear and turned off the road down a smaller one.

'It's a block along here. I wondered, Jocasta, if it would make you happier if I talked to a friend of mine in the police.'

'No!'

'But why not?'

'If Peter has disappeared and it's not because of me, he has a good reason. I don't want to alert the police.'

'I could just make some inquires.'

'No.'

Stephen shrugged and stopped the car.

'Right. Here we are.'

It was a small block of about eight flats, two to a floor. Red stone, nothing exceptional, nicely landscaped into what had probably been the garden of the large house that must have been pulled down to make way for the flats. Stephen let us into a pleasant entrance hall and we took the lift to the second floor. The growing sense of nervousness at seeing the place Peter had never asked me to visit amounted almost to panic as the lift began its ascent and by the time we stopped on the second floor, I wanted to go down again.

Stephen smiled at me reassuringly.

'We won't stay if you don't want to; but now we're here . . .'

'Of course.' I swallowed and stood behind him as he put the key in the Yale lock and the door swung open.

I shivered, there was a penetrating sense of cold, like entering a cave. Yet outside the sun was shining and indeed Peter's flat faced south and the living room, into which we stepped, was flooded with sunlight.

'Golly it's hot,' Stephen said. 'They must have turned on the central heating.'

'I'm cold,' I said. 'I'm shivering.' And I pulled the collar of my coat closer around me.

'It's nerves, girl. Well, here we are.'

It was comfortable enough, but it looked just like a hotel, with the same sort of furniture and the same unlived-in appearance. It had a conventional three-piece suite, a coffee table with some magazines scattered on it, a colour television set, a dining table in the corner and around it four chairs. On the other side was a sideboard with bottles and decanters on it and in addition there were a few occasional chairs. That was all.

Next to this was a small spotless kitchen that looked as though it was hardly ever used either. Typical bachelor, I thought. Opposite the kitchen was a small hall that led to the single bedroom and bathroom. Hotel furnishing again. A double bed, a chest of drawers, a long mirror fixed on the wall, a wardrobe, a bedside table with an alarm clock, some aspirin and an ash-tray. The bathroom was completely tiled and spotlessly clean; toothpaste in a mug, but no toothbrush, shaving cream, plasters and assorted bottles in the cabinet on the wall.

'It looks as though it's just been cleaned,' I said.

'It looks as though no one has lived here for ages,' Stephen murmured, looking in the cupboard, through the drawers. 'There're hardly any clothes here. It seems as though Peter had packed meaning to go for a long time.'

'Yes, it does,' I said. 'Did he say anything to the agent?'

'No he pays his rent and rates by banker's draft. National Westminster, I checked.'

There was a movement at the door and we both started guiltily as though we'd been caught pilfering.

'Oh sorry. I thought it was Peter. I thought he'd come back.'

A woman stood at the door; she was about forty, large and blonde. She was dressed in a housecoat and in one hand was a cigarette while a hostile-looking cat, nestled against her bosom, was cradled in the other arm.

I still felt cold and apprehensive and I huddled against the central-heating radiator while Stephen went up to the woman.

'How do you do? I'm Stephen Baker, this is Jocasta Oaks.'

The woman nodded pleasantly enough but said nothing. She obviously wanted to know what we were doing here.

'Do you know where Peter Ryder is?'

'No, I don't. I'm wondering that myself. I'm his neighbour Kitty Bradshaw, *Mrs* Bradshaw.' She seemed to underline the Mrs as though to emphasize that the relationship was one of the utmost respectability.

'When did you last see Peter, Mrs Bradshaw?' Stephen asked her politely.

'May I ask why you want to know?' She carefully put the cat down and stubbed the cigarette out in an ash-tray. Then she folded her arms and assumed an obdurate expression.

'Miss Oaks is a very great friend of Mr Ryder's . . .'

'Oh?' She looked at me as though what she was hearing was a bunch of lies.

'She was almost engaged to him . . .'

'Oh?' Disbelief as her eyes cooly appraised me.

'He was supposed to meet her in Leeds, over three weeks ago . . .'

She looked at Stephen and got a packet of cigarettes and a flashy gold lighter from her pocket.

'I still don't see that gives you the right to prowl round his flat.'

Stephen was beginning to perspire. He got out a large white handkerchief and mopped his face. I could see he was wondering if he could be struck off the roll for breaking and entering.

'Mrs Bradshaw, would you sit down? We're not here on a fool's errand. Miss Oaks, Jocasta here, is worried about where Peter Ryder is.'

'Oh, Jocasta!' Mrs Bradshaw pronounced my name with a decided softening in her voice. 'Now, he has talked about a young lady in London. I remembered that name, it being so unusual.'

'Quite.' Stephen mopped his face again, this time I sensed with relief.

'And you're Jocasta!'

'Yes.'

Mrs Bradshaw scratched her beehive hair-do and drew on her cigarette.

111

'Well, I don't know what to say, really. It has worried me in a way though he's been gone before, I mean for a long time. You'll know what he does of course, travels, selling and that. But the thing is that Peter is good friends with my husband and myself, and we both thought it very funny he didn't tell us goodbye or anything. He always did and said where he was going and for me not to do anything he wouldn't do. You know we used to have a laugh.'

Yes, it would be a laugh with Peter. I'd had a laugh too. He'd brought laughter into my life. I felt my eyes fill with tears.

'Did he ever go away and not say goodbye?'

'Oh yes. Often we're not in and he has to dash off, you know how it is, but I don't remember him being gone as long as this; not continuously. I mean he hasn't been back that I know, unless he dashed in and out; and then he'd send a postcard if he was on the Continent or in America. This time he didn't.'

I caught my breath; real fear for Peter possessed me now and I wondered for the first time, though God knows why I hadn't before, if some harm had come to him. I was looking at Stephen whose face was grim too.

'He went and stayed at a hotel before he left, on the other side of Leeds.'

'A *hotel*?'

'The Morecambe House Hotel.'

'That's on the way to Skipton, the Ilkley side. Whatever would he do that for?'

'We don't know. But it was almost definitely Peter. The porter recognized his photograph.'

'Well, seemed to,' I said to be truthful. 'He said they had a lot of people coming and going.'

'Oh they do. It's a nice place. Mr Bradshaw and I sometimes go there for a drink if we're running up to the Dales. I've never heard Peter even talk of it. Well, I don't know.'

Mrs Bradshaw looked excited; she was enjoying herself

and got out a third cigarette. The cat sauntered through the door into Peter's bedroom.

'Mrs Bradshaw, did Peter ever talk to you about his business worries or anything . . .'

'Oh no. He didn't have any! Business was going very well. He was full of himself; he was a very happy man, confident . . . Oh dear, we're saying "was" as though he's dead.' A hand flew to her head, 'He's *not* dead, is he? You're not trying to tell me that?'

Now the tears that I'd been holding back welled up again and poured down my cheeks. Mrs Bradshaw looked at me with consternation.

'Oh you poor girl . . .'

'No, he's not dead, Mrs Bradshaw, he's certainly not dead. Jocasta – ' Stephen came over to me and tried to lead me to a seat – 'sit down.'

I wriggled away and clung to the radiator.

'No. I'm so cold.'

'Oh, but it's that hot in here, dear.' Mrs Bradshaw waved an imaginary fan across her face.

'She's in shock,' Stephen said. 'Did he ever mention to you that she was coming up here?'

Mrs Bradshaw thought very hard. The cat wandered back, a crumpled paper in its mouth and began to play with it on the rug.

'I don't think he did, to be truthful. You know, we weren't *that* close, just neighbourly. We'd a drink together, oh, about once a week; either him in our place or us here. Terry, my husband, is racing correspondent for a group of northern papers and Peter would ask him what he favoured for such and such a race. I remember it was near Wetherby races when we last saw him and that would be, on . . .'

'He seems to have gone missing about the eleventh of September,' Stephen said.

'Yes, it would be the weekend before. Joey, stop that.'

Joey, the cat, was catching the hairs of the rug in its claws as it played with the ball of paper. Mrs Bradshaw reached out and took up the paper. 'Now stop it, Joey, or I'll lock you up and you don't like that, do you?' She clasped the cat in her arms and fiddled with the paper in her hand.

Stephen got up and looked out of the window. The trees in the garden were turning brown and gold, and leaves floated down, adding to the russet carpet on which we'd walked to the door. It must once have been a lovely old house set in a park, I thought.

'Peter's drawers are half empty, just a few clothes in the wardrobe. It looks as though he packed and intended to go. He went to the hotel, he didn't meet Jo and then he vanished . . .'

'Oh, it does sound peculiar, doesn't it?' Mrs Bradshaw was smoothing out the paper on her knee. 'Not like him at all.'

'That's what I said,' I burst out. 'It's *not* like Peter. It isn't.'

'He *was* casual, you know.' Mrs Bradshaw's voice had a cautious note. 'I bet he could break many a female heart, but it was him being so friendly with Terry and me and not saying anything . . . Oh look. Now here's something.'

She was staring at the paper and Stephen strode over to her and took it from her hand, looking at it with a puzzled frown. I closed my eyes with dread; it could be anything. A farewell note, a . . .

'It seems to be the time your train arrived. Look.'

Stephen brought the paper over to me. It was from a lined memo-pad and consisted of two columns. It had Euston written in one column and Leeds in the other and there were a few times dotted down. Against one was a question mark.

'Yes, my train left Euston at 10.45 and arrived at 14.02. That was my train.' I looked at Peter's handwriting, the familiar scrawl of a man always in a hurry.

'It looks as though he meant to meet it,' Stephen said. 'I wonder why he didn't?'

Ten

We got away from Mrs Bradshaw with difficulty. Obviously she liked nothing better than a good mystery and, in addition, had plenty of time on her hands. I didn't think, however, she was genuinely worried about Peter and this depressed me; perhaps she knew his reputation with girls and hadn't liked to distress me. He obviously also hadn't talked to her about me as though I was the great passion in his life.

We never knew where the cat had found the paper, maybe under the bed. A woman came to clean once a week, Mrs Bradshaw told us, and all the waste-paper bins were empty. Stephen gave her his card and she promised to ring if she thought of anything. I didn't imagine he'd hear from her again. Still, she was a good-natured woman and it was a good thing to have her on our side.

'What about Peter's mother?' I said as Stephen turned the car in the drive, waving to Mrs Bradshaw, who was following our departure from her window.

'What about Peter's mother?'

'Well, maybe he was close to her, was he? I can understand he might not write to the Bradshaws if he was hiding something, but his mother . . .'

'It's an idea. Where does she live?'

'I haven't a clue.'

'You've no idea where his mother lives?'

'No.'

Stephen's silence meant: 'He hadn't even told his mother about you, you poor girl.' Finally he said, 'Well, I can try my detective skills at that one.'

'She married again. She has a different name.'
'Oh, a stumbling block. When, do you know?'
'A year or so after his father was killed.'
'And they lived up here?'
'Yes. I'm not quite sure where. Ilkley rings a bell for some reason.'
'Then there may be something to tell us at Ilkley Town Hall. I can find that out easily.'
'But she didn't stay there. I think she went south.'
'First let's find the name. Still depressed?' Stephen glanced at me.
'Very. Whatever the answer to this is, I don't like it. It's either because of me; or he's done something wrong; or . . .' I didn't like to say it.
'Or you think something may have happened to him?'
'Yes.'
'Well, I think that least of all. Honestly. I'm not just saying it to cheer you up. If Peter had had an accident, or was, well, dead, we should have heard. That we should know about.'
I felt a sudden sense of relief. 'Oh Stephen! I hadn't thought of that. Of *course* we should have heard. Well, at least he's not dead; but I don't like the other alternatives much either.'
'Let's take Mother to the cinema this afternoon. Like to?'
'Yes, I would! Anything good on?'
'We'll get a paper, and then we'll go somewhere nice to eat.'
I sat back in the car and looked out of the window. We were passing the huge comfortable family houses of nineteenth-century Leeds, set back from the road in ample gardens like the grounds of Peter's block of flats. Now they'd mostly been converted into flats or maisonettes, or one-roomed boarding houses. I thought of the families who had lived there, large Victorian families growing more and more wealthy with the development of the industrial North. Families like the Ryders and the Dabroes . . .
'Jonathan Dabroe,' I said suddenly.
Stephen looked at me.

'Pardon?'

'Jonathan Dabroe. Surely he would have to keep in touch with Peter because of this machine he was importing?'

'Jocasta, we can't go back to him. At least not for a while and by then Peter may have turned up again.'

I got home that night even later than the week before. My Saturday excursions went unnoticed by the Ryders, or at least they didn't comment on them. The house was in darkness, as usual no light left on for me. This always seemed to express disapproval of my behaviour; I don't know why. It was probably fanciful to think that – but a curious state of tension lay between us. One might almost have called it an uneasy truce, as though war was about to break out at any minute.

I couldn't really explain this atmosphere between myself and the Ryders, unless it was that I thought they knew I was still looking for Peter and somehow didn't approve of it. Why? What did they know that they should have told me? Or was I meant to believe that he had jilted me; and was I silly not to? Was it true?

I slept well that night, for a change. Usually I woke at least once during the night and lay listening, or early in the morning to find I couldn't get to sleep again and I'd watch the dawn come up over the cliff and the light slowly permeate the valley, and the smoke appear in the chimneys of the houses nestled in the village, because Yorkshire people are early risers, especially those with farms or who have to travel to work in nearby quarries or even in Skipton. The Ryders never got up early and I seldom saw them before the late afternoon, when I came home.

The next day was Sunday and I lay in bed late, exhausted by the emotional stresses of the week, to say nothing of the hard work I put in at school. After early morning drizzle, the sun had come out and was gently filtering into my room when there was a soft knock on the door and Agnes came in carrying a tray.

'I brought you breakfast,' she whispered and the pungent smell of smoked Yorkshire bacon and eggs and hot coffee suddenly made me ravenous.

'Oh Agnes.' I sat up. 'How kind.'

'I thought you'd be tired. I was chatting to the Rector yesterday and he said how hard you worked in the school. All the children adore you and Mrs Baker doesn't know how she ever did without you.'

I pushed back my hair and smiled.

'It's flattering, but I—'

'I suppose you won't be *thinking* of going now?'

The inflection in her voice had subtly changed as she put the tray on my lap and began to pour my coffee. 'Black or white?'

'White, please. I don't really know, Agnes. It is hard to think of leaving; the longer I stay . . .'

'But when Peter comes back . . .' She trailed off and looked at me.

'*Is* Peter coming back, Agnes?'

'However do you mean?' Her voice had an edge to it and she spun round, almost dropping the cup she had in her hand.

'I find it very hard to believe that he left because of me. He's too keen on his business for one thing, and too hard-headed for another. Also – ' I picked up my knife and fork and vigorously attacked the bacon and eggs – 'I think Peter would have told me. He's too straight. He'd never have fixed everything up for me and just done a bunk.'

Agnes turned to the window, her back hunched and sad. 'It's difficult to believe, isn't it, when people behave badly? I can understand your reluctance.'

'But I don't think it's in character.'

Agnes turned round and looked at me, her face soft, her mouth twisted with pity.

'Jocasta, you knew him such a short time. We've known Peter all our lives. It *is* in character, once you know him.'

'But the business . . .'

'Oh, the business is where Peter is. He takes it with him, as the snail its house. He can write letters and telephone from wherever he happens to be, Germany, France, America . . .'

I finished the bacon and egg and turned to the toast, smearing it thickly with Wensleydale butter and coarse home-made Yorkshire marmalade. The coffee was hot and strong. It made me feel alert and vigorous, reluctant to allow anyone to pull wool over my eyes.

'Do you *know* where Peter is, Agnes?'

It may have been my imagination but even in the bad light I thought she went pale, or was it a defensive movement of her shoulder, an imperceptible stiffening of the body?

'Why should I know?'

'I thought he would tell you, being so close to you. Wouldn't he take you into his confidence?'

'No, not in that way. I mean, Peter could be very secretive about women, you know. And then of course he'd often go off on business without saying anything, as he has this time, I've no doubt.'

'How long had he lived in the hotel?'

She looked surprised.

'A hotel. Peter lived in a hotel? Who told you that?'

'Tim told me,' I said, never taking my eyes off her face. 'Didn't you know?'

She shrugged and made use of her distraite expression again, and the familiar passing of the hand over the eyes as though in anticipation of pain.

'No, I didn't really know where he lived. He always came here. Tim would know where he lived and if Tim says a hotel, then it was a hotel. You can be sure of that.'

Her expression was innocent enough and she looked at me appealingly. 'Give up,' the expression was saying, 'forget about Peter.' But it wasn't convincing, and my determination to know the truth hardened. Agnes suddenly became animated; she really was like a child in many ways, with periods of excitement or petulance as extreme and irrational as a child's.

119

'Look, we wondered if you'd like to come for a drive up the dale with us today; then we're invited to tea with the Fullertons. Karen thought you'd like to see the hall.'

'How very kind. I'd love it.' I jumped out of bed and held the door open for her as she took up my tray. 'Thank you so much, Agnes. You know, I really do feel at home here. You're too good to me.'

I thought she smiled as she went through the door; but it might have been a grimace.

Sometimes I wondered whether it rained more in Yorkshire than anywhere else, or was it merely in this part of Yorkshire, this valley? As I trudged to school on the Monday morning, my wellington boots squelching in the mud on the side of the road and the valley almost entirely hidden by a thick white mist, the cold seeming to penetrate my bones, I thought suddenly of my childhood in Calcutta, of the hot breathless days and of the torrid heat that had driven my mother into the hills and ultimately into the arms of another man.

Later I thought how curious it was that I'd been thinking along those lines when I was to hear that Tessa Dabroe had left her husband and taken the children with her.

At first, apart from marking the Dabroe children absent on the register, Mrs Baker and I didn't even discuss the matter. Monday was busy and particularly this Monday with the children arriving at school, some of them soaking wet and Mrs Baker and I having to amuse them during the morning and afternoon breaks as well as the long lunch break because it was too wet to play outside.

'Now I know the life of a country teacher is dedication,' I laughed as we were tidying up before going home, 'I don't think I've stopped all day.'

'Come home and have tea with us,' Mrs Baker said in a tired voice, massaging her wrists. 'The rheumatism is attacking badly today.'

'Oh dear, it's been so wet. Did you ever think of moving to a warmer part of the country?'

'I've thought,' she laughed, 'and it never went any further than thought. No, Herbert and I are wedded to the North.' She was looking at the register. 'By the way, no word from Mrs Dabroe. Unusual to have both the children away at once.' She frowned. 'Come on, let's call it a day. Lucky I got the car to start this morning.'

As we drove past Croft House she glanced at me.

'Do you want to call in?'

'No. Both Tim and Agnes are out today. I think they went to Wetherby to see some friends. I don't know, I didn't listen properly. They've been very pleasant to me this weekend; took me to tea at Hammersleigh Hall, to Hubberholme for a drink yesterday, right up the Dales as far as Hawes. Tim is very knowledgeable.'

'He is, and very interesting when he gets going. Ah, here we are.'

The lights were on in the house and the door stood open. In the light of our car headlamps we saw another car in the drive and at first I thought it was Stephen's; but Stephen didn't drive a large black Jaguar.

'I think Jonathan Dabroe is here!' I exclaimed. 'Oh dear, I hope the children are all right.' We hurried into the house, leaving Mrs Baker's car in the drive.

Jonathan Dabroe it was, drinking whisky with Herbert Baker. He looked strained, and, oddly for such a meticulous man, appeared not to have shaved. He jumped up when he saw us and as he came closer I saw that his eyes were bloodshot and there were heavy dark circles under his eyes. In short he looked either like a man who had had a sleepless night, maybe quite a few, or was suffering from a hangover.

'Oh, you're both here,' he said, seeing me. 'Good. I'm afraid I have rather bad news, Mrs Baker, Miss Oaks. My wife, Tessa, has taken the children to her mother. She says she intends to leave me.'

We both stared at him and Mrs Baker sat down on the settee next to her husband's chair and took his hand.

'I can only say,' Jonathan continued, 'that I have not the

slightest idea why, or rather I have but I know her to be utterly mistaken. He held out a note and Mrs Baker took it, read it silently and passed it to me. I looked at him and he nodded.

'Please do. Read it.'

It was very short.

Dear Jono,

You must know I've had enough and am taking the children with me. We shall be at Mother's, but you should communicate with me through our solicitor, David Bramley of Chichester.

Yours, Tess

Apart from the terseness of the letter, the thing I noticed was that even at a time like this she used their intimate names for each other, Jono and Tess. I handed him the letter silently.

'What is "enough"?' Mrs Baker asked. 'What does she mean by that. Enough what?'

Jonathan Dabroe looked at his shoes; the muscles of his jaw were working as though he was having some kind of inner tussle with himself; at last he looked up at us and said, 'I have no idea.'

I knew he was lying. The tussle had been whether to tell us the truth or not. He had decided not to. I respected his right to keep the truth to himself. In the circumstances I might lie myself. I knew that Mr and Mrs Baker, bound by their Yorkshire reserve, wouldn't question him either.

'I thought I should tell you the truth,' he said. 'I mean that she has left me. I don't think it's necessary to tell anyone else, do you?' He seemed to be appealing to Mrs Baker, who got up and poked the fire.

'You mean you just want to say she's gone away, some-thing like that? No – ' she shook her head – 'everyone knows your wife has too much of a sense of duty both to the children and the village to go away without a strong reason – leave her committees, interrupt their education?' She gazed at him, the rest left unspoken. There was bewilderment in her face.

'Then what can I do?'

'I wouldn't say anything. It will get around. The other children will say the Dabroes aren't at school, and the bush telegraph will do the rest. You of course will go and see her.'

'I've already spoken to David Bramley on the phone. She left me this note. You see she went yesterday and I was out. I came home late at night and she and they were gone. Cleaned out.'

The Volvo estate car would hold a lot, I thought. Certainly most of their clothes. What on earth had gone on in the Dabroe household to provoke such a reaction? I gazed at Jonathan, respectable business man, Justice of the Peace, wishing, like Peer Gynt, that I could peel through the many layers of this complex personality and get to the core of the mystery. But the faces both of Jonathan and the Bakers remained impenetrable.

'What did the solicitor say?' Mr Baker spoke quietly. Obviously the whole thing, the prying into the personal life of anyone else was distasteful to him.

'He's going to speak to Tessa. He says she wants a few days of quiet; that the children are well and will attend the local school.'

'It looks like she's been planning it, to have fixed up schools,' Mrs Baker said, still looking at him. Jonathan was gazing at his shoes again.

'Yes, it does. Well, I must go. Thanks for the whisky, Herbert. I'll keep in touch.'

I nodded and smiled and Mrs Baker saw him to the door. After I heard it shut, she didn't come back immediately, and I could imagine her thoughtfully preparing tea in the kitchen. Mr Baker said nothing, staring glumly into the fire, and I lit a cigarette. When Jane came in, I got up to help her serve the tea.

'A bit early for whisky, Herbert,' she said tartly.

'Well, dear, I could hardly offer him tea, and in the circumstances . . .'

She smiled.

'Of course. Well obviously it's a woman . . .'

We all nodded. We'd all been thinking that; obviously, it was a woman.

'Any idea who?' I asked.

Both the Bakers looked rather shocked and Mrs Baker bent her head, busy with the tea.

'I'm not meaning to be indelicate,' I said in a tone, I knew, of exasperation. 'But I suppose it *does* matter.'

'Actually I don't know.' Mrs Baker passed me my tea. 'And I don't really care. I'm simply surprised because, as I said to you the other day, Jocasta, I never heard any scandal about Jonathan Dabroe.'

'But did you think they were a happy, united family?'

She looked troubled.

'No. I always thought Tessa looked too sour for that, didn't you, Herbert darling? Busied herself in too many good works.'

'Maybe they simply weren't happy together. A matter of chemistry,' I said.

Mr Baker packed tobacco into his pipe.

'No. Something *provoked* her to leave, in the middle of term. I don't think she'd leave if she were just unhappy. She had too much of a sense of duty. She'd have put up with it. No, we've known or rather we've heard of a lot of women going after Jonathan Dabroe, but we've never heard of him reciprocating, have we, Jane?'

Mrs Baker sipped the hot tea and shook her head.

'I'm sorry for the children,' I said, beginning to rise. 'I must get back. Thanks for the tea.'

'Oh, stay and have dinner. It's only leftovers from Sunday lunch, a sort of bubble and squeak.'

'No really . . .'

'Yes, do. You said they were out and Stephen will be so happy to see you.'

I smiled.

'If you insist. We were having leftovers too.'

It was, I thought, typical of the Bakers to play down something as sensational as the news of the Dabroe split, and not even mention it until we were having coffee by the fire after dinner. The talk had been rather deliberately restrained to the level of school news, the state of the country and Stephen's rugger fixtures for the winter, and as I watched and listened, I thought what a lot Yorkshire people managed to keep beneath the surface, and no wonder that, with such repression, things danced and bubbled like a cauldron under the apparently calm surfaces of their lives, as no doubt they had done with the Dabroes.

In fact it was some cause for amazement that the subject ever came up at all, but Stephen mentioned some fixture or other and Douglas Dabroe, Jonathan's brother, in connection with it, and Mrs Baker looked up half yawning and told him about the visit from Jonathan.

Stephen's reaction, however, was not one of Yorkshire phlegm. He leaned forward and his eyes gleamed in the light of the flickering fire.

'That is very interesting,' he said. 'Most coincidental.'

'Oh? Coincidental what?' His mother, I thought, was guarded.

'Well, I saw Jonathan Dabroe together with a woman a few weeks ago, and it gave me quite a surprise. Quite a surprise.'

'Oh darling, really, I didn't think you could be so gossipy,' his mother said reprovingly.

'Well, Mother, one can't help noticing these things, particularly with the lady in question. I mean there's such a thing about the feud between the Dabroes and the Ryders . . .'

His mother gave a gasp. The news had impressed even her as indeed it did me.

'You mean *Agnes Ryder* was the woman?' I said.

'Yes. They were having a very quiet tête-à-tête in a pub right over Northallerton way; the last people I expected to see. I was with a client. They didn't see me because I was tucked away by the bar in a corner.'

'Well, I don't know.' Mrs Baker leaned back as though winded. 'You think Jonathan Dabroe has been carrying on with Agnes Ryder?'

'It would look like that, Mother, and actually, I know you don't approve of gossip, but other people have seen them too. One or two of the men in the rugger club have mentioned it.'

I could imagine that talk at the rugger club was a good deal less discreet than at the home of the Baker family. In fact Stephen was rather pink by now.

'I didn't like to say anything before, Mother; but there has been quite a bit of talk in the dale. It's been going on for quite some time.'

I thought of what a handsome couple they would make and the contrast with the thin, upper-class and rather bitter-looking woman who was Jonathan's wife struck me with a poignant forcefulness.

'No wonder Agnes has headaches,' I said quietly. 'Keeping all this from her brother, I don't doubt, must be an awful strain. What a lot is now explained.'

'Isn't it just?' Mr Baker spoke quietly. 'Tim was always the one for keeping up the feud. It was he who had a particular hatred of the Dabroes.'

'Why?' I asked.

'He just felt it more deeply, losing his mother. Goodness knows what he would do if ever he heard about Agnes.'

'Do you think he could know?' I asked quietly.

'*Know?*' Mrs Baker's voice was tremulous. 'You think Tim would know something like that and keep it to himself? Why, the whole house would be shaken by the noise of his wrath. No, you may depend upon it, Agnes has kept it from Tim, and that *is* why she's having headaches. Goodness, if this gets round I should hate to think what would happen then.'

The atmosphere in the room now was tense with suppressed

excitement, a sort of explosive force born of a half-hearted reluctance to be intrigued.

'If they were having an affair,' I said, practically enough I thought, 'and Tessa has now left Jonathan, presumably the way is clear for a divorce.'

'A *divorce*?' Mrs Baker said rather in the way I imagine that Mrs Bennett might have treated such a suggestion from one of her daughters. Distinctly improper.

'Oh Mother, divorce is very common now, even in Yorkshire.' Stephen too smiled at his mother's tone.

'But still it's not very *nice*, and as for Tim Ryder . . .'

'Maybe it will clear the feud, and a good thing,' I said. 'Anyway I must go back to the house of secrets.'

Stephen got up and fetched my coat from the hall.

'By the way,' he said helping me on with it, 'I have found out where Peter's mother lives.'

'Oh?'

'Not too far away, we could go there at the weekend if you want to.'

'Oh Stephen!'

'She married a Colonel Cornford and moved to Cornwall.'

'Yes, Peter mentioned Cornwall.'

'Well, he died a few years ago – it appears he was a good bit older than his wife – and she went to live in the Lake District, where she came from. Keswick.'

'Stephen, you're so clever. How did you find out?'

'She was married in Ilkley and the rest I got from Cornford's regiment; he was a professional soldier. Would you like to go?'

'Please, yes. It is three weeks tomorrow since I arrived.'

'It's not long, you know,' he said looking into my eyes.

'It's too long,' I replied, 'much too long,' and I knew that Stephen wanted to know too.

Eleven

Mrs Cornford lived in a gracious house outside Keswick overlooking Lake Derwentwater. No wonder it had inspired so many poets and writers, I thought, as we drove along the lakeside road after what had in any case been a spectacular drive over the moors from Coppitts Green.

The house was called Pines and lay back from the road, so that indeed it seemed to nestle in a forest of pinewood, and the pungent smell as we drove up the drive together with the magnificent view of the lake reminded me of Switzerland.

'Peter must have money,' Stephen grunted.

'It was his stepfather, don't forget, an entirely new family.'

'Still, I smells money.'

A rather ancient maid in brown and cream uniform took us into a drawing room that overlooked the lake to as far up as Buttermere. Mrs Cornford surprised us admiring the view and as I turned round I caught my breath because of the resemblance to Peter. She was about fifty-five, tall and with a well-kept trim figure; she looked as though she rode or walked a lot. She wore a dusky-pink twinset and a tweed skirt, with sturdy shoes as though she had just come in from a walk or was about to go on one. Stephen had, naturally, phoned the day before to say we were coming.

'Miss Oaks, Mr Baker. Won't you sit down?'

'We were just admiring the view, Mrs Cornford.'

'It is beautiful, isn't it? You can see what drove me back to my native county after my husband's death. He was a Cornishman but I, I am Cumbrian through and through.'

'Did this house belong to your family?'

'Oh no. My family were farmers on the Penrith side. This house came on to the market just as I was looking for one. It is large but then my family is still young enough to make use of it and my younger daughter, Jill, still lives at home. Thank you, Phyllis, on the small table, please.'

The maid had brought in coffee and I was glad of it for we had made an early start.

'Now, what has brought you two young people here?'

Since the introduction, the feeling of unease in the pit of my stomach had seemed to weigh like lead, growing heavier all the time. Mrs Cornford had not welcomed me in the way that one would have expected her to if I had been a special friend of her son's. I don't believe she'd heard my name. Peter had never mentioned me to her, and, indeed, he'd hardly ever spoken of her to me.

When one reflected on it, ours had been a very odd relationship. He had told me so little; I had told him so little. How could I ever have thought the kind of passion we'd had could have lasted, turned into love? It was fierce and possessive and life-enhancing – how could I ever have imagined it would be permanent?

'You look pale, dear, are you cold?'

She was looking at me with concern and I even believe that my teeth were chattering.

'Let me explain, Mrs Cornford,' Stephen broke in before I had the chance to speak. 'Jocasta knew Peter very well. Did he ever mention her to you?'

Mrs Cornford looked both amazed and rather disdainful, if it is possible to couple such an expression.

'I don't see . . .'

'Anyway whether he did or not, he invited her to come and stay with his cousins in the Dales, where she was to be the local schoolteacher.'

'Coppitts Green? With Aggie and Tim?'

'Yes.'

'Well, how extraordinary. He never mentioned it to me. But

then of course I don't see a lot of Peter. Even though he was so small when I remarried, he always resented his stepfather, who was so good to him, and of course as my other children came along he resented their place in my affections.' She shook her head and bit delicately on a Marie biscuit. 'Peter was never an easy child. I did all I could; but he was much closer to his Uncle Charles, the father of Tim and Aggie, and seemed to regard them as his siblings more than his own. He loved the North so much, he craved it, so I sent him to school up here and he spent his holidays with the Ryders. Sometimes I wonder if I did wrong.'

'I'm sure you did what you could, Mrs Cornford,' Stephen said gently.

'But I can't understand why you're here. Is something wrong with Peter?'

I could sense the feeling of hopelessness in his voice as Stephen started to explain. Indeed, how to begin when a mother knew so little of her son? We had come on a futile errand.

'Mrs Cornford, Peter was supposed to meet Jocasta at Leeds. He never did and she has never heard from him since.'

'At least he rang, but I wasn't there,' I began until, seeing the expression on her face, I stopped. It was what I can only call a compound of exasperation and pity.

'My dear girl—' she began.

'He's done it before . . .' I finished what she was going to say. 'That's what you're going to tell me, isn't it?'

She spread out her hands and regarded her beautifully manicured nails.

'Peter was very *popular* with women, dear. He did, yes, he did seem to have a way with them. I'm sorry if he—'

'He never mentioned my name to you?'

Again that rather pained expression.

'I'm sorry, dear, but, truthfully, no . . .' Her face softened and she came over and sat beside me. 'It sounds terribly heartless, doesn't it? I can see you've been hurt, to come all this way because you're worried about him. I wish I could say, *do* something to help you. I think it's very naughty of Peter, very naughty, but – ' she nodded her head like a little bird – 'it has happened before. He just whizzes off. You see, my dear, you must try and understand Peter. I do, and I have difficulty even though I'm his mother. A doctor I once consulted about Peter said it does all go back to those early years, his insecurity when he was a baby and I a rather distracted and unhappy widow. Then my affection for Geoffrey Cornford, my other children . . . Peter felt left out, although I loved him as much as any of them. It made him aggressive – ' she shrugged – 'but of course that's why he was so successful in the Army and now at his business. It also makes him rather attractive to women, my dear, and I'm afraid he doesn't always behave as well as he might.' She looked at her watch. 'Oh dear, I am due to play in a ladies' golf match this afternoon. The time has gone so quickly. Will you excuse . . .' She got up.

Stephen had sat listening to her, looking both puzzled and rather angry, I thought. Was he regretting the journey made for nothing?

'Mrs Cornford, just for the record, when did you last hear from Peter?'

Mrs Cornford looked again at her watch.

'Oh, now let me think, towards the end of July he was here for the weekend. Before that I had not seen him for ages. We weren't very close, I'm sorry to say.'

'And you haven't heard from him since?'

'Oh no, but that's not unusual; he never writes and hardly ever phones. I would say about two months since I saw him, yes.' She looked at me and took my arm. 'I'm so sorry, my dear. He has given you such a shock, and when I see him I shall tell him what I think of him in no uncertain terms. But if I were you, I would forget Peter and go back to London. You see, my dear, he did mention the name of a girl to me to whom he was very attached, but it wasn't you. The name was Tessa. In fact he talked about her all weekend. I think

131

he'd just met her and was obviously very taken. Now wasn't that *naughty* of him?'

Stephen didn't speak until we were the other side of Keswick and I don't think I could have uttered a word if I tried. I kept on swallowing and clearing my throat and I was convinced that a great lump had grown and would choke me before I was much older. Finally I gasped in a small weak voice:

'Tessa Dabroe!'

'We don't know for sure,' Stephen growled looking angrily at the road before him.

'Of course it's Tessa Dabroe. It all adds up. Unhappy with her husband, who is carrying on with Agnes, she meets her cousin, a business contact of her husband's. Peter has an eye for a woman, especially a rather bitter, frustrated but still beautiful woman like Tessa.'

'You think they planned to run away together?' Stephen sounded incredulous.

'What else?'

'But surely he'd have put you off, done something to dissuade you?'

'I suppose he thought it was too late. He met her suddenly after he'd arranged everything. Although Peter was physically brave, he lacked the moral courage to behave properly, everyone has said that, or rather everyone who knew him well, his mother and his cousins. Even my brother-in-law, Bob, looked a bit apprehensive when I told him Peter and I were so involved. Now I know why. And I also understand the expression on Tessa's face when I mentioned the Ryders.'

'You thought it was the feud?'

'Yes; but it was me. She suddenly realized who I was.'

'Maybe he didn't tell her about you, being Peter.'

'Oh yes, he did. She knew.'

Stephen had driven into the forecourt of a pub and stopped the car.

'Let's have a beer and a sandwich. You must be exhausted.'

132

'I'm suddenly angry,' I said. 'I realize what a fool I've been. What a fool he's made of me.'

'No, he hasn't,' Stephen said stoutly. 'You've behaved superbly. The thing is, what do you do now?'

'You mean, do we tell Jonathan Dabroe? What do we tell the Ryders?'

'Exactly. We've a lot of thinking to do.'

I sometimes wonder, looking back, how I got through those days – the uncertainty, the shifting suspicion, my work at school, where one had to appear as normal as possible, and above all the irrational terror the house had for me, however much I tried to analyse this emotion.

What was it about the house? In the first place I always had a feeling of foreboding when I looked at it, whether coming round the corner on my way home from school or along the road and across the bridge by car from Skipton, or wherever I had been. I would look searchingly down into the village, trying to pinpoint the house, as though as well as repelling me, it attracted me too. Then when I got to the house I always looked up towards the roof and as I opened the door and stood on the threshold I listened. For what did I listen? What was I expecting to hear?

The thing was that it was a very silent house, considering that it contained two relatively youthful people and a cheerful housekeeper; there was never a bustle of noise, or the sound of a radio or the television. It was like entering a monastery – silent, but not peaceful. There was no peace in Croft House and I think that was what I knew and wondered about, and dreaded.

When I came back from Keswick and Stephen left me at the door before going on to his mother's, I wanted so much to go with him that I knew he sensed it and he looked at me, that unspoken offer of security in his eyes. Silently I shook my head and after thanking him, I went into the house alone.

After all, we hadn't worked out a plan as to what to do on the way back and had decided that a good night's sleep and more thought were required when we should speak again. I was invited to lunch at the Bakers on Sunday, and Tim and Agnes were invited too.

As usual I stood on the threshold listening. It was after four and almost dark but there were no lights on. I put on the hall lights and went into the lounge, but there was no fire in the grate. The place had a bleak desolate air as though no one had lived there for a long time. It was absurd. I put on all the lights I could find and went into the kitchen to make some tea. I hummed a tune to try to cheer myself up.

Suddenly I was aware of someone else with me in the room; my spine tingled and I dared not turn; in the window in front of me I saw a reflection . . .

'I'm sorry, miss, I startled you.'

'Mrs Bargett! Yes, you did. I thought everyone was out.'

'Everyone was, miss. Miss Agnes has her hair done in Harrogate on a Saturday. I didn't light the fire before I left at lunchtime knowing no one would be here. Did you have a pleasant day, miss?'

'Yes, thanks. Tea, Mrs Bargett?'

'Well . . . I won't say no. Saturday afternoons I do my own cleaning and then I saw a light in the house and hurried over, knowing the fire wasn't lit.'

I shivered.

'It *is* cold.'

Mrs Bargett looked at me.

'You surprise me, miss. I thought the central heating was making it very warm. Mr Tim turned it up this morning, but they do like a log fire in the grate, it being October.'

'I expect you're fond of the house, Mrs Bargett, having worked here so long?'

Mrs Bargett paused in the act of leaving the kitchen, presumably for the drawing room.

'Fond, dear? Fond did you say? I love this house. My mother worked for the family before me and I used to come here as a little child and think what a lovely house it was, full of corners and cupboards – lovely little hidey-holes they were. Then, though, I didn't *need* to work of course, Mr Bargett providing for us very nicely; I wanted to when the work got too much for my mother. I feel this is my home just as much as Clive Cottage.'

I looked at her, the soft, tender expression on her face as though she were talking about a lover, and I wondered why on earth I should find the place so antipathetic while everyone else loved it so much.

'Yes, it *is* a lovely house,' I said, 'but it gives me the creeps, do you know that, Mrs Bargett, the creeps.'

Mrs Bargett's expression was comical.

'You don't *like* the house, Miss Oaks? Why, everyone loves the house who comes here.'

'I know. But it frightens me. There, I've said it; and I hate the way the cliff hangs over it so menacingly . . .'

'But the cliff is *miles* away. Oh dear, you're ever so imaginative. Nervy, are you?'

I sipped my tea and took a digestive biscuit from the tin.

'No, I wouldn't say I was a nervous person. I don't think you'd choose teaching if you were; but the house has had this effect on me from the beginning, kind of menacing . . . yes, that's it, menacing.'

Mrs Bargett shook her head.

'Well, I can't understand that, really I can't. To me it's warm and friendly, like a person; it really is.'

'The children, I suppose, love it, and their father loved it too?'

'Why, yes; they were born here. I remember the births, both of them. I helped my mother out; she was here then and I had young children of my own. Mr Charles had so wanted the children to be born at home, so we had to be that bit extra-careful on account of Mrs Ryder had had a difficult pregnancy, with Mr Tim anyway, not Miss Agnes; that was an easy birth . . .'

'Did you like Mrs Ryder, Mrs Bargett. I mean if you don't mind my asking? It seemed such a cruel thing to do, leaving the children . . .'

135

Mrs Bargett was silent as though wondering how much she should tell a comparative stranger about the family she'd worked for all her life. I thought she was going to rebuff me but instead she sat down, clasping her hands round her tea cup as though wanting to talk.

'Well, it's difficult to understand, isn't it? They'd wanted those children, my they had, and lovely babies they were. But Mrs Charles . . . now there was a puzzle. She was quite out of place here, that was obvious from the start . . .'

'How out of place . . .'

'Oh, she was a city lady if ever there was one. The countryside bored her to death. "Oh, I long for London, Mrs Parker," she would sigh to my mother. She was always looking for distraction, if you know what I mean, and of course she found it with Sam Dabroe, and in the end she went off with him but not to live happily ever after if I hear right. She was a very beautiful woman, Mrs Charles. I often think of her and see her in Miss Aggie, not so much Mr Tim – he more favours the Ryders. And she was a very nice woman, but she just wasn't, well, a very *good* woman, was she, to leave those two little children? My mother always had a soft spot for her though and would hear no wrong word about her.'

'And Mr Charles . . . how did he take it?'

'Ah, there was a one; never knew what he was thinking one day to the next. He seemed to freeze up, you know, withdraw into himself like. My mother brought up those children when they were babies. Then as soon as he could he sent them away so as to be as far from the Dabroe children as possible. A very lonely man was Mr Charles.' Mrs Bargett stopped suddenly and looked at the time. 'I must go. And I haven't lit that fire!' She bustled out and I slowly washed the tea things, my head teeming with thoughts. Whoever said that the country was quiet! But that was it; it was quiet, too quiet and the undercurrents of life stirred all the more fiercely for appearing to lie beneath the surface.

When Mrs Bargett came back she had her coat on.

'I came in the front way, so I'll go out that way. Well, it's been a nice little chat though I daresay you'll be discreet about what I've said.' She straightened her hat in the mirror. 'Not but what everybody doesn't know.'

'I'm sure.' I laughed. 'I'll see you out. Are the Ryders home for dinner?'

'No, miss, and I've left you a nice steak and kidney pie, only needs heating up and the potatoes boiling.'

I wandered into the hall with her and stood at the door. The door was ajar but a bunch of keys hung from the lock.

'Oh dear,' Mrs Bargett said, taking them out, 'I've left my keys in the door. I'm that unused to having to use them. I suppose it's your London ways makes you want to lock up after you.'

I was looking at the keys.

'My London ways, Mrs Bargett?' I murmured.

'I notice you always seem to lock the door behind you, dear. It's not what we're used to here; there are no prowlers in these parts, you know, nothing to be afraid of.'

She popped the keys in her bag and waved herself off. I watched her walk down the road, thinking about the keys I'd seen her take from the lock. They were the ones I'd seen on Tim Ryder's desk. There was no doubt about that; a bronze St Christopher medal had hung from a bronze chain – a bronze medal with a blue enamel surround. Mrs Bargett had popped them into her bag.

They weren't Peter's keys after all.

Twelve

O n the first Sunday of the month the Ryders went to church – just for show, Agnes told me as we were getting ready the next morning, because they didn't really believe.

'We have to support the Rector, whom we like, and it does no harm. Come *on*, Tim.' Tim was still hidden behind *The Sunday Times*, which had arrived a few moments before. Agnes seemed in good form that morning – had been when she came in as I was having my morning tea to tell me about church and see whether I wanted to go. She looked as though she'd slept well and for hours and her face was fresh and her eyes sparkled with health.

'You look awfully well, Agnes,' I told her – like a girl having an affair, I thought. And she smiled as though she had a secret.

Tim on the other hand was pale and grumpy at breakfast, just the opposite to Agnes in fact and it almost made me wonder whether he knew what her secret was. But no, surely? I began to think that it was simply that Tim didn't like me and still resented my presence in the house.

'How nice to be having lunch at the Bakers. Tim, you haven't forgotten have you?'

'Of course not,' said Tim shortly.

'All right, don't snap my head off!' Agnes winked at me. 'I think Stephen Baker has taken quite a shine to you, Jo; ah you're blushing . . .'

Yes, my cheeks were hot. The remark had confused me, taken me by surprise. I wondered how much the Ryders knew about Peter. Could they possibly know about Tessa? I searched Agnes' eyes but all I saw was a teasing expression in them.

'I'm glad anyway,' she went on, getting up. 'Sincerely glad.' And I knew she was thinking about Peter and the way he had treated me.

St John's Church was a picture that sunny October morning. Its old stained glass shone like a kaleidoscope, dappling the stone-flagged floor with its colours, its minglings of blues, yellows and reds. Great vases of flowers and autumn leaves stood in the sanctuary and on the altar, and the brass and wood shone. The old stone walls were a warm pink mellowed with age and the plaques and memorials to long past inhabitants of Coppitts Green in marble, brass and stone adorned the walls of the nave. I looked for the names of Ryder and Dabroe as I sat there, trying hard to concentrate on the sermon on thrift, which was being delivered by a story-book clergyman with snow-white hair and the expression of a patriarch, but if there were any memorials to them I didn't see them.

In front of us sat Mrs Baker and Stephen and just before the service started there was a rustle to one side and Jonathan Dabroe sidled into a pew, and the glances that fell his way told me that everybody knew, and that he knew they knew but he didn't care. I found my gaze often straying towards Jonathan Dabroe during the long morning service. Despite the strain on his face and the grim set of his jaw there was a determination about him that made me wonder what he would do to Peter Ryder if ever he should set eyes on him again. For surely he must know that Tessa had left him for my boyfriend?

It then occurred to me that this fact created a bond between Jonathan and myself; we were both the victims of deceit, of illicit love. Really it was silly to talk about 'illicit' love, I thought, in this day and age. It was all very old-hat to talk of deceit and deception. We knew now that it took two people to break a marriage, the husband and the wife, and one wondered what had been Jonathan's contribution to his wife's behaviour? Agnes, surely.

After the service we all gathered outside after shaking hands with the Rector. I noticed that Tim went straight out and into the churchyard while Agnes lingered, looking about her – for what or whom? Of Jonathan there was no sign and I guessed he had slipped out during the final hymn.

'Tim always goes straight to Father's grave,' Agnes said, linking her arm through mine.

'Don't you?'

'Oh yes, I usually drift over; but Tim was frightfully attached to Father.' We were walking along the path that led to the graveyard and Tim was standing by a well-kept grave at the head of which stood a tombstone with a simple description on it denoting the birth and death of Charles Ryder M.C., T.D. The Bakers hadn't lingered; they were walking towards the lychgate of the church chatting to some people.

We joined the Bakers at the gate, where they'd waited for us. 'Stephen suggests you come back for sherry now,' Mrs Baker said, looking at her watch. 'It's such a lovely day and you can sit on the terrace. That sermon has made us horribly late.'

Tim looked at Agnes, who smiled agreement.

'Why not? We've nothing else to do,' and we set off in the direction of the Bakers' house at the top of the village. The sunlight scudded over the fell as soft white clouds dotted the pale sky. It was really very warm for October although there was a definite chill of autumn in the air. I noticed that Stephen escorted Agnes, and that Tim rather sullenly kept abreast with me, not attempting conversation, and only nodding replies to my rather perfunctory remarks.

The spot in the Bakers' garden on the terrace facing the valley and at right angles to the fell was sheltered. Herbert Baker was already there reading the Sunday papers when we arrived.

'I put on the beef, dear, as you said half an hour ago.'

'Oh lovely, Herbert. I must go and baste it. Jocasta, would

140

you give me a hand, dear? Stephen, would you offer drinks, or there is coffee if anyone would prefer it.'

She bustled inside and I hurried after her.

'So, Mr Baker can move about a bit on his own?'

'Oh yes, he's very good. He has a wheelchair, you know, which he only uses when he's on his own or we're by ourselves. He doesn't like people to see him using it. He's very vain. Just like a man. Now, if you'd make the coffee would you, Jo, dear? I'm sure Agnes prefers coffee. I do, I know.'

'And I.'

'Good. Everything else is ready. I'll put the potatoes on and the Yorkshire pudding in just before we eat. I thought Agnes looked very well this morning.' She glanced at me as she shut the oven door, brushing a whisp of hair back from her hot face.

'Doesn't she look well? She looks as though she hadn't a worry in the world.'

'Which is extraordinary really,' Mrs Baker murmured. 'Stephen told me about the visit to Peter's mother yesterday. Did you say anything to Agnes and Tim?'

'Of course not! Anyway I didn't see them until this morning.'

Mrs Baker was critically examining her Yorkshire pudding mixture, which she had taken from its resting place in the larder.

'Well, it's all got to come out some time, I suppose.' She shook her head and by this time the coffee was well and truly percolating and I put the jug on a tray and carried it out on to the terrace.

Stephen was showing Agnes the garden and Herbert Baker and Tim were reading the papers. It was a peaceful scene except that the sight of Stephen and Agnes somehow irritated me. Had I taken Stephen's affection for me for granted? I called to them but they were so engrossed in conversation they appeared not to hear and when I called again I realized my tone was a little sharp and they both looked up at me surprised.

But it was the same through lunch – Agnes and Stephen. He sat next to her and their heads were forever bending close together as he offered her vegetables or gave her more wine or murmured something to her, and she seemed to respond to him so intimately as though agreeing exactly with everything he said or did, laughing, nodding or simply waiting – Stephen's time her time. I remembered then how Stephen had felt about Agnes long before I'd appeared on the scene and I recalled the truism about an old love being the strongest, the most lasting.

Yet apart from this there was an atmosphere at the table that I couldn't altogether place; a restraint, a lack of gaiety as though everyone were somehow locked in private compartments of their own. Tim and Mrs Baker made desultory conversation but there were more silences than words spoken; and although I tried to keep Mr Baker entertained I did not feel I was being very successful. Or was it just me, the feeling that over everything hung an ominous presence, a tangled skein of deeds unaccounted for; words unexplained and things left unsaid?

That night my wakefulness was worse than ever. Although I had no difficulty in getting to sleep – we'd spent an evening in front of the television watching the play of the month and I was quite relaxed when I went to bed, by two o'clock I was sitting on the edge of my bed, listening. Outside, there was a fierce moon and the village appeared to bask in daylight as I looked out of the window and saw that the cliff lay well back in the shadow of the moon, which rose behind it. The peace of the scene quietened me and I prepared to go back to bed. Then I paused, listening. There it was again, the soft uneven footfalls as though someone were limping, dragging a foot or a heavy burden. The hair rose on my neck and my forehead broke out in a sweat; there was something so uncanny, so sinister about the sound in a quiet house where everyone was asleep.

I rushed to the window and threw up the sash. The noise of the beck was gentle and reassuring; it seemed to break in

142

from the outside in a gesture of sympathy and normality. The air was fresh and keen. I drew in a great gulp. And then the moon disappeared behind the cliff and the whole village was plunged in darkness and what had been a scene of serenity became sinister and menacing; total darkness, annihilation. Even the sound of the beck grew to a roar and I hurriedly closed the window as though to keep out its threatening presence.

Inside, all was quiet again; except for the shaded light of my lamp, there was nothing to see or hear. Yet I felt I had to go downstairs; just to reassure myself, just for the sake of . . . peace?

The switch for the landing was outside my door; and before I flicked it on I saw that the light in the hall below was on. I tip-toed along my landing and looked down the stairs. No one there, no sound. But below that, too, the light was on in the hall and more fearful now, but of something more physical than supernatural, I crept downstairs along the corridor and down the final flight of stairs into the hall.

Now I felt afraid and wished I'd stayed in my own room or gone to call Tim. Suppose it was an intruder? Suddenly the light went out and a jet of icy cold air rushed past me. I started to cry, but all I managed was a sort of grunt. I turned for the door to escape this house when a hand seized me and held my arm in a fierce grip. I struck blindly in front of me and a female voice said, 'Ouch!'

'Agnes!'

'Jo! Whatever are you doing prowling about at this time of night?'

The hall light flooded on and Agnes stood there in her nightgown, looking towsled and very beautiful as though she'd just woken from a deep sleep. She was staring at me with undisguised hostility.

'I thought I heard a noise. I wanted to see . . .'

'What makes you so nervous? I was making a drink. I don't sleep well, you know, and at the base of my brain the pain is beginning.'

'Oh, I'm sorry. Let me help you.'

I went into the kitchen, where a pan of milk was starting to boil on the Aga. Now in the better light I saw she did look drawn around the eyes and her mouth had the pinched sour look of pain.

'Will you have one too. Cocoa?'

'I'd like tea if that's all right. Do you often come down here at night?'

'Oh, often. The night is sometimes awful. I just creep along and down here for comfort.'

She looked so forlorn that my heart went out to her in sympathy. Here was a tortured, suffering person; but what tortured her or made her suffer I didn't know.

'Doesn't Tim help?'

'Oh, Tim sleeps like a log. I don't want to get him up every night.'

Of course she would shuffle along, trying not to disturb anyone; that would be the explanation . . . and then something jolted my mind and I looked sharply at her. But the night I'd first heard it I'd been alone in the house, or thought I had. The Ryders had been away . . .

'What's the matter, Jo? Why are you staring?'

'Agnes, I know it sounds absurd; but is there any sort of thing about this house? I mean . . . well the fact is that I often hear a sound like someone shuffling along, limping . . . It's uncanny, ghostlike . . .'

I stopped. Agnes had gone very pale, clutched her head.

'Agnes, what is it? What?'

'Oh, it's just that the pain is getting worse. I'll have to go up to bed, Jo.'

I reached for her arm to give her support.

'Let me help you. Agnes, is it anything I said? About the house?'

Her eyes now were dimmed as though with pain and she appeared to have difficulty in focusing. Now I was seriously alarmed about her.

'No, no. This is an old house, full of noises. No, I am

getting one of my attacks. I've got some pills if you can help me to my room.'

But before I could do anything more she swayed and fell in a dead faint on the floor at my feet.

At first I thought she was dead. I had never seen anything so realistically corpse-like; but I felt the pulse at her throat which was strong and even. I then rushed through the house calling for Tim. By the time I was on the first landing, Tim was there, too, hastily fastening the cord of his dressing gown.

'Jocasta! Whatever is it?'

'Agnes has fainted. Oh, come quickly, Tim!'

Tim had bounded past me down the stairs before I had time to turn round and when I joined him in the kitchen he was bending over his sister. To my intense relief I saw that the colour was slowly coming back to her cheeks and her eyelids were fluttering.

He looked angrily at me.

'What on earth happened? What did you say?'

What did I say? Even then in the heat of the moment I thought it was an extraordinary remark to make. What had I said? Surely it would have been more normal to ask what I'd *done*?

'I didn't *say* anything. She was here making cocoa. I'd heard a noise. She said she felt an attack coming on and then she fainted.'

Agnes was murmuring. Tim put his arms under her and sat her upright. She opened both eyes and looked first at him then at me. It seemed to me that she had no idea where she was or who we were, then recognition slowly came back.

'Did I pass out? I'm sorry. I must have frightened you, Jo. Oh Tim, my head . . . help me.'

Tim got her upright and I took the other arm and between us we shuffled up the stairs, along the corridor to her bedroom. The cover of her bed was turned back and the bedside light was on; but it looked to me as though she hadn't been to bed, hadn't even tried to woo sleep. What did she do if she wasn't sleeping? An awful paralysing fear crept over me as I looked

145

at her and I imagined her creeping along the corridor in the dark, shuffling, feeling her way with her hands. Why?

Was Agnes Ryder going out of her mind? Was she in the grip of something much more serious than she or anyone else thought?

Now we had her in bed and Tim sat by her side stroking her face tenderly. Her eyelashes fluttered and then were still and her breathing was deep and regular.

'She'll sleep now,' Tim said, fastening the cap on the box from which he'd taken two pills. 'I'll leave the light on just in case. But she'll be all right now.'

I crept out in front of him and waited for him in the hall while he gently shut the door. Tim looked drawn and haunted, suffering too, not hostile, and for the first time since we'd met I felt pity for him and the glimmer of something like friendship.

'Tim, would you like a drink? I'll have to go down to the kitchen anyway.'

He looked doubtful, then put his hands in the pockets of his thick woollen dressing gown and shrugged. Tim looked utterly defeated as though he had been fighting a private war against something and had lost.

In the kitchen he sat at the table while I used the milk that Agnes had boiled to make us both cocoa, a drink I didn't usually like but whose effects might provide us with a needed soporific. My nerves were taut as a drum skin and Tim looked as though he needed a sedative rather than a stimulant. I gave him a mugful in silence and then sat down opposite him, looking at him while I stirred my cocoa.

'Hmm it's good,' I said, sipping it. 'Drink up, Tim, or would you rather take it to bed?'

Tim shook his head and sipped the hot brew. It left foam on his lips and made him look like a little boy despite the growth of beard that was beginning.

'You're worried about Agnes, Tim, aren't you?'

'Very.'

'Don't you think she should have a consultation with the specialist again or whoever saw her?'

'The doctor says no. I spoke to him after the spell at Hammersleigh when Karen Fullerton brought her home. The doctor does think it's psychological; I've no doubt about that.'

'She looked so well today at church and at lunch, so animated.'

Tim nodded.

'That usually precedes an attack; she seems terribly well. It's one of the signs.'

Suddenly I wondered if the thought of seeing Jonathan Dabroe, the sight of him at church, had been what had made Agnes seem so terribly well? Could that be it? The sight of the beloved? It would make her excited, exciting, interesting to Stephen . . . men always seem to find women more exciting when they're in love with someone else. Then the excitement would bring on a reaction, a depression, the guilt of Tim finding out, knowing, the sleeplessness . . . Yes, it was probably psychological, I thought.

'Tim, I wanted to ask you,' I said, looking at him suddenly, 'I know it may not be the time or the place but I feel I must ask you something.'

I thought Tim seemed apprehensive as he returned my look.

'Do you *know* where Peter is?'

'Oh dear Jo, I thought we had got over that.'

'Well, I haven't, not by any means.'

'You're not still worried about Peter, are you?'

'No, I'm not worried about him, exactly, hurt yes; but I wondered if *you* knew what had happened to Peter?'

'You sound as though you do.'

'I think I do.'

Now Tim went very pale and gulped the cocoa as though to hide his confusion and give him strength. I suddenly felt a threat, a menace coming from him and I was afraid. Yes, I was afraid of Tim, and of this house. That was it, the Ryders and the house frightened me . . . both of them together.

However, I was not the girl I'd been, the timid little schoolteacher who'd come so confidently and trustfully to the Yorkshire Dales only a few short weeks ago. Time had changed Jocasta Oaks, time and uncertainty and to some extent fear and humiliation; just as love had changed her, love for Peter Ryder, a total, abandoned, life-enhancing passion after which there was no turning back.

I had no one to rely on now but myself. No one I could really trust – even Stephen had had eyes only for Agnes at lunchtime. Suddenly I wondered if there was a conspiracy embracing the whole village, everyone I knew, even the nice Mrs Bargett, to get rid of me and drive me back to London?

Tim interrupted my reverie by going to the Aga and pouring himself more cocoa. I suppose it had only taken a few seconds, yet it seemed like hours – one's life can change in a very few seconds, one can grow up or become a different person. No, I wasn't frightened of Tim, or of anyone or anything. All I wanted was to know the truth and to let everyone else know the truth.

'Well, what has happened to Peter?' Tim had turned round and was stirring his cocoa, looking still very grim but composed. He said nothing.

'I think he has run off with Tessa Dabroe!' I burst out.

Tim first stared incredulously at me, then sat down and began to laugh. It was a fresh cheerful laugh, a laugh of relief. It was not the sort of laugh I expected to hear at the mention of the awful, the hated name of Dabroe. But then I realized why. He'd thought the suggestion so absurd the only thing to do was to laugh at it.

'Peter gone off with Tessa Dabroe! What an absolutely ridiculous suggestion.'

'Did you know Tessa had left her husband?'

'Everyone knows; but she's gone back to her mother, not run off with my cousin. Don't you know about the feud between the Ryders and the Dabroes? Peter would no sooner look at a Dabroe, even one by marriage, than fly . . .'

'Are you sure?'

'Of course I'm sure. Utter loyalty is a mark of our family, and Ryders and Dabroes do not talk to each other. Our father even sent Agnes and me away, much as he wanted us with him, just so that we would never come into contact with the Dabroe children.'

'Yes, I know, but things can change, Tim.'

For the first time a little frown of uncertainty appeared on Tim's forehead and his brow remained creased.

'Do you actually know something, Jocasta, or are you merely guessing?'

Oh, I know, I thought, how much I know; but I was only going to tell him part of it; only part of it tonight anyway.

'I have very good reason to think it; to think that he and Tessa have gone off together. But I do *know* that a Ryder has talked to a Dabroe and for a long time. Peter has been having business discussions with Jonathan for almost a year; now did you know that?'

Tim's jaw hung heavily and I knew he had not.

'But Peter wouldn't . . .'

'Peter *did*. Jonathan Dabroe told me; and if you feel he was being mischievous, this was confirmed by your friends the Fullertons, who saw them together at a Chinese restaurant in Leeds. Jonathan said they both thought the feud was absurd and were doing business together, a machine to make sheep-shearing more profitable.'

'Peter told me about the machine,' Tim said prosaically, as though still trying to slot into place what he had heard, find a reason, a justification for it. 'He didn't tell me he was talking to Dabroe about it . . .'

'But he wouldn't would he? He wouldn't dare. You hate the Dabroes so much, Peter knew it was more than his life was worth to tell you, and then when he met Tessa, became attracted by her . . . why, what else would he do but disappear? I thought you knew where he was, that you had conspired with him; I thought you had his keys, I saw some on your desk, and you were looking after his flat for him. But then I found out they were Mrs Bargett's keys and, I thought, you're just as ignorant as I am, just as puzzled, or are you? Are you, Tim?'

Tim's eyes had never left me, and search though I did, I still could not fathom whether or not Tim Ryder was telling the truth or concealing it. I was struck again by his likeness to Peter and now that I knew Tim and more about Peter, I realized that the Ryders could assume, when it suited them, an enigmatic expression that neither revealed nor concealed but could be all things to all people.

'So,' I said as lightly as I could, though even the telling of the story had made my heart heavy and it was very nearly morning, the light beginning to illuminate the outbuildings in the yard, 'so that is why I think Peter has disappeared and the mystery is solved.'

'I didn't know – ' Tim shook his head – 'I can't believe . . .'

Suddenly we both looked at each other and with one accord started from our seats towards the door. A terrible scream had come from upstairs, just one piercing single scream like nothing I had ever known in my life. It charged the adrenalin and, from feeling tired, I now ran as I had never run before, Tim ahead of me. Up the stairs along the long corridor, pounding along the short corridor to Agnes' room.

Agnes' door was open, but in the dim light we could see her lying on the floor and the bedclothes of her bed were hurled back as though something terrible had frightened her out of her bed and sent her screaming to the door.

Thirteen

Doctor Brasenose had been persuaded by the urgency of Tim's voice that Agnes wasn't just having another of her attacks and had arrived, reluctantly it was true, on the doorstep of Croft House at five in the morning. We'd left Agnes on the floor and covered her with a coat; the pounding of her heart at first had frightened me, but after a while it subsided and it appeared that, whatever it was that had frightened her, had made her faint almost instantly, so that the racing heart continued for some moments until it slowed down.

There was nothing in the room at all to indicate any disturbance apart from the bed and the open door, no sign of an intruder, nothing. Tim had gone downstairs just to be sure the doors were locked.

The doctor knelt to examine Agnes and when he got up, he shook his head, stowing his stethoscope away in his bag.

'It's the same as always; yet this time she has been unconscious for longer than usual . . . ah.'

We looked and Agnes' eyes were fluttering again. How could it be merely psychological, I thought, watching her fight to regain consciousness, to have flaked out twice in one night? What deep mysterious thing was disturbing this girl?

We'd lifted her on to the bed and as she lay there, she opened her eyes and at first turned them to the window; outside, the birdsong seemed very shrill as though they too were alarmed.

'Peter,' she said, just once.

'It's Tim, Agnes, not Peter.' Tim stooped towards her.

'I saw Peter,' she said in a monotonous voice. 'He came and stood by my bed.'

'That was when you screamed?' I asked quietly.

'Yes; it was like Peter and yet not like Peter . . . it was horrible, like a ghost.'

Dr Brasenose looked enquiringly at us, measuring some liquid he'd produced from his bag into a glass.

'My cousin has disappeared,' Tim explained, 'rather we think he's gone abroad; frankly we don't know. I . . .'

The doctor nodded.

'She's got him on her mind; that kind of thing would make someone like Agnes go off again. We'd better have a talk downstairs,' he added quietly and then propped Agnes up while he gave her the medicine. 'There my girl, you sleep for a few hours and I'll come and see you again.'

Almost immediately Agnes closed her eyes obediently and her head rolled to one side.

'It's a knockout,' the doctor said. 'She's exhausted and that will make her relax completely.'

'It's nearly morning,' I whispered tiredly, 'and I've got to teach today.'

'Been a bad night?' The doctor smiled sympathetically.

'Terrible; it started at two when she couldn't sleep. Then Tim and I were talking . . .'

'You're the new schoolteacher. I've heard of you.'

Tim had gone ahead of us and we were walking towards the door; we both paused to look back at the sleeping patient and then went on down the stairs where Tim waited for us in the lounge. I shivered; the fire had long gone out and the central heating was probably primed not to start again until about seven.

'Tim, I do think Agnes had better have further investigation. There may be something we've missed out.'

Tim nodded looking grave.

'Jocasta said something like that earlier on.'

'I still think it's psychological; but that, too, can be very serious. We don't want it to get worse. I think she should go into the Brotherton Wing in Leeds for a complete overhaul, physical and psychological. I'll arrange it.'

'Could it be the house?' I said quietly. Both men stared at me, the doctor about to leave for the door.

'The house?'

'It affects me. It frightens me.'

'But she's lived here all her life—' the doctor began.

'No, she hasn't,' I insisted. 'She was born here and she's lived here on and off; but she hasn't lived here all her life, not a bit; she was at boarding school and then at Cambridge.'

'But the headaches started in Cambridge,' the doctor said, 'not here.' Tim was looking at me, the muscles in his jaw working.

'She seemed to get peace in the house. I mean when the headaches were bad and she came home she got better. I don't think it's the house.'

'How could it be the house?' the doctor scoffed, then he looked thoughtful. 'Although in fact, to be fair, I have known a house affect an ill woman, I don't think she'd mind my telling you. It was Karen Fullerton's mother when she was ill. Oh, years ago, but we had to move her out of the house . . .'

'And later everyone said it was because of a ghost,' Tim said quietly. Tim, I thought, sounded shaken. Dr Brasenose looked at him.

'Oh, you heard that too, did you?'

'We only heard bits of it. Neither Karen or Hugh would ever talk about it. It came through our Mrs Bargett. I don't believe in that kind of thing.'

'Don't you?' The doctor looked at him closely. 'You believe in feuds though, don't you?'

'Oh, that's completely different.' Tim's voice was brusque. Dr Brasenose looked at me and then thoughtfully put on his coat.

'Maybe it's not,' he said. 'Maybe a feud has a presence too. Now, Tim, anyway, I want the girl examined; no nonsense or I'd be evading my responsibilities.'

153

'Of course. Thanks for coming.'

I suddenly felt such an overwhelming exhaustion that before Tim came back into the house from seeing the doctor to his car I fled upstairs. I set my alarm. I could get a couple of hours and still be at school on time.

I so badly needed to sleep.

For the first half of school that day I found it difficult to perform my duties as a teacher. With small children you can't just give them a book as you can with older ones. Stimulating work or activity has to go on all day, which is why infant teachers have really more to do than any other type of teacher. If you've got a headache you can't set them to parsing a paragraph of *Lorna Doone*; even if they paint, you have to supervise the little darlings. By lunchtime I felt all in and I reckoned I looked it. Luckily the fine October weather had continued and the children were able to play outside at morning and lunch breaks.

I'd noticed Mrs Baker looking at me carefully at the coffee break, but it wasn't until we were sitting on the bench in the yard after lunch that she said anything.

'Tired today, Jocasta?'

'I look awful, don't I? I feel it. We were up all night.'

'Good heavens, whatever for?'

'Agnes wasn't well. We had the doctor at five in the morning. She's to go into hospital.'

Mrs Baker looked shocked.

'Good gracious! I didn't realize it was as bad as that.'

'It's very bad. She fainted twice; once for over an hour . . .'

'Oh, that's terrible. I am sorry. But you look more than tired, Jo dear, you look worried.'

'I am. I sometimes feel there's something awful brewing and I don't know what it is or how I can prevent it. Something we don't know.' I looked at Mrs Baker, her own kind face now strained and anxious on my behalf. 'I think it's something to do with the house.'

'The house? But it's a lovely house. Whatever can you

mean by that? Mind you, you've never liked the house. From the beginning, Stephen was telling me you didn't like it.'

'There couldn't be anything about the house that affects Agnes, could there?' I looked at her searchingly.

'Not that I know of,' Mrs Baker said after, it seemed to me, pausing for rather longer than necessary so as to measure her words. 'Of course it may have bad memories on account of her mother. Charles loved the house; he said it had old roots; but there was one thing, I suppose I could tell you.' She looked about. The children were happy in their various playgrounds and from our bench against the schoolhouse wall, we looked straight up on to the sloping hill of the valley, the leaves on the scattered trees burnished in autumn colours, the sheep with their large, fat lambs, almost grown-up, grazing contentedly nearby. Even as I write now, I recall that scene so vividly as though, because of the importance of what Mrs Baker had to say, it was always to be etched on my memory.

'Well . . . no one likes to talk about it much. I never remember anyone in the village even mentioning it, certainly not the Ryders; but everyone knows about it.'

'What, for heaven's sake?'

'Well, it was the reason for the feud between the Dabroes and the Ryders and it began in the nineteenth century. Of course the details now are lost in the mists of time, but it was to do with Matthew Ryder, Charles' great-grandfather, who was born in the house and became the first Ryder to live there all his life. Well, his son Roger Ryder was a ne'er-do-well, the sort that families, especially big ones, always seem to have. He didn't work and he whored and he never had any money and the family decided to make him work in Leeds in one of the mills as a clerk.'

A feeling of excitement started inside me; it was personal, apart from the fact that I loved these old once-upon-a-time stories.

'Well, Roger Ryder was very friendly with Jeremy Dabroe, also a ne'er-do-well and fitting companion for Roger in all his exploits. But Jeremy Dabroe was the son of the owner of the mill where Roger worked and a sort of hostility seems to have grown up between the young men, especially when the Dabroes decided to send Jeremy to America, in those days the land of opportunity. Roger sulked and would have nothing to do with Jeremy for a time, and begged his father to let him go too. But the Dabroe father and the Ryder father were good friends and they decided that Roger must work industriously at home while Jeremy must seek his fortune abroad. Then the time came for Jeremy to leave. He was living at Felton Hall, which the Dabroe family had just bought, rebuilt and enlarged and Roger was at home in Coppitts Green under the watchful eye of his father, Matthew. Now what follows is supposition, for no one has ever known the truth. Jeremy, it is said, decided to say goodbye to his old friend for old time's sake and, knowing his family would disapprove, one night he crossed the river secretly and walked the few miles to see Roger at Croft House. He was never seen again.'

'But what happened to him?'

'Well, this is what no one is quite sure about. It was assumed he had gone off to America, though he hadn't said goodbye to his family and he'd left all his things at his house except forty gold coins, which his father had just given him. Years later, people reported meeting a Jeremy Dabroe in America, where he had set up a business and done well; but you see, Roger Ryder disappeared at the same time and he was never heard of either . . .'

'So?'

'The rumour is that Roger killed Jeremy and changed places with him taking the money for his passage, for he never had any of his own, and that it was Roger Ryder who pretended to be Jeremy Dabroe or called himself by that name. They say that Matthew found Jeremy's body and Roger gone and to save scandal and the family name he disposed of the corpse; so you see, there might have been a murder in the house.'

'Well, what an extraordinary tale!'

'Yes, it is, and nothing is quite certain, you see, not even the Ryders know for sure; but they say there's a walled-up room in the house and that that was where Matthew found the body. Mind you, Charles never believed this. He denied all knowledge of a walled-up room; but a funny thing happened a few years ago. Repairs were being done to the roof of the house and a workman dropped his hammer through one of the chimneys and, do you know, though he searched and searched he never found it in any of the grates. So you see it could have dropped into the walled-up room.'

'I think it's under my bedroom,' I said.

Mrs Baker was now staring at me.

'I beg your pardon?'

'That was one of the first things I noticed when I came there, because I thought I heard noises underneath me, yet no one could tell me what room was underneath. Agnes said it was the bathroom or her room, but the measurements didn't fit. But there's no window from the outside . . .'

'What sort of noise did you hear?'

'Like a limping, dragging sound, as though someone was shuffling along. I thought last night it might be Agnes, who says she's often up at night and if she's in pain I imagined she'd creep about. But the first time I heard it was soon after I arrived and the Ryders were away.'

I thought Mrs Baker had an odd expression on her face and was studying her shoes with a degree of concentration that denoted an unusual preoccupation.

'It's very odd you should say that,' she said, still carefully watching the toes of her shoes, 'but people from time to time have said the house is haunted and that it's the sound of Matthew dragging Jeremy's body, and then they hear a banging which is the room being walled up during the various stages of building and rebuilding. Charles said that Angela, his wife, once heard these noises, but that he never did and didn't believe her.'

'Then the house is haunted,' I said softly. 'I know, don't I? I never heard about Jeremy Dabroe's death but I heard the noises . . . and then to get his own back, to even things off, a Dabroe went off with a Ryder wife, and so the feud continues.'

Mrs Baker was gazing up at the hills as though seeing the timeless things that only land or buildings witness but can never talk about, which is why people say buildings and places have atmosphere: silent witnesses.

'You see, no one knows for sure.' Mrs Baker got up, her hand on the bell hammer. 'It is just supposition about what happened all those years ago. Yet Dabroes believe that Roger killed Jeremy and took his place, and the Ryders by their secretiveness seem to accept it. It's as though they are covering up for Matthew and Roger. So yes, maybe Agnes and you to a lesser extent are affected by the house; maybe the Rector should be called to perform exorcism.'

And she rang the bell with a fierce strident gesture as though casting out the spirits of evil herself.

I don't know whether I felt depressed or elated by the confirmation that my feelings about the house might have some basis in reality. Could it be that an age-old murder had affected Agnes, was affecting me? But what of anyone else who had lived there? Who could one ask?

I'd always been curious about the beautiful Angela, the children's mother, whom I regarded as a rather sad and romantic figure, exiled because of her passion, abandoned by her lover. Shouldn't Angela anyway be asked about her daughter? Be consulted? Stephen would know how to find her; Stephen, whom I was sure still loved her daughter, if his behaviour yesterday was anything to go by.

In a way I was sad about Stephen. It had been nice to feel that somebody else considered me as attractive as Peter had, thought it worthwhile to pay me compliments and attention. Or had Stephen only been doing it in order to get, through me, close to Agnes? It was a thought.

But I felt better, more at peace as I went into the classroom for the afternoon's school. I felt I had a new object in life to replace my hopeless quest for Peter.

Mrs Baker left school as soon as the last child had been seen safely on his way. I thought she looked pale and tense and I wondered if her rheumatism was troubling her more than usual. I often used to look at the poor swollen joints of her fingers, the slow way she walked, and wondered how long she could continue teaching. Then what would happen? Would the school close down, or would I maybe take to this lovely contryside and stay on into spinsterhood as the teacher at Coppitts Green school, a sort of Brontëish character nursing memories of a lost love?

I tidied up, leaving everything straight for the cleaner, then I started getting materials together for a craft session the next day. By the time I locked up and left it was nearly five. I knew I'd lingered because I was reluctant to get back to Croft House. Knowing what I knew, how could I ever sleep peacefully again?

I was standing by the school door, in the shadow as it happened, when a car went by and stopped some way along the road towards Starthrush. A woman got out, bent in to the car as though saying goodbye, then shut the door and began to walk back towards Coppitts Green. I remained where I was, intrigued and fascinated. As she came nearer and passed the school, not looking up, not seeing me, her head set straight towards the village, I thought of the last time I'd seen Agnes Ryder, flaked out, under sedation. She was supposed still to be in bed; yet here she was getting out of Jonathan Dabroe's car, her face aglow as a woman's face is supposed to look after a visit from a lover, swinging her way towards the village.

Soon she was out of sight and I went down to the gate, ready to follow her, only taking care that she should not see me. Then I stopped; the car hadn't moved but remained where it was, pointing towards Starthrush. As I turned and closed the gate the door opened and Jonathan Dabroe walked towards me, his hands in his pockets, his gait easy and casual.

'Hello, Miss Oaks. I thought it was you but I couldn't be sure.'

'Hello, Mr Dabroe,' I looked up at him, suddenly unnerved. Why had he waited?

'May I give you a lift?'

'No, thank you. I prefer to walk.'

Why hadn't he given Agnes a lift, I wondered, why had he let her walk? Because they didn't want anyone in the village to see them. That was why; that was patently why.

'Please let me drive you,' Jonathan continued. 'I'd like to talk to you.'

What could I say? I shrugged my shoulders and went towards the car, nodding thanks to him as he held the door for me to climb in. Once inside, he set off the way the car was pointing, towards Starthrush. Suddenly I was afraid. Knowing what I knew now, was beginning to know about the Dabroes and the Ryders, the suppressed violence of these families, I wondered what he wanted to say to me, why he was taking me away from Coppitts Green? I'd just seen Agnes get out of his car. Supposing he wanted to hide this at all costs, any cost?

Yet Jonathan Dabroe seemed to be smiling as he drove at high speed towards the next village.

'I thought we'd have tea in the pub there. Is that all right?'

'Oh.' I was relieved and rather abashed. I was really becoming too dramatic for my own good. 'That would be nice.'

'Good.'

He said nothing more until we were comfortably ensconced in the old-fashioned lounge of the Walter Inn and we were being served with tea in a large earthern pot and buttered scones and freshly made cakes.

'Why did you want to talk to me?'

'I wanted to talk about Peter Ryder. I understand you think he's gone off with my wife.'

The baldness of the statement startled me. He could only have got this information from Agnes, and he'd known I'd seen her get out of his car. But somehow to talk about Agnes

160

now seemed to me wrong timing. Jonathan was leaning over the table pouring tea for us both as though this was merely a social occasion, afternoon tea in the country.

'It's all because Peter's mother said he was on about someone called Tessa,' Jonathan went on easily, giving me my tea with a smile.

'Yes.' I nodded my thanks for the tea. I felt on the defensive as though I were under interrogation. 'It seems reasonable. Peter has disappeared and Tessa—'

'Has gone to Chichester. You see, Jocasta – you don't mind me using your name, we did agree on Christian names, didn't we? – you see, if they'd have done a flit like Angela Ryder with my dear father, Tessa wouldn't have gone home to mother; and why should Peter disappear?'

'It's coincidental though,' I said.

'Well it is, very.'

Jonathan rubbed his chin and smiled at me sympathetically. His charm lay in making one feel immediately at ease, trustful towards him as though you and he were together in whatever the problem was.

'I don't want to decry Peter at all, Jocasta, I really hardly know him; but he did have a, well, reputation . . .'

'I know,' I said bitterly, 'as everyone keeps telling me.'

'Oh, I don't only mean as far as women are concerned, but he was, is rather, shall we say, an individualist? In the old days he'd have been a pirate, an adventurer. He's brilliant, really; but not reliable. As far as business is concerned he delivers the goods, but his methods are his own. No doubt about that.'

'Do you think he may have done something dishonest?' I whispered. 'Might he be, as it were, lying low?'

Jonathan shrugged, that Continental gesture that you can make what you like of.

'Frankly I don't think that's like him either. If I were you, I'd try and put him out of your mind . . .'

I was about to explode again. Jonathan Dabroe really had a very irritating patronizing quality about him. He saw the wrath on my face and put out a hand.

'Please, don't misunderstand me. I'm just thinking of what is best for you, really. But as for Tessa, no. You see, I know why she left me.'

I drew a breath and looked at him.

'She thought I was having an affair with Agnes Ryder.'

I let the breath go. It was out at last.

'Only I'm not,' Jonathan said, pouring milk into his cup.

'But nothing I could say would convince her. You see Tessa wanted to leave me; she wanted an excuse. Just like Agnes' mother, Tessa hated it here in the Dales and, as for our marriage, it was over long ago. Only, Tessa wanted an excuse to go; so that she could say she'd been provoked into it. Tessa was a very dutiful person; she had been brought up with all the old virtues of duty, right conduct and so on. What Tessa really wanted to do deep down was strip and run naked into the street; she was so inhibited about everything, especially about sex. So to use a sexual excuse to leave me was fine; it would be all right by her mother. Infidelity was the one thing that made it right to leave a man; anything else, no. It's funny, really, when you think sex was the thing she least prized; yet it was the one thing that gave her the freedom she wanted, pretending I was having an affair with someone else.'

As I listened, the bitter years of a sterile marriage slipped by; a tale so familiar from articles and novels, yet here related from real life.

'I don't blame Tessa,' Jonathan went on. 'I would have given her her freedom just for the asking; she didn't have to trump up excuses, to pretend. But Tessa was all pretence; hating it here yet doing all the things the wife of a country notable is supposed to do. I don't blame her for marrying me because for a time we did love each other; we were attracted and we did try, and we loved the children – but we just grew more and more apart as people with different interests do.'

'What did Tessa want to do?' I asked, curious.

'Oh, she wanted to live in Surrey or Sussex, somewhere near London. She wanted to cruise and go to America once a year. She felt she was cooped up in the Dales, with theatres in Leeds or Bradford as the social bright spot of the week. It wasn't social enough for her; or rather it wasn't society. Her father was a belted baronet and society was what Tessa missed. I don't know why she married me.'

I knew why she'd married him, though I couldn't say it.

Good-looking now in his early thirties, ten years ago he must have been the most romantic dish any woman could wish for. I suppose Jonathan could have had any woman he'd wanted; only as one grew older and a marriage matured and romantic love faded, it wasn't enough.

'It's very sad,' I said, 'sad for the children, sad for you. But I find it hard to believe about Agnes, that you're not having an affair, though it's none of my business . . .'

Jonathan sat back in his chair and looked at me, as though calculating, measuring. Then he leaned forward until his head was close to mine.

'I'm telling you what very few people in the world know, and you must keep it to yourself. Do you promise?'

The look in his eyes was intense and my heart beat faster as I felt their gimlet-like, compelling quality.

'I promise.'

'I'm telling you because I trust you and in a way I think you've a right to know. Agnes is my half-sister, the daughter of my father, Sam Dabroe, and Charles' wife, Angela.'

Fourteen

I remember that the lounge where we were sitting had a grandfather clock and that until the profound silence that followed Jonathan's announcement I hadn't heard it ticking, but now the heavy tick, tick of the clock as the ornate pendulum swung backwards and forwards seemed in its intensity to dramatize the importance of what he'd said. Of course it was all clear now, they even looked alike – why had no one ever noticed it before? They were both tall and dark and intense; Tim was sandy coloured, like Peter and quite differently built and complexioned. They both had the same flashing yet merry blue eyes, walked with the same insouciance.

'You see it now, don't you?' Jonathan was watching the expression on my face, or rather expressions, as shock, disbelief and then recognition followed one another in quick succession.

'Yes,' I told him, looking at him thoughtfully, 'I see it now. I wonder everyone doesn't see it.'

'Because they never see us together. They never associate us. The obvious is often not realized just because it is so.'

'And how did you know?'

'Peter told me. He didn't come to see me about the machines in the first place, or rather he used it as the means of affecting an introduction between us. Peter is clever, rather ruthless, you know. Then I asked my mother and she said it was true, that Sam and Angela were always together and that in all probability Sam was Agnes' father; but he'd never said he was; she just believed it to be true

164

and for that reason Charles had been so concerned that the Dabroes and the Ryders should be kept apart. I suppose in case they became attracted.'

'So. Charles had a reason for keeping up the feud?'

'Yes.'

'And you and Agnes have been meeting secretly?'

'Yes. We find we've so much in common, that we like each other's company so much. That—'

'But Tim must be told one day!' I got up and crossed the room, making sure the door was closed and no one could hear this extraordinary conversation.

'Well, he must, I suppose; but Agnes loves him too, she doesn't want him to be hurt. She also thinks he might not care for her so much, if he knew, and I can't look after her.'

'She doesn't need looking after!' I said. 'I think Tim is the cause of Agnes' trouble; if she could break away . . . And I thought she was in love with you.'

'You thought . . . ?'

'People have seen you together.' I noted the expression of concern on his face and nodded grimly. 'Oh yes. I've hardly been here a month and I've heard it. I wonder it hasn't reached Tim. But, Jonathan, if you knew this, why didn't your wife believe you weren't having an affair?'

'Because I didn't tell her Agnes was my sister!'

'Why not?'

He shrugged and got up so that he stood beside me at the window. Cars were beginning to come into the car park and we would not be alone for much longer.

'I just couldn't. I didn't trust her to keep it to herself and maybe, who knows, I wanted her to go.'

I looked at him; his gaze was warm and tender, concerned.

'Why did you tell me?' I said faintly, wondering what on earth was happening.

'I trusted you. I saw you were upright and sincere and caring; that night you came to the house . . . you were so worried about Peter. I thought, What has he done to deserve you? He is insincere, on the make, ruthless . . .'

165

'Oh no, no.' I kneaded my fists to my forehead and shook my head. 'Peter isn't like that. He isn't. Peter has made me into a woman, changed me from an immature, shy, awkward girl. Even for that, I owe Peter so much; even if he is the other things . . .'

I realized I was close to tears and this wouldn't do at all. The onslaught on my emotions was too much. I grabbed my bag and blew my nose vigorously on a handkerchief. Jonathan took my arm.

'I'll drive you home,' he said gently.

It was almost too much to face Agnes after my meeting with Jonathan. I felt she would look at me and see immediately that I knew. Jonathan had asked me not to tell her I knew. I went straight up to my room and bathed my face and then made it up carefully; but when I went downstairs, Agnes was on the phone and she waved cheerfully to me as I came in, pointing to a seat for me to sit down.

'That was Anne Baker,' she said, putting the phone down. 'We were at Cambridge together. She wants us to go round for coffee. You'll like Anne. I wish she was here more but she's doing archaeology and is always travelling.'

'Do you ever miss Cambridge?' I asked, lighting a cigarette and carefully not looking at her.

'You mean, do I wish I'd taken my degree? Yes, I suppose I do. I don't know. Sometimes. I'm lazy, too, and I doubt whether I'd have wanted to get a job.'

'What did you read?'

'History. I specialized in sixteenth-century French and English. I don't know what I'd have done with it.'

She must have been clever to have got into Cambridge in the first place, I thought. To me, it seemed she'd wasted her life; here she was, without a career or a job and on the brink of permanent invalidism. No wonder she was excited by her half-brother Jonathan. It must have been quite electrifying finding out something like that.

'Tim's not in. Thank goodness because he doesn't like Anne. Let's eat.'

She led the way into the dining room. I realized it was the first protracted spell alone with Agnes I'd had. She took off the lids of the silver entrée dishes on the sideboard.

'Good. Cannelloni. Mrs Bargett is awfully good with Italian food. You wouldn't expect it, would you? I must say I'm hungry. Those attacks always leave me famished. Two or three?' She looked at me inquiringly.

'Just two, please. I have to watch my weight. They're delicious but fattening. Thanks.' I took the hot plate and put it in front of me.

'I'm afraid I must have scared you.' Agnes sat next to me, leaving the head of the table free. 'Tim says I did.'

'I was worried, I admit.'

'And anxious, because of Peter?'

I looked at her but saw nothing in her innocent expression.

'*Did* you see Peter?'

'Do you know, I can't remember a thing about it. I don't even remember going to bed last night. But I'm not going into hospital, whatever Brasenose says . . .'

'But don't you want to get better, Agnes? Greens?' I passed her the vegetable dish. She was flushed.

'Of course I want to get better. How do you mean?'

'Well, at the hospital—'

'They won't find anything!' She was angry now. 'They didn't before. I had all sorts of horrible painful tests and it took weeks and they found nothing . . .'

She was becoming heated.

'I'm sorry,' I said quietly. 'You must do what you think best.' And I changed the subject and started to talk about school.

Anne Baker was an interesting girl. One was immediately arrested by her as though she had some intangible quality to offer. She was basic and direct and had the tanned look of someone who spent a lot of time in the open, as she did.

She wore jeans and a T-shirt and made me feel overdressed in my shirt and skirt. She greeted Agnes warmly; but didn't kiss her, as though this sort of gesture didn't come easily to her. She had the look of someone who didn't tolerate fools at all, let alone gladly. She must have thought a lot of Agnes for them to have been so friendly.

'Mother begs to be excused. She's in a lot of pain today, and Dad is watching something special on television.'

'Oh, I'm sorry about your mother.' I had been right to be concerned.

'Shall I go up and see her? You can talk to Agnes.'

'I think she might be asleep,' Anne said, smiling at me. 'Do you mind not?'

'Of course I don't.'

'Mother thinks an awful lot of you; she says she doesn't know how she coped before. But I think she has got worse this year. Don't you, Aggie?'

'I'm afraid I've hardly noticed,' Agnes said. 'I know it sounds selfish, but I haven't been too well myself.'

Anne looked grave and fiddled nervously with the cheroot she was smoking.

'And they still don't know why?'

Agnes shook her head.

'Do you have any idea, Agnes?' Anne was being very direct. I watched with interest to see what would happen.

Agnes shook her head again.

'They're unpredictable . . . take last night. It just happened, didn't it, Jo?'

I was looking puzzled, trying to think back how it had happened. I'd asked her about the house, whether that disturbed her, and it had seemed to make the pain unbearable and she'd fainted.

'We were talking about the house,' I said, determined to emulate Anne's directness.

'The house?' Anne said.

'I said, did anything about the house disturb her. It disturbs me.'

'Really? How interesting.' Anne flicked the ash from her little cigar. 'Do go on.'

'Well, I don't want to upset Agnes, but I felt unhappy about the house from the beginning. Not at peace in it. I thought I heard noises and couldn't sleep.'

Agnes' mouth, I noticed, was beginning to pucker. I wondered whether she was doing her best to try to conjure up that pain again; to try to stop me talking.

'There's nothing wrong with the house,' Agnes interrupted me, but Anne looked at her.

'Now, Agnes, you know that's not true. People have heard noises there before. You know the old story . . .'

Anne glanced at me and I nodded.

'Your mother told me about it today.'

'But it's not true!' Agnes burst out. 'It's an awful lot of rubbish that old story about Roger Ryder and Jeremy Dabroe . . .'

She looked hot and tearful. Of course she was half a Dabroe herself . . . a girl riven by conflicting passions. A terrible heritage, in a way, poor Agnes had. Anne and I were both about to say something when the door opened and Stephen came in.

He looked as though he'd been in court and wore a dark formal suit and a stiff collar. He looked eagerly about for his sister obviously, but stopped when he saw Agnes. I then knew that Stephen Baker was still in love with Agnes whatever he or anybody else said; his face became suffused with emotion and he went over to her and took her hand.

'I heard you weren't well. Are you all right now?'

'Oh yes, thanks, Stephen. How did you hear?'

'I saw Tim in Skipton at lunchtime. He said he'd left you sleeping, and that the doctor had been called. He hadn't wanted to leave you, but had business to do and knew you'd be all right with Mrs Bargett. Anne, darling . . .' He'd finally spotted his sister and went over to kiss her. I think she too had noticed the main object of his interest and she laughed up into his face.

'Mother was expecting you for dinner.'

'I couldn't make it. I was in court all day and had to catch up this evening. Jocasta, how are you?' He was warm and friendly with me, but his voice had lost that intimacy. If I'd ever wanted Stephen Baker I had lost him now.

I smiled and nodded and Anne poured him coffee. Then he went and sat down next to Agnes and started talking animatedly to her. Anne moved closer to me and made a gesture with her mouth.

'We seem to have Stephen enamoured,' she whispered.

'He was once before. I thought it was over.'

'I think she's responding this time,' I said. 'Not overtly but subtly . . .'

'Do you like her?'

'Very much. I'm worried about her though.'

'We all are, if only because she suffers so. I mean, I don't think basically there is anything wrong, a tumour or anything sinister.'

I looked at Anne and was struck by her wisdom, by her sensible tone of voice.

'You must have been at Cambridge when the attacks started?'

Anne nodded and lit another cheroot.

'Yes, I was. I remember it very well. It was just after her mother had been and—'

I felt myself flush with excitement and I leaned forward, whispering urgently, 'Her mother? She saw her mother in Cambridge?'

'Oh, yes. Agnes always had a hankering after her mother, not like Tim, who wouldn't hear her name mentioned. I think she plucked up the nerve to get in touch with her and they met in her second year. Aggie was awfully reticent about the meeting, and afterwards the headaches began . . .'

'Don't you think that's significant?' I was still whispering but Agnes and Stephen seemed totally absorbed in each other.

Anne shook her head and looked at me oddly.

170

'No, I didn't particularly. I mean it never occurred to me. Do you think it's significant?'

'Yes I do, I—'

Stephen and Agnes were both looking at me and I paused. 'Something to do with me?' I asked.

'I was telling Agnes about our visit to Peter Ryder's mother. She said did we know anything more?'

I shook my head.

'But Tessa Dabroe! Why, she is the pillar of moral rectitute.' Agnes was laughing, rather maliciously I thought. 'Still . . .' She inclined her head and gazed at the floor.

She's hiding something, I thought and I said to her: 'Peter never said anything to you? He told his mother but not you? Wasn't that odd, Agnes?'

'You're always asking me questions,' Agnes said petulantly. 'I think you think I live on a bed of lies. You must know that Peter would never mention the name Dabroe in our house; not in front of Tim. If he was attracted to Tessa, we should be the last people to know. Surely you realize that, Jo?'

I realized nothing of the sort except that I couldn't trust anything the Ryders said. This volatile nature of Agnes was almost too wearing – friendly one minute, hostile the next. But I knew that more than ever I had to know the truth about Peter, whether he'd gone off with Tessa Dabroe or not. I had to confront him and find out; only then would I be at peace.

I waited for the weekend to see Jonathan again, mainly because of the difficulty of getting to the house. If it was fine, I could walk. I didn't want to tell him I was coming in case he told Agnes, and she would want to know why. I had to take the risk that he would be in.

He was. It was late morning and he was gardening, dressed in old trousers and wellington boots, digging the soil in the vegetable garden. I stood looking at him as he bent and heaved and when he saw me he leaned his foot on the spade and his face spread into a grin.

'Brought your gardening things? This is a surprise.' He took off his gloves and came over to me. His face was perspiring and he smelt vaguely of sweat. It was nice. 'I was just thinking I could do with a beer.'

He didn't ask why I was there but took my arm and led me into the house. It was a light house, a friendly house. It was an enormous house, though, and I wondered how he liked living there alone. He seemed to read my thoughts.

'I think my mother is going to move back. You haven't met my mother, have you? She very tactfully moved out when I married; but now I need a housekeeper.'

'You don't think Tessa will ever come back?'

'No.' Jonathan shook his head. 'She wants a divorce. I've heard from the solicitor but as she can't cite my sister it will all have to come out sooner or later. I shall have to go down there.'

'Soon?' I said.

'Why?'

'I'd like to come with you.'

I thought for a moment Jonathan looked embarrassed. He must have thought I was being terribly forward, even in these enlightened days.

'Because of Peter,' I said quickly. 'You see I must know about Peter. You can see that, can't you?'

'Yes, I think I can.' Jonathan got up and came over to me; but he didn't touch me. He just stood looking at me. 'You want to know if you're free don't you?'

'Something like that.' I turned away so that he wouldn't see my face.

'You still think he's gone off with Tessa?' Jonathan's voice was by my ear, gentle. I turned to face him and he kissed me; I think, in retrospect, our faces were too close for him to do anything else. It was a keen warm kiss, not lingering. I was aware of the firm lines of his mouth, the strong white bone of his teeth.

'I had to do that,' he said. 'I'm sorry.'

I didn't reply. I was trembling; it was absurd to feel such an emotion. After one kiss . . . He'd think I was a child if he guessed. I wanted to be mature and sophisticated for Jonathan.

'It's an awful mess,' I said at last when I'd regained my composure.

Jonathan sighed and sat down drawing his beer glass to his lips.

'Because of Tessa?'

'And Peter.'

'Even if they're both together it's a mess. But they are not. I know that.'

'I can't understand how you're so sure.' I said. 'I think maybe I should go back to London and everything can sort itself out.'

'I don't think anything would sort itself out if you did that!' I was surprised by Jonathan's fierceness. 'Mrs Baker needs you. Aggie needs you, and I need you.'

'Oh Jonathan! You can't need me. We hardly know each other . . .' I looked at him despairingly.

'You've got such balance,' he said. 'You don't know what it's like after Tess.'

I laughed despite my misgivings.

'I don't think "balance" is very flattering. You mean I'm sane and sensible, rather dull.'

'Not at all!' Jonathan was looking at me earnestly, his expression warm and lovable. 'I feel at ease with you: It's incredible. And don't think I don't find you sexy, because I do. I know that you act as though you're a prim little schoolteacher, but you're not. You can't fool me by that.'

'It's half-term next week,' I said, sidestepping the compliment. 'Let's go and see Tessa and Angela.'

'Angela?'

'Agnes' mother. She lives in Brighton. She's still called Ryder, isn't she? We should find her.'

'Yes, but why? Why Angela, for God's sake?'

'Because I want to solve the mystery,' I said. 'Two

mysteries. Why Peter left so suddenly, and why her mother's visit to her in Cambridge three years ago turned Agnes into an invalid.'

Fifteen

I think my drive south with Jonathan at the half-term weekend was my happiest time since I'd last seen Peter. Maybe I had set out to get him, I don't know. I could have gone down by myself, by train, stayed with my sister. There was something provocative in the way I'd suggested we went together. The old Jocasta Oaks would never have done such a thing. What she was now she owed to Peter, and she owed it to herself to lay his ghost – so that she could face the future without echoes from the past, footfalls in the memory.

It seemed incredible that within two months I'd been attracted to three men – one a deep passion, Peter, one a fleeting attraction, Stephen, and Jonathan? Was I just dazzled by his superhuman good looks, his rakish air? Was I swept off my feet as I'd told myself any woman would be? Was I flattered by his obvious attention to me, by his kiss? Or did I sense something much more profound than I'd known before, something that made me want, if not to bury the past, at least to have it revealed?

Jonathan released inhibitions in me I hadn't known I'd had. I seemed to talk all the way down the M1, and reminisced as we drove through London down the Finchley Road and through Swiss Cottage, where I'd lived, before taking the road towards Chichester from the Elephant and Castle. We had sandwiches and beer on the way and although getting to Chichester from London took almost as long as getting to London from Leeds we enjoyed the lush Sussex countryside, so different from the moors and valleys of Yorkshire, which

I realized I was beginning to think of as home. How could I ever leave it now?

Jonathan had booked us into the hotel overlooking Chichester's lovely cathedral. I'd been in the town before but only for a few hours. We had rooms on different floors as though to emphasize the gap that must lie between us until we had solved at least one part of the twin mysteries that had brought us south. We dined as soon as we arrived, purposely not chatting about anything important and after coffee in the lounge said a brief goodnight by the stairs on the landing where my room was.

We had planned nothing except that Jonathan was to phone Tessa's solicitor, who had known he was coming, the next morning and see if he had arranged a meeting. I wondered what Tessa would say when she saw me? It would confirm her suspicions that her husband was an unashamed womanizer.

I was nervous at breakfast and Jonathan was tense. Whatever ease we had enjoyed the day before had gone. I had dressed carefully in a jersey suit and as soon as breakfast was over, went out and had my hair done. When I returned to the hotel it was nearly twelve and Tessa was in the cocktail bar with Jonathan.

It was not what I would have planned, but in a sense it was the best thing. They'd had time to have a preliminary chat – apparently she had only arrived five minutes before me – and, not expecting her, I wasn't nervous. She looked surprised when I came in as though, although she knew my face, she couldn't put a name to it.

'It's Jocasta Oaks, the schoolteacher,' Jonathan explained, taking an arm lightly as though to give me comfort.

'My goodness, so it is,' exclaimed the elegant Tessa in her haughty upper-class accent. 'Whatever is she doing here? Is she with you, Jono?'

'In a way,' He smiled, at ease with his wife, and with me, a man who took everything in his stride, who wouldn't get flustered, make mistakes. 'I'm going to drink a pink gin, I don't know about anyone else. Tess?'

'I'll have a gin and tonic, please.'

'Jocasta?'

'I will too,' I said, because I wanted to be sophisticated like Tessa, not because I liked the stuff. Whatever she sensed in the atmosphere, Tessa was on her mettle, trying to put me at a disadvantage. She was elegantly dressed in a woollen dress and matching coat and she wore a hat, a thing I bet she'd never done in the Yorkshire Dales. She also looked more relaxed and prettier than I'd remembered her. I turned round, at any moment expecting to see Peter walk in and complete the quartet. Yet as she accepted the drink from Jonathan, there was a steely careful look in her eyes.

'Thank you, Jono. Now explain the mystery.'

'The mystery?' He leaned back in his chair, studying the fresh colour of the gin through the clear glass.

'Why are you both here? You I'd have expected, yes. We have a lot to talk about, the children and so on. But why Miss Oaks?'

'Because she is looking for Peter Ryder and she thinks you might know where he is.'

If I expected to score I couldn't have done better. Although Tessa must have been prepared for something like this, the directness of the remark caught her by surprise and her throat began to crimson. I sat looking at her without saying a word, trying to add to her discomfiture as much as I could, trying to force the truth out of her.

Finally she took a sip of her drink and placed the glass on the table with great care.

'Peter Ryder? Why should I know where he is?'

'Because Jocasta thinks, and nothing I say can dissuade her – which is why she's here – that among the reasons you left me was Peter Ryder.'

'Why should she think that?'

The way they were talking, looking only at each other, I might have been pardoned for thinking that they had forgotten my presence. It was part of the husband-and-wife-at-war game, I decided, the endgame, and the third person was a mere intrusion to the deadly final battle.

'Ask her,' Jonathan said, bringing me into it at last.

I cleared my throat.

'Peter's mother said that the last time she saw him he couldn't talk about anyone else but you—'

'About someone *named* Tessa,' Jonathan interjected and I realized that of course he didn't really want to believe it either, whatever he said, that Tessa preferred another man to him.

'About you,' I said. I was determined not to let her get away on this one. Not to go on covering up for Peter. 'You see, I am so interested because we were almost engaged. That's why I came up to Yorkshire. To see more of Peter . . .'

There must have been a hard, bitter note in my voice because Tessa looked at me as though she pitied me and her haughty, distant features softened.

'I know. I'm sorry.'

Both Jonathan and I now stared at her. Was an admission to be obtained so easily?

'You mean it *is* true . . . ?' Jonathan began incredulously.

'Not exactly. It's partly true.' Tessa blushed slightly and lowered her voice. She looked embarrassed and confused and I almost felt sorry for her; but inside I was exultant because we were ferreting out the truth, at last.

'Go on,' Jonathan said abruptly.

'Peter was attracted to me. You know he is a flirt.' She looked at me apologetically. 'He came to the house once or twice when I was alone to chat me up and phoned me several times, I was flattered. Jono and I hadn't attracted each other for years and no affection or tenderness had taken its place. I felt old and bitter, devoted to the children, good work – oh, those endless committees! Here was a man younger than I, and it made me feel good. But we never had an affair,' she went on quickly, 'I promise you that Jono.'

She was thinking of grounds for divorce, I thought coldly.

'Well, I suppose I talked to Peter and he realized our marriage was washed up, and he told me you were seeing so much of Agnes and that helped. Then he said if I did go away to let him know . . . I think he felt guilty about you.' Tessa looked at me defensively. 'He'd told me of course that you were coming, that he'd arranged it.'

'But that he'd regretted it already,' I said tersely.

'Well, not exactly. I think he thought he'd been a bit foolish, that he wasn't ready to settle and thought he might have given you a false idea.'

'Thank you for putting it like that.' I was swallowing hard, but I was beginning to be more mystified than before. There was something so detached in the way she talked about Peter.

'Anyway that was that. I did go; but I never saw or heard from Peter again. Not yet anyway. He's left it rather late, hasn't he?'

Jonathan and I were both staring at her, in a sort of half disbelief.

'You mean Peter never got in touch with you?' I said. 'He didn't know you were going to leave Jonathan?'

'No. I decided quite suddenly. Or rather I decided one week and left the next. I used as an excuse the fact that Joan Sunderland told me at the hairdressers in Harrogate that everyone knew that Jono was having an affair with Agnes Ryder. She did it to prevent me "being hurt", as she put it.'

'But you never talked to me,' Jonathan said bitterly, look-ing at her, remembering, maybe, how much they had once loved each other, the tenderness they'd shared, the children they'd had. I already felt envious that they'd ever known such intimacy, shared a bed, eaten countless meals together. 'You didn't talk to me to find out the truth, because you wanted to go. Didn't you, Tess? You hated the life there.'

Tessa shrugged and lit a cigarette with a beautifully worked gold cigarette lighter.

'In a way. Joan's gossip was the trigger. I didn't stop to think, only to tell Mother . . .'

'Who would have approved,' Jonathan nodded. 'For that reason only but not for any other.'

179

'What do you mean, Jono?'

'You know what I mean. We didn't get on; our marriage was a farce; but you couldn't talk to me about it in a civilized way for the children's sake. It had to be dramatic to be convincing so that your family could cluck their silly beaks and say, "How awful!"'

Jonathan got up and went to the bar, Tessa's eyes following him with an offended expression.

'He really is most unreasonable,' she said. 'He didn't use to be like that,' she spread her arms out in a gesture of finality. 'Anyway there it is. It is the end, I suppose. I'm sorry, Miss Oaks, about Peter. I've told you the truth. If he's left you, it's not on account of me. That's Peter, you know, he isn't very sincere. I hope he hasn't hurt you too much. You see – ' she looked at me sadly – 'he did seem rather keen about me, very keen in fact and one would have thought that if he'd meant it, knowing that I'd left Jonathan, he would have shown up. But he hasn't.'

Both Jonathan and I believed Tessa. There was no reason not to. Her sad sincerity was proof enough, as though she would rather like to have heard from Peter, having done the deed, and was sorry not to. It even looked as though Peter had meant to continue the relationship, because he hadn't told her that Agnes was not Jonathan's mistress, but his half-sister. He'd seemed to be spurring her on to leave, and then . . . He hadn't taken the opportunity up. He hadn't done anything about it. Whatever his feelings about me, and clearly they hadn't amounted to much, he might have kept in touch with a would-be mistress, a tempting divorcee with time on her hands and the tastes for spending that Peter liked, a woman much more sexually experienced than I . . .

Why hadn't he kept in touch with her? I puzzled over it that afternoon as Jonathan went to meet his children from school and have tea with them and Tessa – and her mother no doubt, to see that all was correct and above board – and I scanned the Brighton telephone directory. I found without any difficulty that Mrs Angela Ryder lived on the sea front near Black Rock and when I phoned her she answered herself and confirmed that yes she was Agnes' mother and if I was a friend, why didn't I come to tea the next day?

Angela Ryder was a beauty, still, despite the fact that she must have been nearly sixty. She had that soft powdered skin, the delicate colouring, the elaborate coiffeur of a famous actress and she wore a purple dress of angora wool and two rows of pearls. She was tall, had a marvellous figure and a grace and dignity that, as she stepped aside to let me into her flat in Sussex Square, already made me feel gauche.

She took me straight into a drawing room overlooking the sea; in front was the well-kept square, ahead in the distance Brighton Pier.

'Luckily the hideous new marina is just out of sight,' she said as I went and stood at the window. 'Have you been to Brighton before?'

'When I was a little girl.' I turned and looked at her, thinking of the boarding house where we'd stayed with my aunt and uncle and the dull tedium of the dreary beach routine every day regardless of weather, and how we hated the hard pebbly beach and longed for the soft sand that other children always seemed to have on their holidays by the sea.

She gave me a bright, rather nervous smile and held out a cigarette box.

'Smoke?'

'Thank you.' I took a cigarette and she lit it with a slender silver table lighter before lighting her own.

'Everything is ready for tea. Tell me when you want it.'

She was looking at me curiously as though aware that there was something beyond mere politeness about my call.

'How's Agnes?' she said finally and I noted the sadness in her voice. 'Is there anything special you came to see me about?'

I stubbed out the cigarette. I was so nervous the smoke was beginning to make me choke.

181

'In a way. She doesn't know I'm here.'

'Oh . . . ?' Mrs Ryder's voice trailed off interrogatively.

'I should explain,' I said, 'that I'm staying with Tim and Agnes and that Agnes isn't very well . . .'

Mrs Ryder's detachment vanished and she too stubbed out her cigarette, got up abruptly and came and sat nearer me, looking at me intently.

'What is the matter with her?'

'She suffers from very bad headaches, periods of amnesia, doesn't sleep . . .'

'But has she had them investigated?'

'Oh yes, but she had to leave Cambridge because of them. It was that bad.'

Mrs Ryder looked into the distance and I wondered if she was looking back also in time, reproaching herself for what had happened all those years ago.

'She is such a lovely girl,' she said softly. 'How I regret the past, Jocasta. I may call you that, mayn't I?'

Looking at the beautiful Angela Ryder, it was so hard to think that her behaviour had amounted to something evil, inhuman – to leave two small children, one of whom wasn't even her husband's. Surely such evil people shouldn't have that ethereal beauty? Then I thought of the beauty of Lucifer, the fallen angel – evil can have the face of an angel. Yet who was I to judge? Here was a sad, stricken woman, her beauty of little comfort to her, living alone.

As though she could read my thoughts she said, 'My memories haunt me, you know. I don't sleep well.'

I should have told her not to reproach herself, but how could I? Yet she should reproach herself, for what she had done to Agnes and Tim.

'I can see you don't approve of me, Jocasta. You do right. I was a fickle silly woman, dazzled by life and attractive men. First, Charles was so attractive. Then afterwards he became rather a dull countryman and all the glamour faded and I felt stifled by the country and the life we led. Sam Dabroe was so vibrant and exciting, such a rogue, a charmer. We

were attracted to each other immediately, and Charles and
Rebecca Dabroe suited each other, funnily enough, but they
were both too dull and upright to see it.' She looked at me
sadly. 'We know so much more today than we did about
child psychology; today you are so much more responsible
than we were in those far-off days.'

'Didn't you feel at all guilty about leaving two small
children?' I asked, my voice scarcely audible.

'Of course I did! I wanted to take them with me, but Charles
wouldn't have it; but he did it so cleverly. First he said I could,
and then he had them made wards of court so that finally when
everything came out and it was established I was living with
Sam, I'd never have had a chance. Then he refused to let me
see them. He turned them against me. It was terrible . . .' Her
voice trailed into a whisper and suddenly she looked sallow
and old. No, she wasn't an evil woman, just a foolish one
and I was sorry for her, very sorry.

She got up and went out of the room, I think to recover her
composure, but when she reappeared it was with the tea tray
and I got up to help her place it on the table and arrange the
cups and plates. She had fresh make-up on, but there were
still tear stains on her cheeks. She gave me my tea in silence
and when we were sitting again she said, 'I've spent my life
repaying for those follies, Jocasta. I am a lonely, unhappy
woman. Sam left me when he found someone younger and
prettier. I'd become dull and maudlin, always wondering
about the children, and although I tried to see Charles, he
always refused.'

'I didn't realize Charles was so hard,' I said.

'He'd been hurt very badly, you see. Agnes, do you
know . . . ?' She looked at me her head on one side.

'Yes; she wasn't Charles' daughter. Did Charles know this
all along?'

'Oh yes. Charles and I hadn't slept together for years before
Agnes was born; but Charles wouldn't throw me out, you see.
He would even have accepted Agnes as his daughter, did in
fact as you know, for the sake of convention. Charles was

always obsessed by the good name of the Ryders and he never got over the old story that a Ryder had murdered one of the Dabroes, I forget names, in the nineteenth century. He spent a long time and a lot of money trying to prove it was false, that it had been a Dabroe who went to the USA and not a Ryder; but he got nowhere. Imagine, such a silly old tale, it haunted his life so that he had to be holier than holy. He pleaded with me not to leave him; but by that time I couldn't bear him and then when he promised he would let me have the children, I left him . . . it was his way of getting rid of me and also being sure I didn't come back. And now Aggie, my dear little Aggie, isn't well and you think . . . it's because of me?' She looked at me, her head on one side again like a little girl who trusted I was going to say it wasn't her fault at all.

'I don't know what the cause is,' I said carefully, 'I'm not a doctor or a psychiatrist. I came to you because the headaches started after you'd been to see her in Cambridge and I wondered if anything you said to her might have caused them. Set them off?'

Mrs Ryder got up and went to the window, perhaps so that I shouldn't see her face. What a comfort the wide expanse of the sea was, I thought; in imagination, one could lose oneself in the depths of the turbulent waves.

'Agnes very much wanted to see me, but she was terrified her father would find out. After she went to Cambridge she wrote to me and we made a lot of appointments to meet but she always put them off. Then one day I arrived unexpectedly and I found her with her cousin Peter Ryder. They'd been out for the day.'

I caught my breath and could hear the rapid sound of my own heartbeat, but I didn't interrupt. She turned and looked at me.

'I don't know if you know Peter Ryder, but he was in the Army, stationed in Norfolk; apparently he'd started to look up his cousin Agnes in nearby Cambridge. I could see they were attracted and after Peter left I stayed on in Cambridge for a few days to be near Agnes so that I could tell her some things she had to know. They were awful things to tell a beautiful normal young girl; things that went back to family misdeeds for which she was in no way responsible. I want you, Jocasta, to understand it as I tried to get Aggie to, to realize that the aftermath of war left us carefree and irresponsible. Well, the fact was we loved lightly too and we hadn't got the contraceptive facilities young people have now; it was something we hardly knew about or thought about. Agnes already knew she was Sam Dabroe's daughter. Charles had told her just before she went to Cambridge and it had upset her dreadfully because the Dabroes were supposed to be such awful people. And not only had their mother left them for a Dabroe but she was a Dabroe's daughter. Tim had inherited Charles' hatred for the Dabroes and Aggie was warned to say nothing to Tim and she kept her word. I think this was why she kept on putting me off though she wanted to see me. She was too confused.

'Well my arrival only added to her confusion.

'I had to tell her that Peter was Charles' son too, so that he was Tim's brother and that neither Peter nor Tim knew it. I said it would be very unsuitable for her to be emotionally involved with someone who was more than a first cousin, almost like a half-brother in fact, and that the sooner she forgot about Peter the better. First cousins can marry of course, but generally it is not a good thing. Not that degree of intimacy.'

'*Charles* was Peter's father?' I exclaimed aghast. 'And yet he blamed you for—'

'Well, Charles and I weren't married then, and Jenny was a very pretty girl. Charles was very dashing, you know, in those days. She and Charles and Rupert all mucked about together and she and Rupert were unofficially engaged. Well, Rupert was away on some kind of business and Charles escorted Jenny to a party and then fell into bed with her afterwards, and before Rupert came back she found she was pregnant. She didn't love Charles, she loved Rupert, and as they were brothers . . . so they got married quickly because Rupert had to go away again. Then he was killed without even knowing she was pregnant.'

'That's why Charles always looked after Peter? Peter said he regarded Tim and Aggie as his brother and sister.'

'Well, there you are. Do you know Peter, dear?'

'He was my boyfriend. Really that's why I'm here . . .'

And quickly I told her about Peter and the events of the past weeks. As I expected, she too had a sympathetic expression when I'd finished, and I could almost echo what she was going to say, so I said it for her.

'That's just like Peter, isn't it?'

Angela Ryder nodded.

'He was always very rash and unpredictable; in this he wasn't Charles' son at all, or Jenny's, who was very correct and pure after her one lapse. I always think she considered Peter somehow rather tainted and never loved him as much as her children by that awful old bore Geoffrey Cornford. Peter always felt an outsider, a terrible outsider. It seemed to give him a chip and he loved his mother passionately at first, to try and make her love him. By all accounts she ignored him, and Peter's love for her turned to hatred. Aggie told me all this. We talked endlessly about Peter after I'd told her, and relived the story of the Ryders and the Dabroes over and over again. She was very upset about the whole thing. She said it made her feel strange, tainted. I did what I could to help her, but after I'd gone she wrote and told me not to come and see her again. She paid me back by rejecting me.'

'Did Peter know he was Charles' son?'

'Not up to then. Maybe Aggie told him. I don't know.'

'So Agnes loved Peter . . .'

'Oh, I'm sure she got over it, dear . . .'

'But if she didn't?'

She left the question unanswered and it hung over us in the air, like a threat.

Sixteen

Jonathan hadn't wanted to meet Angela Ryder; to him her name was too full of bad memories. Even this strong, extroverted man had been marked by the events of his childhood. I never told her he was with me, and he'd waited for me in a nearby hotel. But he was keen enough to hear about her, what she looked like, how she had worn, although he was scornful of my attempts to try to excuse her.

'Sounds as though she got what she deserves,' he said with satisfaction after I'd told him how lonely she was.

'Do we all get what we deserve?' I murmured. 'Should we?'

We were driving straight up the M1, having spent the night in Brighton. Term began for me the next day. It had only been a long weekend break.

After debating what to tell Jonathan about my talk with Angela, I decided to keep from him the news about Peter's father. Jonathan might know it already from Agnes, and it was really not integral to the main point that was obsessing me more strongly than ever. What had happened to Peter? Where was he? Both women had referred to him; he, not Agnes, had really been the point of both visits.

Jonathan and I had lost a little of the rapport we had shared on the way down and enjoyed during our time together. The jolly holiday outing atmosphere of the first days had gone. Now we both had more serious things to think about and our thoughts seem to turn inwards rather than be shared. Jonathan would be thinking about Tessa and the children. I was thinking about Peter.

187

No one really had a good word to say about Peter. He was attractive but unreliable, a womanizer, a go-getter; he was egocentric and let people down; he was a good businessman because the god was money. He had been good in the Army because the goal was success. Yet, to me who had loved him – still loved him, maybe, I wasn't sure – he emerged as the product of his upbringing: the knowledge that his mother hadn't really loved him, resented him, felt guilty about him had made him thrusting and aggressive to prove himself in the world. He repaid his mother for her indifference by being callous towards women, winning their love and then letting them down, as he had me. Had it been different with Agnes? Had he given his heart to her, only to be let down again and, probably, without a reason.

'Very silent,' Jonathan said. 'Peter?'

'How did you know?'

'I know your mind is full of Peter. He has come between you and me.'

'Oh Jonathan, no. It's not like that. Peter seems to have behaved so badly, and yet . . . can't help wondering still if something might not have happened to him.'

'But you said the flat had been cleaned out that day you and Stephen visited it; even the toothbrush was gone. As though he had left for a long stay.'

'But how is it that no one has found out why, or where?'

'Well, you've heard from him. He hasn't disappeared in a puff of smoke.'

'But no one has *seen* him.'

'You don't have reason to think the phone call, the telegram and so on weren't from him, do you?'

'Of course not.' Jonathan was irritating me again; he was trying to prove that I was worried by my own imagination. 'It's the hotel,' I said after a long pause during which I hoped my unspoken disapproval had registered. '*That's* what bugs me. It simply doesn't make sense. Does it?'

Jonathan's face looked dim in the light from the dashboard; but he said nothing.

'It doesn't make sense,' I repeated, 'to have cleared out from your flat and gone to a hotel prior to doing a bunk.'

'I've thought about the hotel,' Jonathan said at last. 'If he was having doubts about you, he might have stayed there for a few days to think it over. Anonymously, you know. Then he'd missed the train, you were in Coppitts Green, he realized he'd behaved dreadfully badly . . . so, why not a few weeks abroad?'

'When will he come back?' I said dully.

'Oh, I expect about Christmas time with a large bunch of holly to say he's sorry.'

'Don't be bitter, Jonathan,' I said. 'It's not fair.'

'Sorry, it was a bad attempt at humour. Cheap, I admit. Jocasta, I want you to forget about Peter. He's no good. Begin life again . . .'

'He wouldn't go to a hotel under his own name,' I said stubbornly. 'It's not like Peter.'

'You didn't know Peter. You didn't really know him at all.'

Jonathan's normal calm voice was over-emphatic and I gazed at him with some surprise. After all, how much did he know Peter? Very little.

'Maybe we should stop in Leeds and go to the police,' I said.

The car swerved, Jonathan cursed, looked at me and roared. 'Oh *Jocasta*! You're the most infuriating person. The police would laugh at you on such flimsy evidence. Now for once and for all put Peter out of your mind. Thank heaven, here is Leeds. How this motorway bores me.'

And we turned off into the town.

Jonathan, thankfully it seemed to me, left me in Skipton and I caught the last bus into Coppitts Green; the late bus, the one I'd arrived on six weeks before. I sat in the same seat and looked out of the same window on to the scene I'd seen before, the valley still clad in the remnants of late summer. Now it was nearly November and the trees, although still beautiful in full autumn foliage, had that slightly forlorn tattered look that said in a month they would be bare; along with the earth they would be resting, gathering their resources for the following spring.

Already I felt that winter in the Dales would not be desolate and barren, but full and hopeful. The countryside still gave up its secrets, astonished us with its mysteries and as I took my little class scavanging in the fields and among the woods and hedgerows we would daily find evidence of the determination of nature to survive, to prosper, renew itself again and again.

In the distance, as I looked, the lights of Coppitts Green beckoned to me; not as a frightened stranger, but welcoming me as one of their own – someone who was coming home.

I got off the bus by the pub and carried my case up the road. I felt cheerful, as though history was repeating itself and that everything would begin again and this time it would be different. Peter would be there, and Tim and Agnes, and everything would be, oh so different, and the events, the uncertainties of the past weeks would be submerged by the thrill of knowing that everything was now all right.

But as I stood at the door of Croft House looking up, the familiar chill stole over me, it crept up on me like a watchful shadow when I had so hoped it had gone, and when I opened the door, the hall was in darkness as it usually was, and I groped for the switch, my fingers trembling.

Nothing had changed. Croft House was as it always had been; and there was no sound of welcoming voices to soothe my anxiety. On the hall table there was a note for me in Mrs Bargett's large, painstaking hand.

> Miss Oaks,
>
> Mrs Baker has been took ill and would like you to go up to the house as soon as is convenient. It is about the school. The Master and Miss Agnes are away and there is a cold supper for you in the larder. It needs heating

up together with veg. I didn't light the fire, but add a
match to it if you want to.
    Mrs B.

If I wanted to. I shivered, looking around. The place was
bleak and cold, spotlessly clean as always, but looking
unlived in, as though I was the first inhabitant for years.
If ever a house had an atmosphere, this one did and it was
rejecting me. Yet only a while before I'd felt so welcome;
so in love with Coppitts Green.
    I looked up the dark stairs, grim and unfriendly, telling me
to go away, and decided not to go up to my room. I left my
case in the hall and, thankfully letting myself out, went up
to the Bakers'.
    There had, after all, been no need to play at charades, pre-
tend I'd been at my sister's, had come back by train. Jonathan
could have brought me back; there had been no one at home.
    By contrast, the Bakers' house was all lit up and as I
pushed open the front door it was warm inside, and the
smell of delicious cooking wafted from the kitchen along
the hall. I called out and Anne came from the drawing room
and ushered me in.
    'How's your mother?'
    'She can't get up, I'm afraid. Her joints are as stiff as
wood. Can you cope at the school?'
    'Of course.'
    'I could help you out. I'm staying here to look after
Mum.'
    She looked worried, as well she might; two invalids in
the family.
    'Won't it interfere with your work?'
    'I'm meant to be in Cambridge on a course. I was late for it
anyway; might as well forget it now. My parents come first.'
    'What about your sister in North Yorkshire?'
    'She has two small children and a farming husband. Mum
may have to go into hospital for treatment. You can't leave
now, can you?'

'Whatever made you think I was going to?'

'Everyone said you'd gone to London to look for a job.'

'I wouldn't be so cruel to your mother,' I said quietly. 'May I go and see her now?'

'Do. She wants to talk to you. And stay for dinner?'

'Love to. Croft House is like a tomb.'

I went up the stairs and into the bedroom, from which light streamed on to the hall.

Mrs Baker was propped up in bed, smiling and looking well enough except that the twist of her mouth betrayed her pain. I sat on the edge of the bed and took her hand. To my horror, she squeezed it and her eyes filled with tears.

'Thank God you're back.'

'But wherever did this ridiculous rumour start that I was going?'

She shrugged and smiled tremulously.

'We don't think you're happy here. You're too unsettled – oh, not at school . . . Don't think for a moment this is a criticism of you.'

'But I'm happy here, I love it here. I already think of the valley as home; I felt almost lyrical about it in the bus, just the sight of it from the high road.'

'Oh, dear, I am glad. It's just Croft House then, maybe because Peter has made you unhappy?'

'Yes, it may be that. I might associate it with not seeing him.' I shivered and hugged my arms, which had suddenly gone gooseflesh. 'I don't know what it is. I've never felt anything like it. Tonight, it was so *unfriendly*. Can you imagine a house being unfriendly? Anyway the Ryders are away.'

'They've gone off somewhere with Stephen. Both of them.'

'*Stephen?*'

'Does it surprise you? He is crazy about Agnes, still. He's talking of marriage, though God knows what he's taking on, if she'll have him. I'm pleased for him in a way, to be so in love, but – ' she pressed my hand – 'I was hoping it would be you; someone normal and someone who would help him. Agnes will be one of those awful invalid wives.'

'She may not be. Leaving Tim may be just the thing for her. Anyway – ' I bent my head conspiratorially towards her – 'I've been to see her mother!'

Mrs Baker clutched my hand convulsively and gave a grimace of pain.

'*Angela?* You've been to see Angela?'

'I wanted to know why Agnes got headaches. You know we all think they're real but psychological. They're ruining her life. I care about her enough to want to know why. Then the other day your Anne said they had started, the headaches that is, *after* her mother had visited Agnes at Cambridge . . .'

Mrs Baker smiled, rather bitterly, I thought.

'And you went all that way to see her? I could have told you what you wanted to know.'

I stared at her and she gave me her twisted pain-ridden smile.

'It all happened such a long time ago. But the evil that men do—'

'—lives after them,' I quoted, 'the good is often interred with their bones.'

'But Charles wasn't evil, and nor was Jenny, and nor were Angela and Sam; but they all did things that left a bitter heritage; they made others suffer for what they'd done. Their thoughtlessness had bad consequences. Charles never stopped regretting it – so much that it made him bitter too. You know over the years I grew quite close to Charles and he often confided in me. He *did* love Aggie, and he hated Angela because he had once adored her so much, of course. I always tried to persuade him to behave differently towards her, let her see the children but he wouldn't. And there was Peter . . .' Mrs Baker sighed heavily. 'Now you know all about him.'

'Not why he's gone,' I said. 'You know there was a rumour – well, Stephen and I thought – he might have gone off with Tessa Dabroe? We saw her too.'

193

'We?'

'I went with Jonathan. He wanted to see Tessa and I wanted to know about Peter. Peter did make up to Tessa but she hasn't seen him since she left. Peter's disappearance is still a mystery.'

'But very Peter-like, I'm afraid.' Mrs Baker shook her head, massaging her swollen wrists. 'He liked to cause trouble. It was the way he brought attention to himself. The more trouble he caused, the more people paid attention to him. But Peter was the apple of Charles' eye; he adored him. He felt he had such a lot to make up for in the way that Jenny behaved. They were both ashamed of what they'd done, producing a child and betraying Rupert; but it didn't make it any better for Peter, who, instead of appreciating what people did for him, used them or abused them if he could. Of course he didn't know Charles was his father and maybe this was unfair; but Charles had promised Jenny, and Charles was very correct like that. But Tim suffered too, because it was so obvious that his father preferred Peter to him. Anyone could see that Charles was irritated by Tim, thought him slow and stupid, didn't appreciate his lovable qualities. Tim is in fact, in looks and behaviour, the image of his father; even his honour of the Ryder name is Charles. Peter couldn't really care less about anyone or anything, certainly not the Ryders. At least he gave that impression . . .'

'He cared about me,' I said. 'I'm sure about that. I wish I could make people see how Peter was with me; he never did a wrong thing, unless being late from time to time was a crime. He was thoughtful, lovable, tender and . . . passionate.' I looked at her, a woman who too knew how to love. 'He brought the greatest joy into my life that I've ever known, and if he was a bounder, if he wasn't sincere, well . . . Peter did all right by me.'

Jane Baker's eyes had tears in them and she was patting my hand.

'My poor child, my poor child, life is very cruel, isn't it? Very unfair, indiscriminating. Maybe you would have done a lot for Peter, you would have changed him; but it does seem that you were deceived, doesn't it, dear? And I am very, very sorry.'

'Did Tim know that Peter was Charles' son?' I asked suddenly, thinking of the effect it must have had on him.

'Well, he knew when everyone knew, or rather should I say, we few intimates knew because the details of the will weren't made public more than they had to be. You see he left Peter the bulk of his fortune, and all he left to Tim and Aggie was the house and some jewellery, and it was after that that Peter left the Army and his money seemed to go to his head and he behaved towards poor Aggie and Tim very badly indeed. Try and forget about Peter, dear, I know it isn't easy; but can't you see, now, what he was really like?'

Anne walked home with me. I'd been so shattered by my talk with her mother that we said little over dinner and then watched television afterwards. On the way home we talked about the school and how Anne would help me out and what duties we should share. Finally we stood together outside the door of Croft House. I nervously looked up as somehow I always did.

'Why do you stay here, Jo? You could have slept at our house.'

'I must overcome this fear. It's irrational.'

'I'll come in with you while you put the lights on.'

I'd left the hall light on and took her into the drawing room. Anne hugged herself in her coat and looked around.

'It is cheerless, isn't it? It's only the fact that the fire's not lit. Do they keep the central heating down low?'

'Maybe they have to, after what your mother told me.'

'Oh, she told you about Charles and the will? It really was an awful thing to do; after all, Tim was his son too. He seemed to think Tim was everything that Peter wasn't, lazy and that he ought to work.'

'Like Roger Ryder,' I said. 'History repeating itself.'

'Strange how it does, isn't it?'

195

Anne got out one of her little cigars and lit it.

'The only thing about that rumour –' she waved out her match – 'is that there's so little evidence for it. Oh, there was a Roger Ryder and a Jeremy Dabroe and one went to America and one disappeared; but maybe Roger wanted to go away anyway from the father who kept him short of money and treated him badly.'

'But they say they found a body in a room.'

'Now, *that* nobody knows the truth about,' Anne expostulated. 'You'd hardly go round telling people you'd found a body and then hidden it. That will never be proved.'

'What about the room, the hidden room?'

'Oh, you've heard about the hammer? That was a nice story that gave the village something to talk about for a bit. Not proven, I say, still.'

'But there is a room,' I said, 'under me.'

Anne puffed at her cheroot and gazed at me.

'Under you?'

'Don't sound so sceptical, Anne. I've heard noises from under my room, but there's nothing there. No room, not that you can see. I've looked at the outside and there's an enormous expanse of wall with no window.'

'But it's a very odd house. The reconstruction was done without any feeling for architectural niceties.'

'Come up to my bedroom,' I said, 'and let's try and find out.'

Anne looked excited and stubbed out her cigar.

'My this is fun,' she said, 'like treasure hunting.'

We were both laughing as, the house bathed in light now, we climbed to my room. The sound of the merriment, the glow of the lights and the thought that I had a companion made me feel almost light-hearted and banished the fears that had haunted me so strongly. Anne wandered round the room and looked out of the window, which was half open.

'My golly it's cold in here. Are you a fresh-air friend?'

'It is cold up here,' I agreed. 'I think it's because it used to

196

be the attic and I'm very near the roof. But it's a cold house. I always feel chilled.'

Anne was on her knees, tapping the floor.

'Under here there is a secret room?' She was smiling.

'Anne I'm not joking. I hear noises. Shuffling, banging . . .'

Anne stopped smiling and looked at me with scepticism.

'You've heard the stories about the Croft House ghost,' she said. 'Makes dragging noises . . .'

'I heard the noises before your mother told me.'

We regarded each other gravely. Anne shivered again and went to the window. I stood by her side as we looked out over Coppitts Green. There was no moon, no sight of village roofs or the cliff; just the sound of the beck gabbling importantly on the other side of the road.

'It's very still, isn't it?' Anne said. 'It *is* kind of spooky.'

'You feel it too,' I said, my heart beginning to beat a little quicker. 'It's the sound of silence, like that song, the sound of Croft House.'

'It's a funny feeling,' Anne said. 'Eerie.'

'I always imagined the cliff hovered over me, threatening. I felt that from the first. Sometimes it seems so near I feel I can put my hand out and touch it.'

'You poor girl.' Anne put down the window gently. 'You have been through it. Let's go downstairs.'

She walked to the door and turned to wait for me, smiling at me encouragingly. She was a clever, strong girl without my fears and inhibitions, yet she understood what had happened to me. I joined her and we went silently along the corridor, down the first flight of stairs to the next landing.

'You see.' I raised my finger. 'This corridor has no door. With an expanse of wall as long as that, you'd expect one, wouldn't you?'

Anne tapped the wall, walking along it.

'Solid Yorkshire stone,' she said. 'What's round the corner?'

'The bathroom and Agnes' room. She says they are underneath my room, but they're both too narrow.'

'Let's look. Do you think she'd mind?'

I shrugged. I was already feeling nervous, guilty at being so curious. We listened outside Agnes' door, goodness knows what we expected to hear, and even knocked. We opened the door and felt for the light switch; a dim light came on by her bed, no overhead light. The room was tidy, the bed made. The top of the window was open and it was very cold; a breeze stirred inside the room.

'My goodness,' Anne said. 'Everyone in this house has a fetish for air. Why, look . . .'

She walked into the room, past the bed. I stared after her and my body gradually seemed to petrify as though I'd walked into one of those giant fridges they have in stores. The door of the fitted end cupboard was open, gently swaying backwards and forwards as though caught in a current of air, it creaked a little on its hinges adding to the atmosphere of impending horror.

'I think you were right,' Anne said. 'Beyond that door is a room.'

Walking through the cupboard was like crossing a corridor, except that it was hung with Agnes' clothes and we had to brush our way past them; the clothes clung round my face and I nearly screamed, thinking of some huge spider's web, so great was my fear anyway. We groped our way towards the place the cross-current came from, which was an aperture in the wall of the cupboard, a narrow opening that would normally be concealed by a sliding door that had been left open.

We now stood so that we faced a room we couldn't see. It was pitch dark and I could feel Anne's arms reaching out, groping.

'There's no switch,' she said. 'I saw a torch by Agnes' bed. I'll go back.'

I clutched at her.

'Oh, don't! Don't go.'

Anne gently detached my hand.

'I'll be here all the time,' she whispered. 'Don't be a goose.'

They call it gooseflesh, that cold creepy feeling: the skin prickles and the hairs stands straight up. I rubbed and rubbed at my arms but no warmth came. I had never known such a feeling of terror, of evil, in my life; never known that it even existed. Gradually the beam of the torch came nearer and I closed my eyes involuntarily before it shone into the room. Anne was breathing heavily beside me.

'It's a horrible little room,' she said. 'It's creepy. I can quite imagine a murder was done here.'

Murder, murder, murder . . . I opened my eyes and stared in front of me.

Murder had been done here. It was a horrible little room, festooned with cobwebs and smelly. And it was full of Peter's things.

Anne was looking at me, understanding dawning.

'*Peter's?*'

I nodded, taking in his cases, his golf clubs, the black briefcase always stuffed with papers; the striped case he'd taken when we'd gone away on our first weekend together and I'd felt like Lola Montez, the Woman of Sin.

'I think I've always known he was dead,' I heard myself saying. 'From the moment I came into the house; his body was here wasn't it? It must have been. It was here all those nights when I was here alone, just under my room . . .'

I think I swayed then because Anne grabbed hold of my arm, her other hand supporting my back.

'He could just have left his things here,' she whispered.

'Here? In the secret room? Can't you smell death, Anne? The Ryders have been covering up traces of Peter ever since I came; they tried to make out he'd left me, to chase me away. The phone calls, the telegram – they were phoney; they were from Tim and, you know, your mother gave me an early clue and I only realize it now. The day after I arrived and Tim came I never heard his car, but I heard it go. It was a very loud car, and then your mother said something like, "I saw his car in the garage." That would be when she was going home after school, *before* me, before Tim arrived. Tim

199

had come back for his car, don't you see? It was nothing to do with Agnes. Tim had driven Peter's car somewhere and *come back for his own*. That's why I never heard it arrive. No one ever *saw* Peter again, Anne. They killed him for his money; to keep Croft House. They killed him because Agnes once loved him, and he was so fickle. They killed him because . . .'

I knew my voice was rising and I was feeling light-headed. The enormity of what had happened to Peter was making me hysterical. Anne's grip tightened on my arm and she led me away from the room, from Peter's things strewn about there. We both jumped as we saw the figure standing by the door and I cried out.

'It's all true,' Stephen said, coming out of the shadow towards us, 'only they never meant it. It wasn't deliberate at all, not in that way; not murder.'

'Stephen!' Anne cried in an outraged voice, 'What on earth are you doing in all this?'

'I've known for some time,' Stephen said, holding out a chair for me, helping me into it. 'Oh, only a week or two, not while I was helping you, Jo, honestly. I could see something was troubling Aggie and Tim, you know how I felt about Aggie? It was happening all over again. But Tim was so odd, so disturbed that Aggie was worried about him; and she wanted to know where Peter was too, and she felt Tim knew something, more than he was saying.'

'*Tim* knew and Agnes didn't . . .' I began. 'Tim killed Peter? But why?'

Stephen shook his head.

'It wasn't like that. Aggie's in hospital. She's had a complete breakdown. But the police know everything and they've been charged today in Skipton. Tim's been released on bail. Look, he's waiting downstairs. He wants to talk to you. Please.'

Seventeen

Tim was standing in front of the unlit fire in the drawing room, his hands behind his back, his eyes studying the carpet. He seemed a long way away and even when we came in he didn't appear at first to know we were there. I could hardly bear to look at him, but something about his utter dejection excited my compassion, if not my forgiveness and I was the first to speak to him.

'Hello, Tim,' I said. 'Stephen has told us.'

Then I sat down heavily, my heart going at a great old pace. Tim heaved a deep sigh and looked up. His eyes seemed to have sunk into his face and he looked prematurely old, but when he saw me he turned his face away and when I thought of all the weeks of lies and deception, iron entered my soul once again.

'I'll make some coffee,' Anne said briskly. I noticed Tim had a small glass of whisky on the mantlepiece. Stephen, who looked very worn, went over to the decanter.

'Jo?'

'I'll have a whisky,' I said. 'It's more the cold than anything else.'

'Peter's dead,' Tim said suddenly as though he had just become aware of the company around him. 'He's been dead for weeks, he . . .'

His voice began to shake and Stephen went over to him and took him by the shoulder.

'Sit down old man,' Stephen said, 'and tell Jo all about it. Try and understand, Jo.'

'I'm trying,' I said; but all I could think of was that Peter,

201

about whom all the terrible things had been said, whose good name had been utterly destroyed, was indeed dead and that his body had been left here in this house with me, the woman who loved him, only a few feet away. How callous could you get to allow that sort of thing? But Peter had been avenged; now I believed in the power of the spirit and the atmosphere of this house, an atmosphere that only affected me, of cold and of death, convinced me that Peter's angry spirit had been asking for revenge. What better revenge, now, than destruction of that good name of Ryder?

Tim cleared his throat and at first his narrative was stilted then, as he became more confident, it flowed more strongly.

'Peter came over here—' he began and Stephen interrupted.

'Why don't you begin at the beginning, with the will, as you told it to me?'

'Well, when my father died he left letters for Aggie and me and Peter. He told us all that Peter was his natural son, conceived in a casual moment, and that he and Jenny, Peter's mother, had lived with the guilt all their lives. They had deceived my uncle Rupert, father's brother, who was a real upright Ryder, and they had brought a child unwittingly into the world whom Jenny found she couldn't love. Dad undertook to look after Peter financially and everything else, but promised his mother he would never let Peter know he was his father in his lifetime. His death released him of his vow and when we were told it was a great shock to us all, especially Peter, who, if he ever had a chip, developed a worse one.

'He felt very bitter that Dad had never told him, and he thought it was unforgivable of his mother to reject him because of it. Although as children we'd always been close, the death of Dad caused a terrible split and Peter became brash and unpleasant, as though we were servants of some kind. He realized also why Aggie, who at one time appeared very taken with him sexually, would have nothing to do with him after our mother had told her the truth—'

'Did Aggie ever tell this to you?' Anne interrupted.

'No; but the knowledge of it made her ill. I wish she had have told me, and then when Dad died and it all came out. Instead of getting better she got worse because of Sam Dabroe and me not knowing about that.

'You see, so much deception and so many lies had afflicted our families, so that we all felt tainted – Peter, Aggie and me. And I felt jealous too because Dad had always so obviously preferred Peter to me, and now I knew why. He left Peter all his money, and to us he left the house and some jewellery, which we were forbidden to sell. Yet I'd always tried so hard to please Dad, be a true Ryder, and Peter had been the very opposite. You can imagine how I felt when I knew Peter was my half-brother . . .'

Tim's voice broke and Anne, who had returned with a full tray and the large silver coffee pot, went up to him and gave him a cup, smiling encouragingly at him. Anyone could see how hard it was for Tim to tell this story. Tim took a gulp of his coffee and continued.

'I tried to please Dad with my books and articles, brandishing my cheques about when I got them; but Dad wasn't impressed. I couldn't do anything to please him, and Peter didn't even try.

'Anyway, then we were on our own and Peter changed. He'd barge in here as though he owned the place, which he didn't, and as soon as Aggie even knew he was coming or heard his voice she'd become ill. In addition to all that she was seeing Jonathan Dabroe who was *her* half-brother, unknown to me. He seemed to give her some relief, away from the unhappy atmosphere of this house. Even Mrs Bargett felt the tension and several times she said she wanted to leave, but we persuaded her for Dad's sake. She'd adored Dad.'

'But why did you allow Peter here at all?' Anne said, lighting one of her small cigars.

'Well, he was my half-brother, Dad's son, and, well, he did give us a small allowance, which was arranged immediately after Dad died, and we were all on more friendly terms, though Aggie and I were terribly upset by the terms of the will. So in a way Peter had a right to be here, and he made that clear. But it was getting worse and worse, and I was desperate to do something to free us . . .'

'Like killing him,' I said bitterly.

Tim went suddenly scarlet. 'No, Jo, not like that at all.'

'Wait, Jo – ' Stephen frowned at me – 'don't anticipate.'

'No, I wanted to raise a mortgage on the house and get a job with some paper or publishing organization in Leeds or Bradford. I was having talks about it as a matter of fact. But there was Aggie. She was terrified at the thought of me having a job and leaving her, because she was beginning to be truly frightened of Peter. Irrationally or not, she hated him because of the effect he was having on our lives.

'Then a few months ago Peter told us he had a girlfriend in London whom he really fancied – ' Tim looked apologetically at me – 'and that she wanted to come up here to be near him. She'd heard that the school needed another teacher and we knew how true this was and how badly Mrs Baker needed help. But we knew nothing about the girl, Jo, except I'm afraid we thought she couldn't be much if Peter was fond of her.'

I blushed hotly and felt close to tears. Anne took my hand and pressed it.

'We were terribly wrong, as it happens,' Tim said quickly, 'but of course by then it was too late.'

'You killed Peter because of *me*?' I said incredulously.

'Hush . . .' Anne whispered. Tim continued as though he hadn't heard me.

'However, Peter wanted the girl to stay with us and we had to agree, though Aggie hated the thought of a stranger in the house. I said the girl, Jo, might be very nice, but Aggie was very apprehensive. Everything, you see, was building up to a climax inside Aggie's brain. She hated Peter, she was afraid of the girl, she was terrified of me knowing about Sam Dabroe and Jonathan . . . it was an awful breakdown of trust on my part that she didn't think she could tell me. I'm partly to blame for what happened.'

Tim cleared his throat; he was beginning to sound hoarse and Anne gave him some more coffee. I was aware of how late it was, and what a macabre unrealistic tableau we must have made, me sitting impassive, the other two listening, Tim confessing to murder . . .

'Well, a few days before Jocasta was due Peter came over unexpectedly on the Sunday; he'd just returned from London. He was very brash and aggressive, saying that he wanted to make sure everything was all right for his girl. We had dinner and he had quite a lot to drink and then he started going on about Tessa Dabroe, saying what a miserable so and so Jonathan was and how he couldn't satisfy her, obscene things like that which was ghastly enough by any standards but Aggie had had a headache all day, since she'd known Peter was coming, and she was looking terribly haggard when we came in here for coffee. Peter started on the brandy. I was of course horrified even to hear the name of Dabroe uttered in this house and here was Peter making disgusting remarks about Jonathan Dabroe's wife, implying he'd already been to bed with her . . .'

I closed my eyes and bit my lip and I could feel the pressure of Anne's hand on mine.

'I said what was the point of having this girl, seeing that we didn't want her and it looks as though he didn't.' Tim's voice was becoming hoarser.

'I also said I didn't want the name Dabroe mentioned in this house and he well knew why. At that, at that . . .' Tim stopped and put his head in his hands . . . 'Peter came and stood in front of me, leering at me, and he said there was an awful lot more about Dabroe that I didn't know and he was about to tell it to me. Then . . .' Tim's voice gave out completely and he started sobbing instead.

'Aggie took up that brass Buddha that was standing by the fireplace and threw it at Peter,' Stephen said dispassionately. 'It caught him on the temple and he lost his balance. As you know, he was a big man and he fell heavily against the fender and seems to have broken his neck.'

'He was dead almost immediately,' Tim whispered, 'and as I looked incredulously at him, Aggie came and, seeing him lying there, fell across his body and I thought she was dead too. It was like the other night, Jo. I didn't know what to do. I went to phone Sergeant Melchett and then I thought, what would happen? I'm sure Aggie hadn't meant to kill Peter, just stop him talking, but who would believe it? There'd be an awful court case and the Ryder name would be in all the papers, as well as the sordid details about the parentage of Peter and Aggie and the connection with the Dabroes. I couldn't bear it. I just couldn't face it, alone. Then I remembered the room.'

'The secret room,' I whispered, imagining the horror of that night.

'Well, it was a bit of a family joke, actually. We used to play in it as children because it was such a funny little room, a hidey-hole. It had no windows and no chimney and seemed to be forgotten, a sort of architectural gaffe when the house was built on to so many times. It was a large cupboard really. Then, of course we didn't know about the nineteenth-century scandal about the house and the room, and when we were older and Dad told us about it, we said what about our secret room? And Dad said it was nonsense because that part of the house was reconstructed in his time and his father was furious with the builders for being so incompetent.'

'If it has no chimney the story about the hammer is out,' Anne said. 'It looks like a story that was partly true but not completely, and you keeping it a family secret added to the mystery.'

Tim was looking at her impatiently and Anne stopped.

'Anyway before Aggie came round I managed to drag Peter's body into the the wretched room and left it there. Then I got Aggie to bed and just as she recovered consciousness, I gave her her medicine which sent her off again. When she woke the next morning she didn't remember a thing and when she asked where Peter was, I said he'd gone away and she said thank God. You see she didn't remember hitting him, I know she didn't. The way she acted was like a sleepwalker, someone in a trance . . .'

'That will be very useful in court,' Stephen murmured.

'But she did remember that he'd been going to tell me something and she asked if I knew. I knew already it was something about the Dabroes, but she wouldn't tell me any more. She closed up.

'Well, I was in a terrible sweat. Jocasta was due in a week. What was I going to do? I decided to go to Peter's flat and make it look as though he'd gone away. We were very alike to look at so I thought if someone saw me I'd get away with it. Then the likeness thing made me think of establishing a sort of alibi, that Peter had been alive when in fact he was already dead. I know it was amateur and silly but I registered at the Morecambe House Hotel and a fair carry on that was with me trying to be seen, but not too much.

'Then what was I going to do about the body? Supposing Mrs Bargett found it? She knew about the room though as far as I knew she never went into it. There was Peter's car which was in our garage; there was Peter's business; there was Jo about to arrive. It was ghastly.

'Then there was Aggie. I think at the back of her mind she was trying to remember and she was suspicious about why Peter had left so suddenly. I was terrified that if she knew she'd killed him she'd go insane.'

'Peter's body haunted me, and I really mean haunted. Peter seemed always to be there as though his presence had taken over the house. Well, as you know, Jo came. Aggie hadn't wanted to be there to meet her; she couldn't face it and I wanted Aggie out of the way so that I could get Peter's car out of our garage. I felt it was incriminating if anyone missed Peter, and I should get the body out of the house before Jo came. But when I got back, she'd arrived; only my car was in the garage. I'd taken the train back from Leeds, where I'd sold the car to a shady secondhand dealer who asked no questions, and then a taxi from Skipton. He left me a mile outside the village. I said I felt sick and wanted to walk.'

'I never heard your car arrive, but I heard it go,' I said dully, horrified by the whole story. 'I only recalled it tonight. If I'd have remembered it before it might have saved a lot of misery because I always thought you were covering up something. But not a body . . . not . . .'

'I'm terribly sorry, Jo.' Tim addressed me directly for the first time. 'Sorry about everything; sorry to have inflicted this on you. Anyway one day you were talking to Aggie about Peter and said he'd lived in a hotel. Aggie knew perfectly well he didn't and she taxed me with it. She said I knew where Peter was and then, suddenly, she remembered the evening and what he'd been about to say to me, but after that it was blank. She then told me all about Sam Dabroe because she thought I'd heard she was seeing Jonathan, and how she was his sister and had known it for years and the knowledge was killing her because of what I'd say. I never felt so bad in my life, that she'd suffered so much for my sake. The feud seemed silly and trivial compared to Aggie's health, and I thought how everyone had suffered because of the Ryder pride. So – ' he glanced at me – 'I went to Jonathan Dabroe.'

'You went to s-see Jonathan?' I stammered.

'I had to. Aggie or you or Mrs Bargett were always around and I couldn't get the body out by myself. I hated thinking of it next to Aggie's room under Jo's. After all Jonathan was Aggie's brother. I told him everything about the row, the blow, the body in the house. He was awfully shocked, but . . . he agreed a scandal was in no one's interest, that it might finish Aggie and he helped me move the body. You and Aggie were with the Bakers, Jo, and we did it that night and buried it on the moors above Pateley. We didn't know how long we could conceal all this, but time seemed the important thing.'

I thought of the night we'd met Anne. Thank goodness Tim wasn't there, Agnes had said. He and Jonathan were lurking somewhere, waiting for us to leave the house. And that was the night Stephen had paid so much attention to Agnes.

'I owed it to my sister,' a quiet voice said and Jonathan came into the room. I wondered how long he'd been at the door listening. No one would have heard him. 'I had to do it for her.'

Jonathan had his coat on; he looked worn and tired and went over to stand beside Tim. He pressed his shoulder as though they too were brothers, and I thought at last Ryder and Dabroe were united.

'I heard in Skipton you'd been in court,' Jonathan said, 'and I went straight to the police. I'm to be charged tomorrow. Today, rather.' He looked out of the window and indeed the dawn was beginning to break, early as it does in winter months in northern England.

'But what are you to be charged with?' I said.

'Abetting a crime. It's a very serious offence.'

'I should never have involved you,' Tim said. 'You acted with honour. I'm sorry.'

'Then I saw Aggie in hospital. She was awake and much calmer. I gather you and Stephen had a time today. I think she's resigned now although of course the knowledge that she killed Peter is horrifying to her.' Jonathan looked at me, came over and took my hand. 'I'm sorry,' he said.

I let my hand drop limply. I couldn't look at him.

'I don't know how you could,' I said. 'Knowing he was dead, acting like you did. *Pretending* to me.'

Jonathan was silent for a long time.

'I couldn't tell you he was dead because I'd promised not to. But I was aware of the agony of the situation, believe me, dear Jo. It was awful for me, seeing you suffer. I thought the best help to you would be knowing what Peter was really like and, although he's dead and it ill behoves us to speak ill of the dead, he really was a swine. He *did* have an affair with Tess, she told me when we had tea with the kids later that day; he crept into my house when I was away and made love to my wife. I don't blame her for that but at the same time he was

209

making love to you, saying he loved you.' I winced. 'And he was telling Tess he loved her too. He was blackmailing Tim and Aggie, moral blackmail, preying on their fears and Aggie's ill health. Peter was an awful swine, Jo, and although I don't think he deserved to die as he did, I think the world is well rid of such as he.'

I was silent, aware that everyone was looking at me. I felt tired and vaguely sick, disgusted with the whole business, the sordid tale. Everyone had deceived me – Peter, Stephen, Jonathan, the Ryders. The village had ganged up against me, an outsider, to protect their own, and I thought that where family and deep loyalties were involved, concern over other human feelings didn't really count.

'You took Aggie and Tim away to make them see sense?' I think Anne was rather amazed at her brother's behaviour.

'I'd been suspicious about what had happened to Peter too, and everything did point to the Ryders, including Tim's resemblance to him. I thought he could have passed for Peter in the hotel. The hotel puzzled me such a lot. Like Jo, I thought it was very unlike Peter in *character* to disappear. Jo always believed that, and she was right; she followed her psychological instinct. I finally had it out with Tim and he was ready to go to the police; he'd had enough, the guilt, Aggie's ill health. I promised him that once it was all straightened out everyone would feel better Aggie included. "Face the music," I said "and get it over with."'

'You'd better represent me in court tomorrow,' Jonathan said. 'It will be quite a field day; the Chairman of the Bench charged in his own court.'

I got up. I felt terribly tired.

'Come back with me tonight,' Anne said. 'You can't stay here.'

I nodded.

'I'll go and pack a case.' I went out of the room by myself. I wanted to be alone for those few last minutes in Croft House, for I would never sleep here again.

I went slowly up the stairs, along the corridor, touching

the wall beyond which Peter had lain, up the further flight of stairs to my room.

I looked out of the window. It really was dawn and the sky over the cliff was pale. I looked at the cliff for a long time, but it seemed so peaceful now in its place watching over Coppitts Green as it had done for hundreds of years regardless of our follies.

I stepped back and listened, but the house was peaceful too. It would go on creaking and sighing as old houses do. I hoped they'd open that room somehow and put a window in.

I hoped they'd banish the ghost of Croft House; lay it to rest.

For those who like neat endings, and most people do, let me say that the ending was far from neat. It seemed to go on for ever and involved a spectacular trial at Leeds Assizes, where the Ryders and the Debroes got more publicity than they had imagined in their wildest nightmares. It was the lead story every night in the Yorkshire papers and even the national dailies did a good job too with pictures of the accused and everyone remotely connected with them, including me. The setting, and the feud between the families made such good copy.

The main evidence centred round Agnes' state of health and here she had good counsel backed up by expert medical witnesses who had no doubt that Agnes suffered from an acute form of neurosis which caused blinding headaches and amnesia; the pressures that had built up inside her had become too intense to bear. But it was treatable and the prognosis was good.

The judge was very sympathetic towards Agnes and in his summing up gave a very clear exposition of her condition and said that he had no doubt she had acted under extreme provocation and hadn't known what she was doing either before or after the event of Peter's killing. He directed the jury to return a verdict of manslaughter under diminished responsibility and put her on probation for three years provided she received medical treatment. He was very kind to her and smiled encouragingly at her as she was led from the dock.

He was less kind with Tim and Jonathan, especially the latter, who, he said, as a magistrate should have known better than to abet in the concealment of a crime. He had a lot to say about people of standing who went about burying bodies on moors late at night, and as he spoke, I thought of Matthew Ryder and how he must have done the same thing. How often one repeats the patterns of the past, recreating the same events in each succeeding generation. Almost every detail of the recent tragedy had some echo in the nineteenth century.

So in fact the sensation of the trial was not what happened to Aggie but what happened to Jonathan and Tim, who were each given prison sentences, which were sustained even on appeal.

After a time they were sent to open prisons and I began gradually to visit Jonathan there, and then my visits became more regular. Because I felt that, for all he'd done, I owed Jonathan hope; the hope there would be someone to care about him afterwards and, in getting to know him afresh, starting all over again, not dazzled by his name or his looks, I grew to love him in that deep private way, that sturdy lasting love that shared tribulations sometimes brings.

I should say here that Peter's body was removed from its moorland resting place and given a decent burial. But most of the following year I spent at the school, running it while Mrs Baker made a long slow recovery, and helping her back to health by living at End House. And as I had felt I should, I grew to love the Dales even more than before because, as with people, knowing a countryside is like knowing a person's moods – my growing love for Jonathan and the valley where he'd been born were complementary. You take the rough with the smooth, the good weather with the bad, the cold and the heat; the imperfections of life are all around us, yet life is nonetheless satisfying for that.

Thus it was inevitable that when Jonathan came out of prison we were married very quietly and we both really started to begin life again. By that time Mrs Baker had retired and I was headmistress of the village school. Slowly Jonathan gathered together the threads of his business and his life in the country, because Dales people were good people and they hadn't thought he'd committed any real crime except perhaps one of stupidity.

Tim sailed for America as soon as he left prison; he wanted to make a new start, as Roger Ryder (or was it Jeremy Dabroe?) had all those years before.

But strangest and most touching of all the things that happened during the following years was Stephen's devotion to Agnes. He visited her in hospital, he reunited her with her mother, with whom she recuperated when she was ready, and when the doctors really thought she was cured and the bad part was behind her for good, he married her and brought her to live at Croft House, which, despite its memories, she loved because she had been born there and now she was the only Ryder left.

But if the actual name of Ryder has vanished from a dale where it flourished for so many hundreds of years I don't think it's too bad a thing; for it meant the end of the feud. But then I'm a Dabroe, and I feel one through and through. The valley has seeped into my blood and in time our children will go to where, so many years ago it seems, I first came as infant teacher to the school in Coppitts Green.